KU-321-510

QUEEN MUM

Ally and Juno are neighbours. And more than that they're best friends. For Ally, life in Cestrian Park, Chester, a world of verdigris planters, antique French wall clocks, Belfast sinks and Farrow & Ball colour charts, is a long way from where she started out. For Juno, beautiful, confident, curious, life with her family is perfect—her household runs with a contented hum, its mechanism lubricated with organic olive oil.

But then Juno suddenly makes a surprising decision: signing up for a reality TV show, *Queen Mum*. For two weeks, she will be going to live with another family in another town, while her opposite number will be moving in next door to Ally. Juno is excited, but Ally isn't quite so sure; how will she manage without her best friend? But that isn't the only reason why she's worried. She doesn't like change. Because she knows from experience how something precious can be lost in a moment.

QUEEN MUM

Kate Long

WINDSOR
PARAGON

First published 2006
by
Picador
This Large Print edition published 2006
by
BBC Audiobooks Ltd by arrangement with
Pan Macmillan

Hardcover ISBN 10: 1 4056 1464 1
           ISBN 13: 978 1 405 61464 1
Softcover ISBN 10: 1 4056 1465 X
           ISBN 13: 978 1 405 61465 8

Copyright © Kate Long 2006

The right of Kate Long to be identified as the
author of this work has been asserted by her in
accordance with the Copyright, Designs and
Patents Act 1988.

All rights reserved.

British Library Cataloguing in Publication Data available

20173803

MORAY COUNCIL
LIBRARIES &
INFORMATION SERVICES

Printed and bound in Great Britain by
Antony Rowe Ltd., Chippenham, Wiltshire

To Simon

Many thanks, for their feedback and support, to Kath Pilsbury, David Rees, Peter Straus, Ursula Doyle and the wonderful WW girls

CHAPTER ONE

Video night last Monday. Manny's been going through a surrealist phase so we had a selection of Luis Buñuel films. Juno had made her own crisps out of parsnip shavings and black pepper and put them in a wooden bowl in the middle of the rug. Tom and I supplied the wine—huge row in the middle of Tesco's about that. 'I'm not spending so much,' Tom had said. 'It's only bloody Juno and Manny next door.'

I was out of the lounge when the first film started, so I didn't see the title.

'What's this one?' I asked Tom.

'*Large Door*, apparently,' he said. I could tell he was hacked off. He's an action-thriller man.

Juno stretched across with the video case for me. *L'Age d'Or*, I read. I caught her eye and she smiled indulgently; luckily, Tom didn't see.

After a while the woman on screen, who looked like Clara Bow, started rolling her eyes and sucking the toe of a life-size male statue. I got the giggles then, I couldn't help it. Tom started to laugh too, then, after a while, Juno joined in. By the time we got to a scene with a bishop being thrown out of the window, I was helpless. My cheeks were wet and Tom's face was flushed and shiny. So the evening was going to go well after all.

The video finished and Manny switched the TV off. 'I never thought of it as quite so hilarious,' he said, smiling, and there was just that edge to his voice.

So, I thought, got it wrong again.

1

*　　*　　*

Cestrian Park's a place of hidden codes. You think, when you buy a house, it's yours to do up as you see fit. But it's not. There are, oh, *things* you have to have. Basket of logs, verdigris planters, antique French wall clock, Belfast sink, one of those granite pestle and mortars on your kitchen top. Your curtains are Sanderson, Zoffany or Osborne and Little; Laura Ashley if you're slumming it. And that place you go and sit in to watch the TV, it's the drawing room, not the lounge. This is Farrow and Ball country.

I remember standing outside, just after we'd moved in, looking at this double-fronted Edwardian house, twice the size of the one I grew up in. I stood on the gravel drive and I thought, It's ours. I can't believe we've been so lucky.

*　　*　　*

The afternoon following our surrealist evening, Juno came round buzzing with excitement.

'Ally,' she said as she stepped over the threshold, 'I've been a naughty girl.'

'I find that hard to believe,' I said. 'Sainthood's your stock-in-trade.'

We went though and sat in the front bay window where I could watch for Ben coming home from school. She knows I need to do this.

'I had a phone call this morning,' she went on, brushing her wavy hair behind her ears. 'You'll never, ever guess.'

'No, you're right, I won't. Get on with it.'

2

She was hyper, more than usual. Her skin's quite dark so it doesn't often show when she colours up, but it did now. 'It was a TV company.' She put her hand to her mouth as if the news was almost too shocking to be let out. 'Ally, listen—I'm going to be on television!'

'Oh my God.' I caught myself mirroring her movements, brought my hand down and gave her a hug instead. 'Really? When? What for?'

'You won't believe it . . . I'm going to be on *Queen Mum*!'

I gaped at her.

'Have you seen it?'

'Where the women swap houses and then the viewers vote for who's the best mother? Bloody hell, Juno. I'm, I'm amazed. My God.'

'Why?'

'Well—what can I say. I wouldn't have thought it was your cup of tea.'

She giggled. 'To tell you the truth, it's compulsory viewing in our house. It's the only early evening programme Manny watches. He finds it fascinating from a sociological point of view.'

I could imagine him saying this. 'Will he be fascinated to be in it, though?'

'Good question. No, he'll go mad at first. He doesn't even know I've filled in the application form.'

'Juno, you crazy girl. He'll have some kind of Gallic fit.'

'He will, won't he? But he'll come round, given time and flattery.'

Emmanuel Kingston on television; I could see him, but more reading the news or presenting an

3

arts programme, Thinking Woman's crumpet. Reality TV?

'You're dangerous, you are,' I laughed. 'So how come you've managed to apply without telling him? Don't you have to both give your permission?'

She took a deep breath. 'OK, I'm ahead of myself. I filled in the form on the Internet weeks ago, and I had a call back this morning to say we're through to the next stage, which is an individual telephone interview. I've scheduled that for Wednesday night, so I'll have to tell him when he comes home this evening.'

'And what do you reckon he'll say?'

'Oh, I'll talk him into it, I always do.'

That was true. The adventures they'd had were all instigated by her. Skinny dipping in the Indian Ocean, being extras in *Robin Hood, Prince of Thieves*, taking a midnight picnic in a haunted house. Bungee jumping on their tenth wedding anniversary, which she'd have done on her honeymoon if she hadn't been pregnant.

'OK. Then what?'

'If the phone chat scores top marks, they come round to the house and do a more in-depth interview. Suss out the neighbourhood; check *you* over, probably.' She grinned and touched my knee. 'No need to worry. There are loads of applicants, the guy was telling me. We may not get accepted.'

'You will.' I knew she would, too. Things happen for Juno. 'When's it kick off?'

'They'd start filming next month; it airs six months later. So, what, August? September?'

An old lady walking past outside looked in and waved. Mrs Beale. Waving at Juno, not me, because Juno runs her to the nursing home every week to visit her husband. There was no way Juno was going to lose at *Queen Mum*. She does everything, and does it well.

'God. Cameras in our street.' I wondered what the neighbours would think. I could just picture Tom's face when I told him. 'Can I ask you something?'

'Sure.'

'It's just . . . ' I paused, not sure how the question would sound. 'Why are you doing it?'

'For fun.'

'It seems like a lot of effort, commitment—'

'Risk?'

'No, I didn't mean that. It'll be very *public*, though.'

'Do you think I won't be any good?'

'Get away. You'll win the whole series. Everyone'll vote for you. *I'll* vote for you about ninety times.'

She laughed again, throwing her head back, her eyes glinting. 'Bless you, Ally. It's a good question, though. I'd better get it straight by the time Manny comes home, hadn't I? I'm doing it because I want to, basically. Because it'll be an Experience, and I'm always up for one of those. Plus I'll get the chance to re-evaluate my relationships with everyone. It'll make Manny and the girls realize how much I do for them—'

'Depends who you they get in your place,' I said mischievously. 'Won't you be nervous you might get *supplanted*?'

I saw a little frown cross her brow.

'I suppose so. Actually, no. Manny and I are really strong together, and, how can I put this

5

without sounding like a crashing snob? They do tend to pair you up with a, a contrasting sort of family. So a woman who wouldn't be anything like me. Makes for more exciting TV. And the things that Manny loves about me, this other woman wouldn't have them. And she'd run the house in a way he wouldn't like.'

I thought about this. What would be the opposite of Juno? A woman who didn't care about anything; a slob, a slut, someone with no style or charm. The sort of woman who sits back and lets life happen to her.

'I get you. You're banking on a twenty-five-stone fishwife.'

'With halitosis, yes.'

'And Manny'll be begging you to come back within hours.'

'Let's hope so.' She pulled a comic-distressed face.

The front door banged and I jumped, even though I was expecting it.

'Ben? Ben!' I heard the sports bag drop on the floor and the sound of feet thumping up the stairs. 'Had a good day?' I called after him, uselessly. He never likes to talk when he first gets in; I know this, but it still makes me sad.

'I should go,' said Juno, rising from the sofa and pulling her camel sweater down over her neat cream cords. 'Pascale and Soph'll be next door, and I've got to get the sauce made for the chicken. We're eating early tonight because Manny's booked tickets for *The Birds*.'

'The Hitchcock film?'

'The play. Aristophanes. You know.' She saw I didn't. 'Greek guy. I'd never heard of him either,

6

Manny's the culture vulture. It's an updated production, supposed to be really funny. We're taking the girls along so I hope it's not too blue. Can I scrounge some sage as I go past? I think the cat's been lying on mine, it's gone all ropy.'

I saw her out, back to her happy house, and it was as if she'd taken a little of the light with her. I imagined her next door, dancing around the kitchen to Charles Trenet or Manny's Breton folk CDs, the girls floating in and chatting about how school had gone.

I dragged myself up off the sofa and went to look in the freezer.

*   *   *

Title sequence to **Queen Mum**

Music: brass over techno; funky electro-beat incorporating the initial six-note riff of 'God Save the Queen'.

Visuals: deep blue background, cartoon head and shoulders of a black woman wearing police uniform. The camera pulls out to show she's holding a baby in one hand and typing on a laptop with the other. The baby reaches up and grabs her hat so it tumbles off, to be replaced by a crown dropping down from somewhere above. The words 'Queen Mum' in a scintillating pink font scroll into the top half of the screen from the left. A cartoon hand from the right appears and snatches the crown from the policewoman; the camera follows to show a white brunette in a teacher's gown holding in the same free fist a dog's lead and a set

7

of toddler reins. The teacher puts the crown on her head, only for it to be whisked away immediately by the figure on her right, this time an Asian woman wearing a suit and holding a GameBoy, with a thermometer poking out of her top pocket. The letters 'Queen Mum' evaporate in a pink mist, and the presenter's name now runs along the top of the screen, while below the crown is taken once more from the right, by a white, blonde woman in overalls holding a diploma bound with a red ribbon, while a pair of grey underpants dangles from her middle finger. Suddenly a magpie swoops down and catches the crown up in its beak, flying to the left and over the heads of the dismayed women. The last scene is the magpie sitting on a tree branch and winking at the camera, the crown still dangling from its beak. The camera moves in closer and closer until the edge of the crown forms a circular frame, through which we pass, into the opening shot of the actual programme.

*   *   *

In the dentist's waiting room I ended up mentally filling in a magazine quiz. What Kind of a Pal was I? As if I didn't know.

When I was at school I had three best friends. The teachers used to joke about us going everywhere together. It was our big fear that we'd be put in separate classes. Then, when we were in the third year, my best-best friend Gilly moved to Oxfordshire because her parents were separating and her mum needed to be near Gilly's grandma. After that the group weren't so close and Amy, who was always more advanced than us, got

8

involved with a boy and drifted away. I didn't understand why she preferred him to us, I wrote long letters to Gilly about it, and about Dad going. So I went around with Sarah and that was all right, but by the fifth year it had become clear she had ambitions I didn't have; she was going to university and then to live in London and have a riverside apartment with iron girders in the roof. Some dawn she wanted to hang her fur coat on spiky railings and drop her pearls down a grid. That was being Metropolitan. All I wanted was to get married and have a family.

Conclusion: 30–45 points—*You might find it difficult making friends initially, but once you have decided you like someone you are very loyal.* That was normal. No worries there, then.

'I came out as Alice Average,' I told Tom over the evening meal. Ben was on the phone, letting his chops go cold.

'There's a surprise,' Tom said. 'Have you heard any more details about this malarkey next door? Is it one of those shows where they come in and lecture you, or the sort where they just give you the rope to hang yourself and let you get on with it?'

'Don't be so bloody pompous,' I said, getting up and swiping him on the back of the head as I went past. 'Juno printed out the Web page for me. Here. It's the show presented by Abby Cavanagh. Don't pretend you haven't watched it.'

'I've seen it. Not the same thing.'

I leant my head on one side trying to read the text upside down. 'Funny, it sounds like an African TV company, Umanzu. I wonder if the producer's got African connections or something.'

Tom scanned the page, then looked up, half-smiling. 'Not U-*man*-zu, silly. *Yoo*-man-*zoo*. Human Zoo, get it?'

'Oh.'

Ben walked in, yawning. When he stretched I could see the tendons in his neck and the blue veins under his skin. He was as tall as me now. 'I know it's a stupid idea,' he said, 'but is there any chance I could go diving with Felix in the summer? No? Didn't think so.'

'Just eat your chops,' I told him.

*   *   *

Juno [Voiceover]—I think I've got a lot to give to another family. Fresh ideas, lots of energy. As, obviously, another woman coming into the house would inject into mine.

How do I spend my days? I get the breakfast ready for everyone, because Manny has to be out of the house early, and we, the girls and I, have a look at the papers if they're there on time, otherwise we listen to the *Today* programme, because it's important for them to be informed, I don't want them growing up in some middle-class bubble. And sometimes they do a bit of violin before we leave the house, if they've got a lesson that day. Next it's the school run, that's nearly an hour by the time you've parked up, and probably someone'll want to discuss the PTA with me or something, a cake sale or second-hand uniform. Two mornings a week I do a stint at the hospice shop and the days I'm not doing that, I'm either being a taxi for Age Concern or catching up on housework. In the afternoons I'll often have a drive out to

10

the farm shop to pick up supplies. A lot of people don't realize how much time it takes to source and prepare good-quality food. I'm not fanatical about it but I do try to see that we eat organic where we can.

The girls come home and I give them a little *goûter* to see them through till dinner. It's what they do in France, my husband's half French. And the girls go and get their homework out of the way and I write any letters I need to. We all gather round the big table together, it's very Jane Austen. When Manny comes in we sit down to eat and have a lovely chat about the sort of days we've all had. The girls always clear away and load the dishwasher, they're very good. Then it's TV time, and we all slob on the sofa together and the girls get to choose a programme they want to watch, even if it's tosh. We chase them off to bed about ten, and Manny and I have some catch-up time on our own.

I think Manny and I work because we've got the same world view. The same interests, the same aspirations, more or less.

I see *Queen Mum* as an opportunity to explore my marriage, my family, to understand the balance of power, the way different components, people, work together. It'll also give me an insight into myself as an individual. Which can only be a good thing, no?

CHAPTER TWO

We were in the front room having a row when we spotted the TV van arrive. I saw Tom's expression and I thought, that'll add fuel to the fire.

He thought the *Queen Mum* stunt was pure attention-seeking, he'd told me as we lay in bed one night, and it would all end in tears. He actually used that phrase.

Now we were arguing about Ben.

'You have to let him go,' Tom kept saying. 'All his mates are going. You'll make him look like a complete loser if you say no. What's he going to tell them at school, Ally? Mummy says it's too dangerous, I've got to stay home and hold her hand?'

'But he doesn't want to go.'

Tom sighed and flopped back against the sofa. 'Jesus. He's only saying that because he knows it's what you want.'

'He wouldn't do that. He's got a mind of his own, for God's sake. You should hear him when I ask him to take a break from his PlayStation.' I tried a little laugh.

'It's not quite the same thing, is it?' Tom drew a hand across his eyes. 'Ally, he's scared of you.'

'You what? You must be kidding.'

'I mean he's scared of hurting you. He knows what you're frightened of, he's an intelligent boy. But he does want to go away with his mates, which is perfectly reasonable.'

I knew it was, but I couldn't get past the fear. 'Look, if it was just a day trip to look at a rock

12

formation or something, that would be fine.'

'Would it?'

'Yes! But they'll be, what did it say on the letter, climbing, abseiling, building bloody rafts . . . That's the whole point of an adventure holiday, isn't it, the risk factor? Otherwise it would be a lounge-about-in-comfort holiday. And five days away from home. God knows what they'll get up to. There'll be booze, there always is, no matter how carefully the teachers check the luggage. Lads, drunk, at night, with mountains and lakes all round; you can't expect me to slap him on the back and say, Off you go, Ben, I'm thrilled.' I came over and sat on the arm of the sofa, but not so near I was touching Tom. He shifted over, though, and placed his hand gently on my thigh.

'They'll have qualified instructors. Good God, schools are so twitchy about litigation these days, they won't go exposing them to any real danger. Anyway—'

I knew, *knew* what he was going to say. Don't! I wanted to shout. Stop now!

'—daily life's risky enough. You don't have to throw yourself down a mountain to . . . '

By a huge effort of will, I made myself not think about the day Joe died; instead I saw him sitting on the bottom stair the day we moved in, gouging pellets off the blown-vinyl wallpaper to create a localized snow shower on the floorboards. I'd said to him, Stop that, but Tom had walked past and muttered, It makes no odds, we'll be pulling it all off soon. Then Ben had joined in, sitting on the step above, only Joe didn't realize that his brother was secretly scattering chips of vinyl in his hair. Little flecks of white in the dark

13

blond. It's his hair I miss the most, in tactile terms. It's the part of an infant you see and touch the most.

'Have you seen that?' When I came back to earth, Tom was turned round on his seat, staring out of the bay.

The van parked on next door's drive had the Umanzu logo on it and two young-looking men were climbing out. One was carrying a briefcase or a laptop; both wore black sweaters.

'So she's really going ahead with it?'

I shrugged, defensive. 'Looks like it. I don't see what your problem is with it. It's their life, not yours.'

'It impacts on ours,' said Tom darkly.

'I don't see how. It's not *Neighbour Swap*. You don't have to be anywhere near a camera.'

'But our street'll be on national TV. You'll have burglars tuning in to check the layout of the house, passers-by gawping . . . No one's asked us if we mind, have they? I feel as if my privacy's been invaded, and all so Manny and Juno can show off how bloody marvellously functional their family is.'

'You know what you sound like?' I began.

But then Ben walked in.

'Wow,' he said, edging past me to go right up to the window, so close his breath made a mist.

'Come away.' I pulled at his shoulder. He stepped back about six inches.

'You and Dad are having a good look. It's cool. Soph says she's having her hair cut for the filming. Juno's been on at Manny to get the downstairs loo repapered quick as well, I heard them arguing about it.'

'They should have gone on *Changing Rooms*,

14

then, shouldn't they?' said Tom.

'You heard them arguing?'

Ben detached himself from the view and wandered over to the armchair opposite, where he dropped and sprawled. 'Not really arguing. I dunno. Can I get a job, Dad?'

Tom glanced across. 'What's brought this on?'

'I thought it was about time. Jase's got a paper round, Chris does gardening with his uncle. They've got cash to spend; I haven't.'

'So is this, in fact, about a pocket-money raise?' I asked, smiling.

'No, it's about getting a job, Mum.'

That told me. 'I don't know . . . '

'Sounds a good plan to me,' said Tom. 'Let me know when you've sorted something out. I can give you a lift at weekends, if you need one.'

'Excellent.' Ben swivelled and put his long legs over the arm of the seat. He looks older than fourteen sometimes. He grabbed the TV guide and started to scan the listings.

'Would you like to be on telly, Ben?'

'No, Mum,' he said without looking up.

Tom shot me a satisfied sort of glance, then rose to his feet and went out. I heard the kitchen radio start up.

'Ben?' I said. 'Do you really want to go on this Lake District holiday with school?'

He raised his eyes for a moment, and they were the saddest eyes I thought I'd ever seen.

'I don't know. I don't know.'

Juno's Top Tips for Coping with School Trips

1. Discuss your worries with your child.

15

There's no need to hide your anxieties if they are reasonable ones.

2. Ask for a copy of the school's risk-assessment document relating to the trip's activities. The head teacher should be happy to show you this.
3. Have a chat with your child's form tutor or head of year to set your mind at rest that the company behind the trip has been recently vetted by the school.
4. Accept that you will be worried while your child is away from home, because that is a perfectly natural reaction for a caring parent.
5. Congratulate yourself when your child comes home bursting with confidence and having had a wonderful time!

I took myself upstairs to our bedroom and sat at my dressing table for a while, imagining it was me on screen being interviewed about family life. Don't anyone think about swapping with me, I told the mirror.

When people ask me how many children I have I always want to say two: sometimes I do. Joe might be dead but he's always around, memories of him pinging up suddenly, the way leaves do after a heavy shower.

I wondered a lot about Ben these days, how he'd have turned out if Joe was still alive. He was always going to be a quiet one; six when his brother was born, used to playing alone. But there'd never have been this weight at his centre.

And Tom was always angry; with me, it felt like. Everything he did was shot through with fury, so that opening a jam jar became a vicious fight in which the solution might be shattering the pot against the edge of the unit. He laced his boots in anger, shaved in anger, cleaned the car like he wanted to scrape the paint off the metal. Yet I remembered his careful movements wiping blood away from Ben's lip after a tricycle accident; I could see Ben now, sitting on the kitchen worktop with his legs dangling, a pile of screwed-up tissues next to him. And the way Tom had lifted back my hair from my face the first time we ever kissed. Years and years ago. His fingers curved round Ben's baby skull, round Joe's.

The phone rang and it was Mum, to check we were coming up on Saturday and also to ask whether I'd heard about the terrible school-bus crash in Austria. 'They're still fetching bodies out,' she said. I swear she keeps a scrapbook of disasters.

'You wouldn't want to come into my home,' I told the camera as I put the receiver down. 'I promise you. I'd stick with next door and normality.'

*   *   *

Juno celebrated the good news from Umanzu by holding a small drinks party for the street. 'A PR exercise, if ever there was one,' said Tom when I showed him the invite.

'You're not going, then?'

'Depends what's on telly that night,' he muttered, bending back over his computer keyboard. He surfs bike sites, creates mammoth Watch lists on eBay motors. There are pictures of

17

Ducatis and Kawasakis all round the shed walls; a pennant over the door, *Free with every bike: you*. I live in dread of him ever actually buying one.

'Don't you think it'll look rude if you're not there?'

He didn't answer, so I turned to go. As I was walking through the door I heard him say, 'OK, then. But let's not be the first to arrive, eh?'

In the end, we were the last by miles; the party was all but over by the time we got there. I'd been ready at eight but then a huge sense of depression and tiredness came over me and I had to lie on the bed for a while till it passed off. Ben poked his head in the room at one point and said, 'Have you got a migraine?'

'Yes,' I said because it was easier than trying to explain that I'd lost my nerve.

'Shall I get Dad?'

I told him no, and he clicked his tongue and went out again.

I lay there and wished Juno had said, 'Just you and Tom for drinks,' rather than inviting twenty-odd neighbours. Tom had been right. But when he came up at ten, saying it was too late to make an appearance now, I felt a huge surge of irritation and jumped up, miraculously cured.

'I've been waiting for you,' I snapped.

He looked hurt. 'I was only downstairs, not halfway up the bloody Amazon. Do you really want to go now?'

'Yeah.'

'OK, then. Jesus. I'm not putting a tie on. Or changing.' So what's new, I nearly said, but I couldn't cope with an argument.

Walking into Juno's house is like stepping off a

plane into a warmer country. Ben went off to find Sophie and Pascale, while Tom and I stood about in the hall, wondering who was going to be in the living room.

'Come through,' said Manny. 'I'm afraid most of the spread's been demolished.'

'Ally didn't feel too good,' said Tom, his hand on my back protectively.

'Just a migraine. It's gone now.'

'Oh, Ally. You OK?' Juno looked up from where she was sitting with May Owen. May smiled in my direction but didn't meet my eyes.

'Mmm.' I thought it best to be noncommittal.

'Come in the kitchen and see what's left of the buffet. If you're up to eating?'

I let Juno take me through. 'Has it been busy? I'm sorry, nearly everyone's gone—'

She cut me off with a cheery laugh. 'Every single person I invited turned up, when does that ever happen? Just as well I made all this olive bread. Can you manage a mouthful? What can I get you to drink?'

'White wine, please. Just a drop. So how've they all been with the news? Any dissenters?'

'No, no. Everyone's been charming about it, they all say they'll vote for me. I thought some people might be sniffy but perhaps reality TV's so much a part of our lives now, it has a certain cachet. Quite a few of them wanted to be in it, milling about in the background, that sort of thing.'

'What did you say?'

'That it wasn't up to me. It's not, either. We're all supposed to carry on as normal, that's the brief.'

'I bet there's some serious dog-walking goes on past your window while the camera crew's here,

19

though.'

'You bet. I did wonder about you popping round one day.'

'What, while they're still filming? You are joking?'

Juno shook her head and took a handful of peanuts from the table. 'Thing is, we're always having lunch together, aren't we? And they don't want me—this other woman, rather—to stop any of my usual routines.'

'Oh, but . . . '

'It probably won't be shown, anyway. They film for two weeks and edit it down to an hour, that's thirty minutes for each mum, so you'll almost certainly end up on the cutting-room floor.'

'Suits me.' Christ; me on telly. 'I'm not sure, Juno. I'm not the type.'

'Look, if you really hate the idea, forget it. Just a thought.' She gave me a big warm smile to show she wasn't cross.

'Let me think about it,' I heard myself saying.

May appeared in the doorway. 'I was telling Manny, I'd better be off. I was about to leave nearly an hour ago. And I'm JP-ing tomorrow, Family Court.' She was grinning madly, goggle-eyed. I know that nervous rictus. *OH GOD, YOUR SON DIED AND I MUSTN'T MENTION IT!*

As Juno showed her out I stayed where I was and picked olives out of my bread. When she came back, I said, 'Have you heard anything about the family you're swapping with yet?'

'Mm, yes. She's a secretary in a timber merchant's, and he's a builder. Kim and Lee, they're called. From your neck of the woods, actually. I mean, where you came from.'

'Bolton?'

'Yeah. And they're slightly younger than us, and they've got two teenage boys. That's all, really. We haven't seen pictures or anything.'

'What, of the brickie and his brood?' said Manny, strolling in and sitting himself at the pine table.

Tom stayed in the doorway, sipping whisky.

'Don't be so snobby,' said Juno. 'Don't you dare say that sort of thing on TV, they'll crucify you.'

'Just stating facts. The man lays bricks for a living. Nothing wrong with that. But that's what he does.'

'Some might say it's a more useful job to society than funding arts projects,' said Juno, smiling sweetly. 'Building homes for people, offices for them to work in. It could be argued that his taxes pay for your council-funded job.'

Manny smiled back. 'I wondered how long it would take you to construct that particular argument. You're the one who's been wondering if Kim'll be able to operate the Gaggia and whether she'll remember to buy Fair Trade bananas.'

'That's not being snobbish. Is it?' Juno turned an open face to us but Tom had picked up the free paper off the fridge and was leafing through it. I shook my head.

There was a thumping noise above us, as if something heavy and solid had fallen over, and a bass beat started.

'God. That'll be our lovely children. I dread to think what they're doing. Manny, could you pop up and have a word?'

Manny's chair scraped across the quarry tiles as he got up.

21

'Don't worry,' said Juno to Tom, 'I'll tell the girls to turn it off when you go. You don't want Rawshock blasting into the night air, do you?'

'No,' said Tom.

Over our heads, the music stopped.

'Ben's into ambient stuff at the moment; some of that's quite pleasant. His problem is, he gets an obsession with the same song for weeks and he plays nothing else. At the moment we have that miserable "Shamed" track whenever he's fed up, it's pretty wearing. But he went through his top-level screaming-vocals stage when he was eleven or twelve.'

'Lucky you. I play classical in the afternoons, it's lovely and peaceful, then the girls come home and it's thud-thud-thud. Still . . . '

What sounded like shouting was coming through now, Manny's deep boom. I couldn't make out any words though because Juno started talking again.

'Do you miss Bolton? I know you go up to see your mum, Ally—'

'It's where we met, where we married, where we had the boys,' said Tom. 'I'd go back and live there like a shot.'

'Would you?' I was amazed. 'I never knew you felt like that.'

'There was never any point in saying it. There's no point now. I have to go where ICI send me, and they sent me to Ellesmere Port.'

Juno was watching me.

'I thought you liked your job,' I said.

'I do. I just . . . We had some happy times there.' The happiest, I knew he was thinking. 'Those years I was at UMIST and you were working at Skittles doing your NNEB. We'd just got married and

22

everyone was saying, It won't last, you're too young, why don't you wait and finish your education. And we didn't care, did we? That bloody minute bathroom and that God-awful carpet. There was mould in the kitchen where the extension hadn't been put on properly, and no water pressure in the evening. But it didn't matter.'

'You were poor but 'appy,' said Manny, walking back in and looking pleased with himself. 'I've told Pascale that if the noise starts again, I shall take a boat trip along the Dee and throw her CDs into the water one at a time. I would, too.'

'I know you would,' said Juno.

I wanted to ask about Ben, was he OK, was he behaving himself. Instead I said, 'Of course, Chester's a lot more aesthetically pleasing than Bolton. Lots of history. Nice shops.'

'Oh, nice *shops*,' said Tom.

'And you like Meadowbank,' added Juno. 'I know you love working there. You've said lots of times how much nicer the kids are.'

'Toddlers are toddlers. They're all nice, anywhere.'

There was a clattering on the stairs and, seconds later, Sophie burst into the kitchen followed by Pascale and Ben.

'Can we light the garden flares, Dad?'

Manny opened his mouth to speak but it was Juno who answered. 'Absolutely not. It's too cold and too late. Soph, are you wearing lipstick?'

Sophie scraped her top teeth over her lip and grinned. 'Only gloss. Anyway, you said I could, round the house.'

'You don't need make-up,' I said, stroking her long dark hair as she leaned against the unit next

23

to me.

'You mean she's too young.'

'I mean she's too pretty.'

Sophie flicked her head back in a model-pose and pouted.

'Gorgeous, darling; give me more,' said Pascale, clicking an imaginary camera.

Girls are so much older these days. It seems like only last week that Sophie was a little stick-girl running about wildly in the garden. Now, at thirteen, every move is studied. She could easily get into any night club. Pascale, at fifteen, could pass for twenty, no probs.

Sophie dropped her head back down and glanced at Ben from under her lashes in a moment of pure flirtation. It had occurred to me before that she might have a tiny crush on him—he's a nice-looking boy—but I didn't know whether he'd noticed or even whether he'd be interested. I wasn't sure how he saw the girls, for all their charms.

I didn't know my son at all, really.

Pascale pushed forward and came to sit at the table, where she picked up the near-empty bowl of hummus and began scraping her finger round the rim.

'Oh, honestly,' said Juno. 'You'd think they'd been brought up by wolves.'

Pascale smacked her lips together. 'Yum, love that stuff. Can we have some more wine, then?'

Juno rolled her eyes but slid the bottle forward on the table. She believes in them drinking alcohol young. That way, she reckons, they'll learn to handle it sensibly. The girls have been having watered-down wine with their dinner since they

24

were eight, or something.

Pascale wiped her fingers on a paper napkin, then reached across and caught the bottle by the neck. 'Ben?'

Ben's eyes swivelled to me. 'Yeah.'

'Soph, you'll want some, won't you?'

Sophie nodded and leaned forward to take the glass.

'Anyone else while I'm here?'

'Top me up,' said Manny.

I saw Pascale's slim bare arm extended as she poured, her skin smooth and brown, and for a moment she made me think of when I was her age. All that energy and excitement and drama and joy; waking up every morning with my mind fizzing. Not that I was ever half so self-assured as Pascale. 'We don't push ourselves forward,' was Mum's mantra, 'we don't draw attention to ourselves.' Whereas Juno tells her daughters, 'You go for it! Of course you can do it!' No wonder they're so confident.

'Cheers,' said Sophie, knocking her glass against Ben's. Impossible to read his expression, lips turning up at the corners but whether with embarrassment or happiness I couldn't have said.

'Yes, cheers to you all,' I said, raising my glass. 'To a successful coronation, Queen Mum.'

'Thanks,' said Juno. 'I think we're on our way now.'

Afterwards, back home in bed, I imagined talking to Ben about the girls.

—Sophie likes you, you know.

—Does she?

—I think so. Yes, I'm sure; properly likes you. Fancies you.

—Yeah?

—Do you fancy her?

—No.

—She's beautiful. And she's nice with it. And clever. She's got everything going for her.

—She's thirteen, Mum.

—Too young for you?

—Sheesh. I don't know. Get off my case, will you?

Next to me, Tom shifted under the duvet and sighed. His eyes were closed but I didn't think he was asleep. We could have talked; I'd have liked that tonight.

—Would you mind me being on telly?

—What do you think?

—It wouldn't be a big deal. A walk-on part, at most. I'd like to support Juno.

—Of course you would. Do it if you want. As long as I'm not involved in any way, shape or form. I've told you what I think about it.

—Tom?

—Yeah?

—Do you really want to go back to Bolton?

—I'd like to go back to that time. Wouldn't you?

As we walked away I'd looked back at the house and seen Manny and Juno through the stained glass of their front door, kissing.

—Yes. Good God, yes. Like a shot.

*   *   *

Sophie—Mum's always on the go, she's always
    dashing around—
Pascale—She goes, 'I'll meet myself coming back
    one of these days'—

26

Sophie—Yeah, I reckon she chews that guava gum, Buzz Gum thingy, to keep herself going—

Pascale—No, she's addicted to caffeine, that's how she has all this energy. She's always on about drugs—

Sophie—God, yeah, is she ever—

Pascale—But she's the biggest junkie of us all. She's just in love with that espresso machine.

Sophie—Amphetamines for the middle-aged.

Pascale [Giggling]—Oh, God, Soph, you can't say that on TV—

Sophie—I just did!

Manny [To camera]—Juno'll cope fine wherever she is. She's got such a positive attitude. She'd have been great in, you know, the war, cheering people up in their bomb shelters, knitting socks for the boys at the front. She gets on with everyone. She meets all types in her charity work. Old ladies, single mums, low-income families; she never bats an eyelid, just asks what she can do to help. I suppose she is competitive, but in the nicest possible way. Anyway, competition is what drives the human spirit, isn't it? My idea of hell? A wife who sat around all day, I think. Someone who expected to be entertained, who whinged a lot. Because Juno's got this household running like clockwork, like an army camp. We all, any time of the day, know where we're supposed to be and what we should be doing. She never stops. Never.

Juno [Voiceover]—I'm hoping it's going to be a sort of cultural exchange. Like going to France. Or something.

27

CHAPTER THREE

After Joe died I went back to work at Meadowbank. 'Is that sensible, wanting to carry on there?' Mum's neighbour said. It must have seemed like the most painful place I could have been. Joe's coat-peg sticker was there still from the six months he spent at the nursery before starting big school. His outgrown anorak was in the spare-clothes box.

All I can say is, being among children felt as right as anything could have done. I could stroke all the little heads I wanted in there. Light, innocent contact, not the touching of someone who's rigid with guilt, or so full of their own pain that they duck away from your arms. Just normal, unthinking fingers curled round yours.

Tom had been worried I might do something crazy. 'Are you sure it's wise, Ally?'

'You mean am I about to go on the run with a toddler under my arm?' I'd yelled back. I'd been so livid with him that I'd broken the door off the ice compartment in the fridge, then lain on Joe's bed and thought about taking an overdose. It was my good luck that Juno turned up as the frenzy was passing. Anyone else, I'd have pretended I was out, but she'd got a special doorbell ring—her idea—so I went down and let her in. When I told her what Tom had said, she scoffed. 'Utter tosh,' she said. That was all, but I felt instantly better.

'Yeah it is, isn't it?' I said, wiping my eyes on her hanky. 'Can I put a bag of oven chips in your freezer, by the way?'

The look on her face had made me laugh, for the first time in a month. It was still two days before I spoke to Tom, though.

Not that I am ever on my own with the nursery kids. But this is because I'm in charge of pre-schoolers and there are too many children for one carer, the legal ratio currently being one adult to eight under-fives. I don't know if any of my colleagues know about Joe. There's a high staff turnover in this profession, lots of young girls coming and going, and two years ago we had a new boss. I suppose it might be on my file that I lost a child, but no one ever mentions it. So, perversely, Meadowbank's the one place where I hardly think about him. I'm always too damn busy.

I'd been working alongside Bethany for a month, wondering how long she'd stick it. I didn't dislike her, not at first. I thought she was funny with her impractical manicure and her thick make-up. If there hadn't been a uniform, she'd have been arriving in crop tops and hot pants. Nursery was just an interruption in her clubbing life. But she was cheerful and smiley, not an ounce of sulk in her, and the children loved her. The girls used to queue up for her to do their hair and she did her best not to spike them in the eyes with her six-inch nails.

She was thrilled to hear about Juno's TV experience.

'God, I wish I could trade my mum in. Nag nag nag, like she's got no other interest. I keep telling her to get out there, meet some men, but she'd rather stay home and whinge about the length of my skirt. Does your mate have any say in who she wants to swap with?'

'No. They get a few details in advance, that's all.' I picked up a foam ball that had come rolling to my feet. 'It's mostly a surprise.'

'But what if they match her up with somebody weird? One of these insanely jealous types, a bunny boiler, or a right, you know, ess-ell-ay-gee. Isn't she worried about leaving her husband with a strange woman? I would be. If I was married, I mean.'

'She says not. Their marriage is pretty strong. Plus they do these police checks, and I suppose there's cameras round all the time. No one would be able to get up to anything seriously nutty.' I picked up Daisy Fuller, who was running a crayon up and down my trouser seam, and stood for a moment with her in my arms watching Bethany confidently slotting together pieces of Tweenies jigsaw. 'Let the kids have a go, Beth. It is Ryan's puzzle.'

She giggled. 'I get carried away.'

They'd taken her out of the baby room because she nearly let a six-month-old fall off the changing unit. 'Keep an eye on her,' Geraldine, my boss, had told me. 'She doesn't mean any harm, but she doesn't think.'

It was exactly six weeks after Juno's party, and two days after Ben had left with the school for the Lakes, that I hurled a child's plastic lunchbox at her head and cut her brow open. Jesus, you could have blinded her, said Geraldine later. So? I nearly replied. It would have served her right.

I was on my morning break—only fifteen minutes, but you do need it in this job—and I'd slipped out to stand and look at the river while I drank my coffee. Lovely spring day, nippy but

30

sunny, some blossom starting to unfurl. I was imagining what Ben might be up to on his Adventure, but all I could picture was him falling into icy water or hurtling off the side of a cliff. So I thought instead about how I must finally get someone in to service the boiler because the water wasn't heating up enough, and then in a flick I was in the hallway of the other house, Joe running round with only a T-shirt on, British Gas rep at the door, Joe telling him not to step on blue because that was sea. Then it was in the dining room at Cestrian Park, Joe bursting in to let me and the decorator know that he'd made a giant snake on the floor, and it had turned out to be a two-metre stripe of toothpaste down the landing carpet. White footprints everywhere. Everything in my head leads to Joe, eventually.

Bethany met me at the door. 'There's been a call for you.'

My heart jumped in fear. 'Was it Ben's school?'

'It was, er . . . I wrote it down. They said it was quite urgent. I did look for you but you weren't . . .'

My blood was hammering already as I followed her to the office.

'Here you go,' she said cheerfully. 'Mr Hannant. Said to ring him back as soon as possible, but not to worry.' Mr Hannant, Ben's new form tutor. So something was wrong. 'He said not to worry.'

'They always say that!' I snapped, grabbing the scrap of paper out of her hand and barging past her. 'Oh *fuck*!' The outside line was engaged. 'Geraldine must be—I can't—'

Bethany looked shocked; I don't suppose she'd heard me swear before. 'Hang on, you can lend my

31

mobile,' she said, disappearing.

But then the line came free and I stabbed buttons, shaking. First of all I hit the wrong ones, then I dropped the receiver. On the third attempt I got it right.

The number you have dialled has not been recognized, came the voice. I went cold with panic but I hung up and tried again. *The number—*

'Bethany!' I yelled down the corridor. 'Bethany!'

A door down the corridor opened and Mo from Little Toddlers put her head out.

I dialled Ben's mobile number, even though I knew from the fact sheet we'd been given that the hostel was out of reception. *It has not been possible to connect you—*

'BETHANY!' I screamed.

She came out of the toilets looking white.

'You've taken the wrong number down!'

'Oh, did I? I'm sure I wrote down what he said. I've got my phone, anyway.' She was close now, holding out her hand with the tiny mobile in it. 'Sorry, I just went for a pee.'

It was then that I picked up the Lion King lunchbox and threw it at her face. It connected with her forehead and she let out a cry of surprise.

Mo darted out and pulled Beth into her room. I stood there trembling for a minute, then tried the number again.

I heard doors opening and quick footsteps, more doors, crying. Then Geraldine was in the office, cold and brisk.

'Go home, Ally.'

'It's Ben,' I said. 'There's been an accident and I can't get through. He's on an adventure holiday—'

'Go home,' she said. 'Now.'

I ran to the car park, didn't even stop for my coat. I'd have the number in the letter rack, on the information sheet the school had sent out. I just had to get home.

As I swung into the drive I could see Manny over the hedge getting into his Subaru. He gave me a wave but I ignored him. I flung open the car door and almost fell onto the gravel, scrambled up and made for the door. Bloody key wouldn't go in. I fumbled and stabbed at the keyhole, tears of temper spilling over. I wanted to kick the door down or beat it open with my fists.

'Ally? Are you all right?' It was Manny crunching up behind me. 'Ally, for God's sake, what's the matter?'

I couldn't answer him, so he took the keys off me, opened the door straight away and helped me in. I pushed him to one side and snatched up the letter rack, tipping it upside down onto the table.

'Is it something to do with Tom?'

I shook my head.

'Ben?'

I managed a strangled noise.

'Oh, right. Is he at school?'

But I'd found the sheet with the number on it and I didn't want to speak to him, I just wanted Mr Hannant.

He picked up straight away. 'Mrs Weaver?' He let out a breath of relief. 'You got my message. Nothing to worry about, Ben's actually fine.'

'Is he?' My voice was quavering; Mr Hannant would know I was crying but I couldn't stop myself.

'Oh, yes, absolutely fine. Well, in the sense that he's uninjured. Feeling rather sorry for himself, but then, that's what happens when you drink too

33

much.'

'He got drunk?'

Beside me, Manny was watching, listening, his body taut. When I said 'drunk', I saw him relax slightly.

'Very much so, I gather,' Mr Hannant went on. 'I don't think the alcohol belonged to him, if that's any consolation; actually, I don't know if it is, because I gather from what the other boys are saying that Ben helped himself to it from a class-mate's bag. So they're both in trouble. We did stress at the parents' meeting beforehand that alcoholic drinks were strictly banned, and that anyone caught with them would be sent home immediately.' There was a pause. 'So that's really it in a nutshell. I need you to come and collect him today if at all possible, and—'

'So he's not hurt?'

'Hurt? No, not in the slightest. He's been sick, but even that was, what, an hour ago, no, nearly two. And of course he's got a headache. He didn't have enormous amounts, about a quarter of a bottle of whisky, but then he's not used to it.'

My whole body wanted to give itself up to sobbing, but I held it together for another thirty seconds. 'Can I speak to him?'

Mr Hannant gave a mirthless laugh. 'He's lying down at the moment. I should think by the time you get up here though, what'll it be, early afternoon, he'll be feeling more himself.'

I put the receiver down and wept. Manny made a hot drink and then went out of the front door, where I heard him talking to someone.

'Is Juno there?' I asked when he came back.

'No. She's at the hospital with Mrs Beale. A scan

or something. Do you want to phone Tom?'

'I just want to get Ben back first.' Manny looked surprised. 'I'll call him when Ben's home safely.'

The Gallic shrug. 'OK. We'd better get moving, then.'

I drew my sleeve across my face and frowned. 'What?'

'You're in no fit state to drive, Ally, are you?'

'I'll be fine.'

'You do want to get to Ben as soon as possible, don't you?'

I nodded.

'For a start you're twitching around so much you probably won't be able to find the gears. And, with respect, your teeny Daewoo isn't built for high-speed dashes up the motorway. You want something that's going to eat up the tarmac.' He turned to look out of the window.

'Aren't you needed at work or something?'

'I've been sorting out a project from home all morning. On the skive, really. I've just rung in to say it's taken longer than I expected, so they won't see me till tomorrow now.' He came back to where I was sitting and stood over me. 'Look, Ally, if you really don't want me to come with you, that's fine. But I still don't think you should drive alone. Let me give Tom a bell.'

I did a quick calculation in my head; how long it would take Tom to get out of work and drive back here for me, then up to the Lakes. Too long. I could have let him go alone, but no. I had to see Ben for myself as soon as possible.

'You drive.'

'Sure? Right. Is there anything you need?'

'No. Let's go.'

For the first ten minutes or so he tried to chat; how did Ben like the school, what had he chosen for his options, but after that he didn't talk to me, which is what I wanted. Instead he played a Bach CD which I started off not minding but grew to hate. It became like an army of ants in my brain, running round and interfering with my thoughts. Over it all I could hear Joe's voice asking repeatedly, Does he get saved? which is what Joe always wanted to know the minute there was any on-screen conflict. No, the Dalmatians don't get made into coats, the sharks don't eat Nemo's dad.

The hostel was a slate barn in the middle of moorland. I couldn't see any other houses around. Manny parked on broken-up tarmac, reversing, going forwards, reversing, till I wanted to reach down and yank the handbrake on myself. I spotted Ben as I got out; he was peering from an upstairs window. He must have been watching out for me.

Mr Hannant, awkward in jeans rather than his suit, met me in the hall and said he wanted a chat before I went up. I ignored him. I never used to be so rude. I ran up the stairs just as Ben was opening the dorm door. He stood, hanging his head, and I pulled him into me. He smelt of mints and sick.

'Sorry, Mum,' he muffled into my jumper. There was an untouched plate of toast on the bedside table and I remembered how, for a fortnight after Joe died, Ben had made Tom and me breakfast every day; we used to have to bin it on the sly as neither of us could eat.

'Are you all right?' He moved away and we went into the room. 'Bit pukey.' He sank down on the end of a bed, and I went round and sat next to him.

'Not hurt or anything?'

36

'No. No; did Hannant tell you I was?'

'He said you'd been very drunk. He said you'd stolen some whisky. Last night?'

'Yeah. Are you really cross?'

I let a breath out slowly. 'I need to know what happened, Ben.'

He turned his face away for a moment and I wondered if he was going to cry. 'It wasn't just about drinking, Mum. I mean, the thing about the whisky's right—'

'Did you steal it from home?'

'No. God, Mum, check when you get back. Your booze cupboard's intact.'

'Mr Hannant said you'd taken it from another boy's bag.'

Ben nodded. 'Oh, yeah. That's true. Felix's sports bag's like a portable cocktail cabinet. They're supposed to have searched, but Felix just kept moving his stash around. Anyway, he won't mind. He said—'

'Hang on.'

I could just make out voices from below.

'Wait here a minute,' I said, rising, and crept out to the top of the stairs.

'You should have window locks, then,' Manny was saying angrily. 'These are teenagers. Of course they're going to try it on. It's your job to be one step ahead of them.'

Mr Hannant's voice was lower and placatory. Manny's scary when his temper's up. 'But at fourteen we would expect them to be developing a sense of personal responsibility. The students had been warned—'

'What, and you expect them simply to do as they're told? Get real. How long have you been a teacher? You and your staff are in loco parentis; that means you have to bear the responsibility for this.'

'I'm well aware what the phrase means,' said Mr Hannant.

I came down the steps to where they were standing in the hall. Mr Hannant hadn't moved from the spot where I'd left him.

'Come on,' said Manny when he saw me. 'Let's go. Has he got his case?'

His gaze travelled over my shoulder to Ben behind me, rucksack dangling from his hand.

'But I need to speak to Ben's teacher,' I said.

'Please, Mum,' I heard Ben mutter. 'I want to go home.'

Manny strode over and reached up for the rucksack. 'Let's get this lad back. I'll fill you in on what's been said.'

This is ridiculous, I'm his mother, I wanted to say. Then I felt Ben lean wearily into me and I knew I didn't have a choice.

'I'll phone you when I get home,' I said to Mr Hannant, who pressed his lips together and spread his palms. Do what the hell you like, the gesture implied.

I ran back up the stairs for Ben's suitcase and came out into the yard to find Manny bundling him into the car. As Manny started the engine, Mr Hannant appeared in the doorway looking small and sour. I tried not to look at him as we drove away.

When I thought I could speak, I said, 'Why did he tell you the story? Why didn't he wait for me to come down?'

'He thought I was your husband. I didn't say I

was, he just leapt to conclusions.'

'And you didn't explain?'

Manny stared straight ahead. He began to speak, but the car clamoured over a cattle grid and I didn't catch the words.

'Manny?'

'I said, I didn't disabuse him of his error.'

I turned in my seat to look at Ben. 'Hannant says I'm going to be suspended,' he said.

'He won't suspend you,' said Manny. 'Trust me.'

'Why not?'

'Because I told him if he did, we'd sue him for lack of proper care.'

Ben smiled faintly and I leaned back in my seat, my stomach churning. What in God's name was I going to say to Tom?

*   *   *

Juno—I'd say I have a very special, a very close relationship with the girls. Yes, we do argue, but you tell me a family that doesn't. And a lot of difficult situations, we head them off at the pass. We have these, it sounds rather, oh, now I say it—we have a lot of Family Conferences. OK, not a *lot*, and it's not as if they're scheduled or anything, although in practice they happen about once a fortnight, maybe. But they're not formal affairs. It's chatting, really. With rules. And anything we have concerns about, or the girls are worried about, we all talk it over. It's very civilized.

Interviewer—What kind of things would you talk about?

Juno—Oh, things like, Sophie wants to have her

navel pierced, she's been on about it for six
months. I suspect there's some rock star she's
trying to emulate. So we'd sit round and look at
the pros and cons, and I'd make her do some
research on the Internet about the dangers of
piercing, and we'd talk about, say, peer pressure
and media images and why it's important to
make one's own decisions in life.

Interviewer—So what would you do about the
piercing?

Juno—Then, I suppose, if she'd done all the
research and had a good think about it and she
still wanted to go ahead—in this actual case—
I'm afraid I'd still say no. Bad example! But I'm
not apologizing, putting one's foot down is part
of being a parent. Young people need their
boundaries. Otherwise, God knows what they'll
get up to.

*   *   *

I phoned Tom's work as soon as we got in and left
a message without going into detail. Manny had
the good grace to leave us on the doorstep, and
Juno's car still wasn't in the drive, so it was just me
and Ben. I installed him on the sofa with a bucket,
because he still looked greenish, although he
hadn't been sick in the car. He sat hunched at one
end with his back to the arm and his stockinged
feet up on the cushions.

'Do you want to tell me what happened?'

'Not really. Look, I'm not being cheeky or
anything.' He glanced over at the bucket, then
away again. 'But if I do tell you, will you go
through it all with Dad for me? I can't face a

double dose of disapproval.'

He'd thought that line up in the car, and decided it was safe to use with me. Not with his father, though.

'All right.'

'It was a dare.'

I sighed. 'A dare.'

'Yep.'

'And?'

'That's all.'

'You know I'm going to call Mr Hannant as soon as we've finished, don't you?'

He nodded and swallowed. 'OK. You must promise not to drop anyone else in it, though? 'Cause it wasn't just me, drinking. Only I won't tell you their names if you're going to pass them on.'

'Oh, Ben, what do you take me for?'

'Right.' He took a deep breath. 'What happened was, this boy, well, Felix, said he could drink more than me and I said he couldn't, so we did this game where you threw, flicked, little balls of wet paper, paper you'd chewed, off the end of a ruler, at the light shade and you tried to get them to stick. Stop looking at me like that, Mum, or I won't tell you the rest. And every time you missed, you had another swig of whisky. So it got, it got more difficult to aim the balls. And I ended up drinking loads more than Felix; he may not have been drinking at all now I think about it, it could have been a set-up. And then Mark said there was a forfeit if you lost, and I said it was the first I'd heard about it, but they all swore it was true. And the forfeit was to go outside and lie on the grass for half an hour. Except the doors were locked at nine, we'd been told that. But Mark said he'd

41

checked the kitchen window when we were washing-up and it didn't have a lock, so I could go through there. Climb into the sink, and out. And that's what I did. And it was so nice lying there on the moor, it wasn't cold like you might think, that I went to sleep there, and Mr Cottrell found me in the morning.'

I felt suddenly sick myself. 'So you could have died of hypothermia, in fact?'

'Not in this weather, Mum.'

'You weren't to know that. It could have dropped icy. Oh, God.' I put my hand to my brow and pinched the skin hard. 'Your dad's going to go up the wall.'

'I know.'

We sat in silence for a while, then I sent him to his room and phoned Mr Hannant.

I haven't the energy to be angry any more. Tom does angry in our house.

'What the bloody hell were you all playing at?' he stormed at me. So many people to be pissed off with. 'Did it not occur to you that I might have wanted to drive up there with you?'

If I could have lied about Manny being there, I would have. But I'm a useless liar, and Juno or Ben might have let it out at some point, and then it would have sounded *really* suspicious. It's crossed my mind in the past that Tom thinks I fancy Manny.

'I've already told you, I didn't want to waste any time getting to Ben.'

'Poking his big bloody nose into our business. I bet we'll have Juno round tonight, dispensing advice.'

I wanted to tell him that without Manny, I'd have panicked myself into collapse, that Manny had saved the day. But that would have been a very bad move.

'The main thing is, Ben's OK,' I said. 'At least he's safe. And all teenage boys drink too much from time to time. It's a rite of passage.'

'But wandering off! What a bloody idiot.'

'I know. I've been on to him. He does realize how stupid he was.'

'I should bloody hope so.'

'We all do daft things.' I thought of Bethany and the lunchbox, the clunk of impact and the way she'd jolted her head in shock; there was that to face tomorrow. 'He wouldn't be a normal teenager if he didn't get himself into trouble from time to time.'

Tom frowned. 'Hmm. S'pose so. Not like those freaky Stepford girls next door. They never put a foot wrong. Not yet, anyway.'

'I like Pascale and Sophie.'

'I know you do.'

'Are you going up to see Ben?'

'Uh-huh. Pour us a drink first, though, will you?' said Tom, the thin end of a smile on his face.

Later, about ten, I went to Ben's room myself. He was lying flat out with his headphones on, gazing at his map of the world stuck to the ceiling.

'You're going to have to come back downstairs again at some point,' I said, lifting one of the pads from the side of his head. 'Tomorrow morning would be good, so you could go to school.'

He switched his amp off, pulled the phones from his skull and sat up. 'So I'm definitely not suspended?'

43

'Mr Hannant never mentioned it to me. Anyway, the Head would have phoned us and told me not to let you darken his doors. I expect he will want to see you, so be prepared.'

'Do I have to go in? Half our year's still at Crawdale.'

'And half isn't. Including Felix, probably.'

'Yeah, he's home. I had a text off him an hour ago. Hannant found his gin supply round the back of the sink.' He grinned half-heartedly. I took the opportunity to hug him and he didn't protest.

'Go in tomorrow, get it over with, I say.' I smelt the cleanness of his hair, felt it with the skin of my cheek. 'Ben, is anything in particular troubling you?'

He broke away at once. 'No, Mum.'

'So I won't find you laid out on our back lawn at midnight tonight?'

'Mum?'

'Yes?'

'It wasn't just the dare, why I went out.'

I sat very still, like a naturalist waiting for a rare animal to come close.

'Mark did dare me, but I'd have told him to, you know, get lost if I hadn't wanted to do it. I wanted to be outside, sometimes I need to get out.' He closed his eyes. 'Does that sound mad to you?'

'Not at all,' I said.

CHAPTER FOUR

Two vans from Umanzu parked in Juno's drive tipped us off that the real filming had started.

'I thought you weren't going for another week?' I said to Juno when she came round to moan that one of them had backed into the outside tap and split the pipe.

'They're doing establishing shots, apparently. Some of the cameras are fixed, some of them are ones that you carry about, then there's a big thing on wheels. The one in the back bedroom is for Kim to talk to and record a video diary. There'll be another for me at her house.' We settled into the bay to watch the crew trailing wires around her porch. 'Listen, I came to ask, what happened at Meadowbank? What did Geraldine say, in the end?'

'Do you mean, have I still got a job? Yes, but with the proviso that I don't ever throw anything at anyone ever again. Which will be easier because Beth's now with Big Toddlers.'

'You've been separated?'

'One of the dads complained she was yakking on her mobile while she was supposed to be supervising playtime.'

'God.' Juno rolled her eyes. 'She's an accident waiting to happen, isn't she?'

'Geraldine says she's on her last warning, but that was still no excuse for lobbing a lunchbox at a trainee's head. She said I could have had the nous not to do it in front of an adult witness, because that meant her hands were tied. So I got a written warning, which is pretty severe, really.'

'You should contact your union.'

'I can't be bothered. Do you know, it all fades away to nothing in the light of Ben being OK; all of it, the whole awful day.'

A grey-haired man stepped out of Juno's front door and walked backwards across her lawn, scanning the roof.

'What's he doing? Counting jackdaws?'

'That's Kieran the producer,' she said, a little smile playing on her lips. 'I shouldn't say this—for goodness' sake don't repeat it to Manny—but I think Kieran and I have rather hit it off. He's terrifically charming.'

The man went in again.

I said, 'So, are you all packed?'

She blew at a hair that was lying across her face and smoothed it back behind her ear. 'It's not so much the packing, there's all sorts of preparation.'

'What, stuff they tell you to do?'

'Some of it. But a lot of it's just me. Such as minor redecorating, because you would, wouldn't you, if your house was going to be on TV? That back bedroom had marks all along the wallpaper where we used to have the blanket chest. And I wanted to stock the kitchen up with new herbs, because those old dried bunches by the sink have been there for eighteen months and they're more dust than plant. Just before I go I need to remember fresh flowers for every downstairs room, and I want to stock up the freezer, in case Kim can't cook.'

'Won't that be defeating the object? You don't want to make it too easy for her.'

'That's what Manny says. But I can't bring

myself to leave the house without topping up the food stores, call it a mother's instinct. Maybe I'll just get plenty of staples in; pesto, tomato purée, couscous, that sort of thing. Then anyone can throw a meal together.'

'Are you allowed to take food of your own?' I imagined her struggling out of the car with an armful of baguettes.

'No. But I can pack my echinacea and my evening primrose capsules. So if they have no fruit in the house when I get there, my immune system'll still cope. And I've been reading up.' She looked pleased with herself.

'On what?

'*Raising Boys*. It's this book by Steve Biddulph. It talks about how boys are different from girls and have specific parenting requirements.'

I couldn't help laughing at her earnestness. 'What, other than not kitting them out at Claire's Accessories? Oh, Juno, I could have told you that. Requirements such as, you don't ever ask them what they were up to in the bathroom all that time, and you don't go rooting under their beds, or hassle them when they first come home from school. I could write a bloody book on it.'

'You should!'

Only Juno could make a suggestion like this seriously.

'OK. Chapter One: never let them run out of deodorant. Chapter Two: don't buy own-brand coke. Chapter Three: on no account touch them in front of their friends. I'll ask Ben for you, get him to list the worst parent-crimes.'

'Ben's a sweetie. So low-maintenance.'

Well, I thought, apart from the odd drunken

midnight crawl across the moors.

'He's not a bad lad. But, Juno, you'll be fine. They're going to love you.'

She pulled a scared face. 'I hope so. I've spent a fortune on smartening myself up; cathiodermie facials, some new clothes—'

'Which you don't need.'

'And I've got to take Fing to the vet's tomorrow because he's definitely looking iffy, and it would be awful if he died on air. And I've just thought; I'll de-flea the carpet while I'm at it. Can you imagine if this Kim rolls up her trouser cuffs and reveals a rash of flea-bites to the nation? I'd never, ever live it down. Let me . . .' She took a pen off the table and wrote F on her hand. 'I'll get the girls to throw out some of their old magazines, too.'

'Juno?'

She swung her head up and smiled at me. 'Yes?'

'You're not regretting this *Queen Mum* project, are you?'

'No way.' She laughed. 'It's like Manny says; it's going to be an adventure.'

* * *

Lee—[To camera] The thing about Kim is, she's very warm, a very warm person. And easy-going. There's not a lot rattles her, really. I think she'll get on and have a good time, wherever she's going.

Oh, yeah, I think she'll get her own way. She's, I don't know, quite sneaky. God, she'll kill me for saying that! But what she does is, she asks you summat and you think you've decided one way, then a few weeks later, you find you've said the opposite. It's like magic. David Blaine. Except she swaps round words instead of cards.

She is quite strong-minded, she'll not suffer fools gladly. Mind you, neither will I. Life's too short to spend it pissing up a rope, oh, am I allowed to say that? Can you scrub that? What the hell; too late now. You've to take me as you find me.

Kim's mum [To camera]—I'll tell you two stories about our Kim. First, when she was about six, yeah, she decided she wanted some lipstick so she went rooting in my make-up bag and helped herself to some of mine. And she was parading round, you've never seen anything like it. I took it off her, I wiped her face and I said, You're not having that, you're not old enough, but we'll get some lip gloss tomorrow when we go to the shops. Thought that would keep her happy. Then I saw her two hours later with this bright pink mouth. I was all set to give her a good hiding when she goes, It's not your lipstick, Mum, I've made it myself. And she had. She'd mixed poster paint and Vaseline together in the top off a can of spray polish. So you see, she's always been determined. *[Becoming voiceover]*

And I'll tell you another: she'd just started in the juniors and she had a new friend, a lass who'd come from Malaysia. And we had this girl round to tea and Kim took a fancy to these hair slides she was wearing. They'd only have been plastic, but they had glitter mixed in so they were sparkly. I told Kim I'd get her some next time I went into town but she said you could only get them in Malaysia. So they went off to

49

play together and then when it was time for this Malaysian to go home, no hair slides. They'd been playing hairdressers, Kim said, and she'd taken them out. We looked all over the house, all in the garden because the girl was so upset, and I did wonder, actually. But I didn't say anything. And it was about, ooh, six years later I came across them in the bottom of Kim's jewellery box, hidden under the lining of a watch case, quite ingenious, really. So I said to Kim, 'Why did you take them? Because you must have known you couldn't wear them.' And she didn't have an answer.

[To camera] She won't thank me for telling you that. But it's true. She does like her own way, our Kim.

Kim [Voiceover]—Lee's a great bloke. We're a lot alike, I think that's one of the reasons we've stayed together. He works hard, and I do; we both like to chill out at the weekend; he's a home bird, and so am I. I'd say I take more of a pride in my appearance than he does, but that's just me. I wouldn't go out without lipstick on. No, he's very easy to live with. We don't argue so much, or if we do, it's usually over summat daft like whose turn it is to walk the dog. If I'm being honest, I do wish he'd help out round the house more, but then again, he's not as bad as some. And he does work damned hard in the day.

Lee [To camera]—Kim's a smashing mum. She knows when to back off, and you've got to with teenage lads; they don't want their mother

50

standing over them watching everything they do, do they? 'Cause I reckon that's the best thing a parent can do, don't you? Get them apron strings cut. Otherwise you're never rid. Kids'll be hanging round the house in their thirties. I can't wait for our two to leave home. *[Laughs]*

*   *   *

The night before Juno left, I got myself into a panic. Two weeks she'd be away. Which was absolutely not worth getting into a state about; good God, they once went to France to see Manny's mother and they were gone for a month. 'Yes,' said Tom in my head, 'and you were like a lost soul. *I* was counting the days till she came back, never mind you. Honestly, Ally, I think you'd rather it was me going away than Juno.'

I shuffled on the sofa next to him but he didn't look up from his magazine.

'Mrs Twitchy.'

I tried to concentrate on the TV but I'd missed the start of the programme, the crucial ninety seconds where you glimpse some important scene from the main character's past. I couldn't tell if he was the murderer or not and all the irony was falling flat.

'Can I text you?' I'd asked her.

'Not allowed. I communicate by phone or email, or meet anyone except Kim and Lee's immediate circle.'

'God. Do they have you under surveillance or something?'

She'd given an odd sort of giggle. 'It's what you sign up for,' she said. 'It's in the rules.'

51

Tom said, 'Are you watching this? Because if you're not, I'll turn it off. That music's getting on my nerves.'

'Has he killed that young girl?'

'Haven't a clue.' He sighed and flexed his magazine.

'OK. Turn it off if you want. Hey, what do you think this Kim's going to be like?'

'She'll be working class, won't she? That seems to be the general idea. Class War.'

'Do you think she'll spend the whole fortnight wearing trackie bottoms and eating pizzas out of the box?'

'Darling, your roots are showing.'

'How do you mean?' My hand went up to my scalp even though I knew he wasn't talking about hair dye.

Tom put the mag down across the arm of the sofa. 'You. You lived in tracksuit bottoms at one time, I seem to remember. And you've had your share of takeaway pizzas.'

I shrugged. 'Yeah, all right. You know what I mean, though.'

He didn't reply; his eyes flicked across to the glossy picture of the Bonneville next to him. He was thinking, Where on my garage walls can I put that? Or maybe he wasn't. Maybe he was thinking of the time we sat in front of the gas fire at 24 Crawshaw Road with me balancing a pizza box on my pregnant belly, that would have been just before Ben was born. The box kept jerking as the baby shifted. He said to me, 'There's a song, isn't there, like this; something about sitting by the fire with little kicks inside her?' 'Squeeze,' I'd said, "Up the Junction".' He'd dug it out and played it

52

and said, 'That won't be us, will it, splitting up after a couple of years?' We thought that was the worst that could happen to us.

'Do you think she'll be nice?'

'Who?'

'Kim.'

'No, because that doesn't make good TV. She'll be a certifiable harridan who'll spit at us over the fence and swear at Ben. I expect she'll bring her own Rottweiler.'

'Don't say that!' I was really alarmed.

'All right, keep your hair on,' Tom laughed. 'She's not moving in permanently, is she?'

'No, but I'm supposed to be popping in for lunch one day, keep the normal routine going.'

'So you said. As long as I don't have to have anything to do with it all, bloody circus.'

'What'll I do if she's really aggressive and horrible?'

'Forget it,' he sighed. 'I didn't mean to wind you up. She's going to be perfectly normal and balanced. If she was a total nutter they wouldn't have accepted her for the programme, would they? They've all had police checks and psychometric tests done, Manny was telling me about it.'

'So you think she'll be OK?'

'Oh,' said Tom, back in his mag, 'yeah, bound to be.'

'Honestly?'

'Oh yes.' He flicked a page and frowned. 'Not as nice as Juno, though. Obviously.'

I think he was joking with me, but I can never tell these days.

That night I couldn't sleep for queasiness. It felt as though I was waiting to sit an exam.

53

I was watching from the window the next day when Kim came. Tom said if I kept that kind of behaviour up I'd turn into one of those sad old women who sit around all day and spy on people with lives.

They filmed her walking down the drive and putting a key in the lock. She wore a fitted black jacket and blue jeans; a short woman with blonde hair, and a curvy figure, what they call a pocket Venus. When she bent to pick up her suitcase again, she paused, looked down by the doorstep and then plucked a piece of rosemary and sniffed it, before throwing it away. I was instantly outraged. Who was she to touch Juno's plants? I waited till the door closed, then went back into our kitchen and made some Horlicks, pacing around while the kettle boiled. I wanted so much to go round there and see what was happening.

Saturday morning; Manny would be at the computer, surfing the Internet or finishing a project. The girls would be cleaning out the rabbit, or getting ready to go shopping, or helping Juno strip the beds. I guessed she'd have sorted bedding out last night.

I hoped they were being kind to her in Bolton.

*   *   *

Kim—Hiya! Anybody home?
Sophie—Hi! Paxo, she's here! Dad?
Pascale—Hello. Can I take your bag?
Sophie—Dad'll be here in a minute. He's just
    putting some coffee on.
Pascale—Do you want to put your coat up there?

54

Here's Dad.

Manny—Lovely to see you. Come in, come in. Pascale, can you go and put the croissants in?

Sophie—Did you have a good journey? Oh, mind the cat, he always sits in the most inconvenient place, I'll shift him onto the piano stool then he'll still be in the sun. There. Do you want to sit down, Kim? Dad's making some coffee, how do you take yours?

Kim—Two sugars.

Manny—Soph, finish off in the kitchen, will you? Good girl. So, Kim, nice to have you on board. As soon as you've drunk your coffee, the girls will take you on a guided tour, not that there's a great deal to see. *[Laughs]* You certainly brought the weather with you. You wouldn't think it was only February. How was your journey?

Kim—Fine, thanks.

Manny—Here we are. Oh, Soph, you could have brought a tray. Never mind. Where've the mats gone? Who keeps moving the mats in this house? Tell you what, Kim, pop your cup on this magazine for now.

Kim—Nice room.

Manny—It needs redecorating, but that's Juno's department. She's the one with all the creative ideas. She's got an eye for style. Spends ages looking through her catalogues, sourcing door handles and the like. Are you interested in interior design? Ah, here come the croissants. That was quick, Pascale. Have you brought plates? Excellent. Kim, if I could pass that one to you. Would you like butter? And there's blackberry conserve. Help yourself. Don't worry

about crumbs, they're unavoidable with—
What's the matter, Soph?

Sophie—We've got that thing.

Pascale—Yeah. You know, Dad, that thing Mum worked out with us. For Kim. Soph, shift the cat will you so I can get at the piano?

Soph—Out, Fing. Go catch some rays. Shoo!

Pascale—OK. Are you ready? Hang on, I've got jam on my fingers. That's better. Right:

Sophie and Pascale [Singing]—

> We know you won't be staying long
> But here's a silly little song
> To say you're very welcome here
> We're friendlier than we appear
> Here's hoping, when we come to part,
> You'll keep the Kingstons in your heart.

Manny [Clapping]—Well done, girls! Did you make up the tune yourself, Pascale?

Pascale—It was the opening part to my Grade Four study, don't you remember?

Kim—Very nice.

Manny—Smashing. Aren't you keen on croissants, Kim?

Kim—Yeah, I like them. I'm not that hungry, I had a big breakfast. Lee cooked it me.

Manny—No problem. But your coffee's all right?

Kim—Fine. Actually, can I use your toilet?

Manny—Soph?

Sophie—Come with me. I'll show you where it is, and then we can take your case up to your room and you can unpack.

Pascale—And then we get to give you the guided tour.

Sophie—Yeah, the guided tour.

Kim [To video diary]—Well I'm here, for better or worse. First impressions: they seem very pleasant, very chatty. In fact I can't really get a word in. I'm worried I haven't come across right. I'm not a shy person normally, but I just got this barrage—Anyway, you can't say they're not making an effort. That song! It's like the bloody von Trapp family. It's a beautiful house, though. I should say there's some money here.

They're quite an exotic-looking family. Those girls, they're like gypsies, real head-turners, but they don't make the most of themselves. He's a bit full of himself, I'd say. Dead hairy too, you can see it coming out of his shirt at the neck. Mediterranean type; Greek, maybe? He kissed me on both cheeks, I've never had that before. Very nearly nutted him. Which wouldn't have been a great start.

No, I quite like the girls, I think we're going to be friends. Not sure about him.

Manny [To camera]—She seems a perfectly pleasant woman. Quiet, doesn't say a great deal. I expect we'll hear more from her tomorrow.

*   *   *

'I hope they're being nice to Juno,' I said to Tom as he helped me drain the rice. 'She's such a sweet person.'

'So go on, then, how are they managing next door?'

'Don't know. Haven't seen a sign of life since Kim walked up the path at ten o'clock. Have you?'

'You know I've been working in the garage all

57

afternoon. I've got better things to do than spy on neighbours.'

Ben came in, sniffing the air. 'Is tea ready? Or can I have a cheese string?'

'Yes and no. Stick these forks on the table and go sit down,' Tom told him.

'I know they'll be lovely with Kim, so it'll be easy for her. Juno ought to win, because she's such a good mum.' I tipped the stir-fry onto the plates. 'But if they're mean to her . . . '

'If the other family are horrible, then Juno'll get the sympathy vote. You know that, you've seen it in action. There was that dental assistant you told me about on the first series who cried because the kids kept hiding her stuff, and everyone felt sorry for her and rushed to the phones. She romped home. And she was in every tabloid, afterwards, spouting forth on manners; you showed me her etiquette column. No, the best way to show up the shortcomings of the new mum is to be ultra-pleasant. Reverse psychology. Not that I'm at all interested in any of it.

'So I ought to be hoping that Lee's a bit of a bastard?'

'I give up,' said Tom, and took the plates through.

It was six days later I got the email.

CHAPTER FIVE

Lee—You've to take us as you find us. If the
  Queen walked in here now, I'd be just same
  with her. I would. I treat everyone alike, me.
  'Cause that's fair, in't it? We're all equal if you
  strip us down to our underwear. *[Doorbell rings]*
  Hey up. Here we go.

Juno—Hi!

Lee—Hiya. Come in, come in. Smashing. Nice
  to—Good God, love, is that all your luggage?

Juno—I'm afraid so.

Lee—What, all them bags too?

Juno—Ooh, is this your doggy? Hell-o, sweetie.
  What's your name? Oops, ha ha, mind where
  you're putting your nose.

Lee—Get off, Marmite, for God's sake. Gyaah!
  Down! Kitchen! Aw, sorry about that. He's a
  devil for crotches. Has he marked your
  trousers?

Juno—Not to worry, I was going to change anyway.

Lee—They've no manners, dogs. I think he likes
  you.

Juno—I think he does, yes.

Lee—Oh, I see what you mean. Go on, out, you
  dirty devil! Never mind putting your sad face
  on. I dunno, if it's not your kids letting you
  down, it's your animals. Come through,
  anyroad. Boys? Hey, Chris, Marco! She's here!
  Are you coming? They'll not be a minute. We've
  been putting a fence in at the bottom of the
  lawn, where the tree fell down. So, is it what you
  expected?

Juno—I'm not sure what you—

Lee—This.

Juno—Oh. I think it's lovely. Lovely practical furniture. And a great view.

Lee—That's Belmont on the skyline, the moors. The view's not so great when you get closer to home. I bet it's nice where you live.

Juno [Laughs]—We like it. Hello! My goodness, you two look as if you've been working hard.

Lee—You could have washed your hands, lads.

Juno—Not to worry. Now, who's who?

Lee—Say hello.

Marco—Hello.

Chris—Hello.

Lee—Well? I give up. This is Marco and this is Chris. Men of few words.

Juno—It's nice to meet you both. I've got two daughters—

Lee—Hey, wait a minute, where are you off now?

Marco—Look at a motorbike with Martin. He's just rang, wants us go with him. It's over in Farnworth so we won't be long.

Lee—Can you not stick around for a while?

Marco—No, it was in *Loot*. If he hangs about, it'll be gone.

Lee—I don't know, it's not great timing, is it? Bloody bikes. You'll turn into a bike, you will. Go on, then. But be back for your dinner.

Marco—He might want us to go see another, after.

Lee—Tea, then. Honest. Lads. I bet your girls aren't in and out like a pair of tomcats.

Juno—Are they old enough for a motorbike?

Lee—No. But their mate is. I've told Marco I'll pay for his basic training when he hits seventeen; he's desperate. Chris is more into cars. Do your two drive?

Juno—They're much too young. Sophie's the older and she's only fifteen.

Lee—Same with Marco. Them two years'll fly past, you see. Mind you, the lads are very mature for their age, like. Can I get you a cup of tea?

Juno—That would be nice.

Lee—I'll show you the kitchen while we're at it, I know you'll want to have a good shufti round all the cupboards. Feel free, have a poke around. You can bet that's what Kim'll be doing at yours. Milk? Tell you what, I normally go out on a Saturday, but I'm staying in today. 'Cause of you, that is. You're honoured.

Juno—I see. Lovely. What do you do? When you go out, I mean.

Lee—Varies. Car audio competitions, football, scrap-yarding, all sorts. Kim goes off shopping, or round her mum's or her mates'. We like to do our own thing.

Juno—Right.

Lee—We all fall out if we're under each other's feet.

Juno—Oh.

Lee—Watch yourself, love. Dog's just behind you.

Juno—So what do you do together, as a family?

Lee—Good question. Let me think. Erm, not a right lot, now you ask. Christmas, holidays, that sort of thing, the normal bash. But the boys are growing up now, they need their space, and I reckon we've done our bit, more than. At the end of the day we're a family, not a ruddy string quartet.

Juno [To video diary]—OK, an interesting start.

61

Lee seems nice, fairly chatty, kind of . . .
uncomplicated. My room's fine, lots of
cardboard boxes and an exercise bike right next
to the bed, which might come in handy, you
never know. No, it's great, really. I've nowhere
much to hang my clothes, so I might be doing
quite a lot of ironing over the next fortnight.
Looking forward to catching up with the boys
again. I might do a pissaladière tonight for us
all.

It's going to be fun. Definitely.

Lee [To video diary]—I'll say one thing for her;
she's very tall.

That's about it.

*   *   *

First of all I had a dream that Dad had come back
and I was still a little girl. He was wearing a Red
Indian costume, headdress and all, and Mum was
anxious that we didn't mention it in case it drove
him away again. Then he turned into Peterson and
I realized why I hated him so much. When I woke
up, cross and thirsty, recalling the dream became a
real memory of the time Dad had taken me down
Great Fold Lane to teach me to ride a two-
wheeler. 'I'll hold onto you,' he'd said. 'I promise I
won't let you fall, trust me.' So I pressed on the
pedals and lurched away, weaved about for a while
and fell, breaking my wrist. When I looked back
through the tears he was waving at me.

*   *   *

Interviewer—What are you doing?

Lee—Good question. I'm scraping face-cream out of the kitchen bin. Does that answer you?

Interviewer—Why is there face-cream in the bin?

Lee—Because I thought I'd play one of my best jokes on Juno, welcome her to the madhouse, like—and she didn't appreciate it.

Interviewer—What did you do?

Lee—It's dead funny. Most people would have laughed their socks off. I don't know why she got so . . . God, look at that. Bloody great hair in it, now.

Interviewer—What happened?

Lee—Eh? Well, what you do is, you scoop out their Nivea or what have you and you fill up the pot with natural yoghurt or summat like that, summat you can eat. Not squirty cream, because it all goes to nowt. Plain yoghurt's best. Then you put it back and you go in later when the lady in question's at the dressing table, say she's getting ready to go out, and you go, Ooh, I'm hungry. And you—oh, I should say you have a teaspoon in your pocket—and you whip this teaspoon out and take the lid off the pot of face cream and dig in. You go, Mmm, delicious. It's hysterical. Should be.

Interviewer—Juno didn't find it funny?

Lee—Not exactly. She goes, Where's the original contents of the jar? Because that's Clarins Super-Restorative-something-bollocks and it's fifty quid's worth. I said, What, in that little pot? I said, You're having me on. The stuff Kim uses you get about a pint for two ninety-nine. So she goes, I hope you haven't thrown it away and I said, No, I put it in a margarine tub. Which was

63

obviously a lie. As you can see. Bloody hell, look at that. Do you think that's worth fifty quid? It's got tea leaves in it, that bit. Never mind, stir it round, it'll be fine.

*   *   *

There's no point fighting the night; I've learned this. So I always get up when I can't sleep.

I went downstairs in the dark, eyes pricking, and tiptoed across the cold tiles of the kitchen to fill the kettle. No lights on next door. What was Juno doing, now? While I waited for the kettle to click off I watched the shadows on the wall of the branches outside, remembered how baby Joe would sit transfixed at the sight of catkin-shadows on the blinds of the old house. 'That's his television,' Ben used to say. 'Channel Tree.'

I poured myself a cup of hot water and took it through to the front room where the computer is. I used to sit here a lot, in this tall, leather-backed chair in front of the glowing screen. There was one period where I got myself hooked on a bereavement forum, distraught parents posting their stories, swapping tragedy, one awful tale after another. I was thinking it helped. I wanted not to be the one who stood out in a group, to talk to people who might understand. Tom knew and didn't approve. But he let me get on with it until I became compulsive and started going on at all hours.

That was years ago, now.

I clicked on the Internet icon and dialled up, Googled the *Queen Mum* site to see if there was any news, although I knew there wouldn't be, not while they were still filming. Next I had a look at Friendsreunited—I am registered, but I haven't bothered with a profile because what the hell would I say?—but none of my classmates had done anything startling since the last time I looked. The current Favourites list was all Tom's bike sites and Ben's music, plus some soft-furnishing stockists I'd bookmarked yonks ago when we were doing up the front room. I thought I'd give up the Net as a bad job and go watch dead-of-night TV, but before I shut down I clicked on mail, just to see. Mainly Tom gets bike spam, Ben gets messages from his online fanzines, and I get advertisements for LaRedoute sales, penis enlargements and opportunities to make £££! from collapsing foreign dictatorships.

Plink. There were two emails; one went into Allison's Folder and one into the general inbox. I went to mine first.

MOV 232

was the title,

J   X

the text. I didn't recognize the Hotmail address of the sender, mymatemarmite, but I knew for sure who the *J* was. She must have got to a computer after the cameras were switched off. I read the title again. *232*? *MOV*? Nothing was making sense about that, so I went to the general inbox to see if there was any enlightenment to be had there.

Big Red-Hot Boys Ready 4 U! said the pulsating banner. A young man with his fringe in his eyes pouted underneath. *The BEST Gay Action!*

We hadn't had gay porn before. I scrolled down curiously. The page was set out like a teen-mag photo-story and the plot was two men in a garage

65

taking their vests off. Towards the bottom of the page they'd got to the stage of putting their hands down each other's pants. *To See More, Click Here* it said. *Get It All For Just $1!*

Then; *Please note: You have been sent this offer because your email was entered on our database.* Like hell it was, I thought. Bloody scam. Manny had told me how these things worked, the trawler programs that nicked your address off legitimate sites. *If you wish to unsubscribe, please check the box below and press Send.* Yeah, and then get twenty more from other dodgy porn-merchants. I added Bigredhotboys to the blocked-sender list, then deleted the page. Finally I went back to Juno's message, but it was still as cryptic as ever, so I shut the machine down and went to see what was on television. Gay action indeed.

*   *   *

Juno—See, I can understand there being no anchovies or Parmesan in, but really, who doesn't keep a packet of bread dough in the back of their cupboard?

Marco—Is it a pizza?
Juno—Sort of. It's called a pissaladière.
Lee—Oops, mind your language!
Marco—I don't like fish. Are they fish?
Lee—Scrape them off, it'll be all right. Hells bells, there are a lot of the little buggers, aren't there?
Juno—I used mature Cheddar instead of Parmesan because—
Marco—I hate it when I can see their eyes. Yuk. Like a big pile of slugs.

Lee—Come on now.

Marco—Who wants my slugs? Do you want them, Chris? Here you go, yum yum.

Chris—Get off.

Juno—If you don't want them, go and scrape them into the bin. Thank you.

Lee—He's never been keen on fish. Although he'll eat sweet and sour prawns in batter.

Juno—All right now?

Marco—Sorted. Yagh, you can still taste them. Slimy slime.

Chris—Can I have mine without olives?

*   *   *

By the time I came back to bed my feet were frozen. It was only 3 a.m. so the room was still dark, except for the red glow of Tom's digital clock. I lay down next to him, pulled the cover up to my neck and curled my body round his back to get warm.

It was then that I began to wonder.

*   *   *

Juno—So, ha ha, welcome to our family conference, and can I say right from the word go, this isn't about me and My Rules, it's about the family agreeing together and reaching a compromise. Because this week is about negotiation and not imposing. Yes? All right, then. First on the agenda is the cooking.

Lee—The boys are sorry they didn't eat your pizza.

Juno—It doesn't matter, honestly.

Lee—Fussy buggers, both of them. I don't know

where they get it from 'cause I'll eat anything, me. I was the only one who'd eat squid last year when we were on holiday.

Juno—Really, it doesn't matter, forget it. Only, I think . . . you see, what we do in our house is to give the girls an opportunity to get involved with planning and making the meals.

Lee—You hear that, lads? I bet I know what's coming.

Juno—Because there are all kinds of benefits. They're made more aware of the cost of food, and sourcing it, and within their budget they have to compare the qualities of various items, and then they're learning to cook, and to consider other people's tastes and requirements, I mean if somebody's a vegetarian or can't eat gluten, and I tell you, it doesn't half make them intolerant of faddy eaters when they're having to take into account so-and-so doesn't like pineapple and so-and-so's off mushrooms.

Chris—So you want us to cook your meals for you, then?

Lee—Hey up, lads. *[Laughs]*

Juno—No, no, certainly not, not all of them. But I think one a week's quite reasonable, don't you? Oh, come on, there's no need to look like that. It'll be fun.

Lee [Still laughing]—I agree. It's about time they stirred their stumps.

Chris—Thanks, Dad.

Juno—Great. Shall we say, then, Wednesday nights?

Chris—Both of them?

Juno—Yes.

Lee—Juno and I can put our feet up and watch telly while you slave away over a hot stove. Sounds good to me.

Lee [To camera]—I think it's good her making them get off their backsides and help out. Kim dun't do that, she leaves them to their own devices. Anything for a quiet life. But I don't think they know how to boil an egg, to be truthful. They can stick summat in the microwave, that's about it.

    Thing is, though, Juno's got their backs up. It's, I don't know, the way she speaks to you, I can't explain. And she definitely shouldn't have told them to take their posters of Jordan down.

Juno [To video diary]—I said to them, and I was quite reasonable; if you can justify the role of porn in society, you can keep your girlie pictures up. But they just went off in a strop. What can you do?

    That dog's been on my bed again, as well.

*   *   *

Looking back, did I set out to dislike her?

Before Kim and I met for our one and only lunch date, Kieran the producer came round and had a chat with me, talked about the aims of the programme, the target audience, the great feedback participants had got in the months after their episode had aired. I asked if he knew how Juno was getting on and he said no, that was in the hands of his colleague at the other house and they didn't communicate during filming. Liar, I

69

thought. So I asked how it was going at Cestrian Park. 'Good,' was all he gave me.

'How's Manny doing?' I said.

'Great.'

'And the girls?'

'They're great too.'

After a whole week there must have been something more to say, but he wasn't giving it up. He did tell me that they'd film Kim and me for about an hour, then edit it down to a couple of minutes at the most.

'You understand, we may even cut you out altogether?' I said I didn't mind. 'So, as far as you can, try to ignore the cameras. Do what you'd do if Juno was here,' he told me lightly.

I still expected it to be Juno when I walked into the kitchen, which is mad, I know. By rights I should have been nervous about being *on TV!* but I wasn't; the weirdness was not the men in black standing around with electrical equipment, but Kim being in Juno's place. She was sitting at the table but she got up straight away and came over to give me a hug. Her hair smelt of cigarettes. I wondered what Manny thought about that.

'Come in, come in,' she was saying, as if it was her house. The cameras wheeled back as she crossed the floor. 'Let me make a brew. I'm doing cheese on toast for us, is that OK? Or I can open a tin of soup.'

Her voice was husky, her tone friendly, and I should have liked the familiar Bolton cadences. But she was just wrong for the place.

'Cheese on toast is fine. Have you worked out where everything is?'

'Oh yeah. I had all the drawers and cupboards

70

out on the first day. She's a load of gadgets, your friend, han't she?'

As Kim moved round the room I took in again her shape—smaller than Juno, curvier—and her fair colouring. Unlike Juno, Kim wore full make-up, and her hair was sleek and straight. A good cleavage, and she wore her faded jeans well, with little black boots. I got the impression she was enjoying the cameras on her.

'How are you getting on with the girls?'

'Oh.' She turned from the grill. 'Brilliant. They're smashing. I tell you, we get on like a house on fire.'

My heart swelled with pride on Juno's behalf. 'They are lovely, aren't they? Very polite, and mature.'

'Yeah, I said to Lee before I ever came, I'll get the girls on my side from the start. Everything else'll follow.'

You seem pleased with yourself, I thought.

Over the meal I got chance to look at her face more closely. She had a few lines round her eyes and her mascara was too thick. But she'd been pretty, in an obvious sort of way.

'And how do you get on with Manny?'

'Oh, Manny.' She flicked her hair back over her shoul-der. 'Yeah, he's coming round. He was a bit . . . you know, stand-offish at first.'

'That doesn't sound like Manny.'

'I think it was just, we'd got off on the wrong foot. He didn't like me smoking in the house, fair enough, so we agreed I'd go outside, I'm trying to cut down anyway. But then he picked up this book I'd brought, 'cause I knew Juno didn't work so I thought I'd be sitting around a fair while, and he

71

sort of sneered at it.'

I thought of Sunday lunches we'd had together at the pub, Manny sharing out the paper, separating the supplements and passing them round. 'Which are you most in need of,' he always said to Tom, 'Style or Culture?' Great joke.

I shrugged. 'I'm sure he didn't mean to. He sometimes looks stern even when he's happy.'

'Whatever. He came in later with another book and said'—she put on a posh voice—' "Have you ever read Emily Lincoln? She writes the most amazing characters, and they're from your part of the world." '

'He recommends her to everyone. He met her on an arts course once, that's all.'

'Oh.' Kim licked the edge of her hand where the cheese had caught it. 'I see. Anyway, Tuesday he goes, "Let's watch a video," and he showed me this black-and-white film about—I couldn't tell you what it was about, to be honest. There was a cow on a bed at one point. Bloody weird.'

I smiled. 'I know the one you mean. It's part of a surrealist collection he has. He's got a thing about them at the moment.'

'Then we went to the theatre, that was Thursday, and saw this play about a woman who was kept in a box because her dad had been a bear. That was the plot. I clapped at the end but I can't say I got what was going on. So, all in all,'—she leaned across the table to me and lowered her voice, which was a pointless exercise with microphones everywhere—'I'm feeling thick.'

I wondered what would happen if I went, 'Yes, you probably are.' I said; 'You shouldn't feel that way. It's just that Manny has this tremendous interest in the arts because of his job. It makes us all feel inadequate from time to time.'

She beamed. 'You're a love. He's all right, I'm having a nice time. But, I tell you what, do you know what I said to him when we came out of the theatre? I said, "This isn't *Educating Rita*, you know." I was laughing but I sort of meant it. I think he's under the impression I spend all my time watching *Coronation Street*.'

'I'm sure he's not,' I said.

While I filled a washing-up bowl, Kim went to the back door for a cigarette.

'So, tell us about your friend,' she said over her shoulder. 'How do you think she'll be coping round at mine?'

Where to start. 'I was hoping you'd be able to give me an idea about that, actually.'

Kim raised her eyebrows but said nothing.

'Well, you know she doesn't work. But she's not idle. As you'll have found out this week. She does a stack for charity—'

'I know, I've been in the hospice shop all morning. I've had ironing up to my eyeballs, like I don't get enough with Lee and the lads.'

'—and she gives a lot of time to the girls. She likes home-making, gardening, cooking. She's fairly tidy and organized. She's a very kind person and she's, oh, bristling with energy, all the time. She's a terrific organizer. Say, if you wanted to throw a party, Juno would have the ideas and the drive to make it go with a swing. Last year she did a Mexican one with a piñata hanging from the beech and we all had to take turns—'

'I prefer my parties spontaneous; you know, everyone piling back after the pub. I can't be doing

73

with too much planning.'

'Juno's spontaneous too.' I knew how stupid I sounded. I tried a different tack. 'So, what changes have you made this week?'

'Oh!' she laughed. 'Nothing specific. You spend a few days just sussing out how everything normally works, do you get me? Like, the way Juno's got them all in a rota with the washing-up and meals, fantastic. So I haven't mucked about too much with that. But they've a funny set-up with the TV, I think they only watch one programme a night or something. And they're always, what, *around* you. My lads, they spend three-quarters of their lives shut away in their bedrooms, you wonder what they get up to, or perhaps you're best off not knowing. I'd say, generally speaking, they need to loosen up.'

'Who? Sophie and Pascale?'

'All of them.' Kim exhaled smoke into the garden. 'I've got some ideas up my sleeve for next week. Should shake them up. In a fun way.'

'Oh,' I said. 'Right.' I wanted to argue that Juno was fun too but I didn't know how to say it without it sounding limp. 'Listen, from what you know of Juno and your family, what do you think she'll be doing in your house this week?'

Kim gave a half-smile and leant her temple against the door jamb. 'Banging her head against a brick wall, I should think,' she said.

Blue smoke curled up above her, off into the sky.

*   *   *

Juno—I don't find this funny.
Lee—Yeah, but, you've got to give them ten out of

ten for initiative. And there's no washing-up, so it's also labour-saving.

Marco—And you did a pizza. How come your pizza's OK but our pizza's wrong?

Chris—'Cause we even got a variety of toppings, so if somebody dun't like chilli—

Lee—He's got a point. Very thoughtful, lads.

Juno—The whole idea, and you know this, was for you to plan and shop for ingredients and then to cook a meal from scratch. Not to pick up the phone and have it delivered ready-made to your door. Apart from anything else, it's not cost-effective. How much was all this?

Marco—Did you get any change, Chris?

Chris—Three quid.

Marco—Twenty-two pounds.

Juno—You see, you could have cooked an absolute mountain of pasta, popped in some lovely fresh veg, for about a quarter of that, do you see? I'm not being snobby here, it's not that I have a problem with fast food per se—

Lee—Where did you get the money?

Marco—It's ours. Our allowance. She should be grateful we spent our own money on her.

Juno—How much money do you give them a week, Lee?

Lee—A tenner each.

Juno—A tenner? Each? My girls get half that, and they have to do jobs to earn it.

Marco [Whispers to Chris]—Poor buggers.

Juno—Thank you for that.

Lee—Look, love, I'm going to say summat now, and I don't want you to think I'm being rude, but I earn a good wage and I'm blowed if I'll see my lads go short. 'Cause why else do you work, if it's not to treat your family? They're good boys, on the whole, but they want to go out with their mates, enjoy themselves while they're young.

Juno—But don't you think it's teaching them money comes too easily? Do you show them how to budget at all?

Lee—I think the best way to learn with money is to make your own mistakes. And, I have to say, Juno, I know what your husband earns and I think you could afford a sight more than a fiver a week on your girls. I'd be the last person to accuse someone of being tight with money, but, honest . . .

Chris—I got you olives on your pizza, see.

Marco—She's crying, Dad.

Lee—Oh, bloody hell.

Juno—It's all right. I'm fine. It's just been a long week. I'm missing Manny. I'm fine.

Lee—Come on, love. Marco, pass us some kitchen roll.

Juno—Why won't you work with me?

Chris—I got a Viennetta for afters.

CHAPTER SIX

That night Tom and I had the sad, clinging-together sex that we sometimes have these days. There were months when, after we went to bed, we lay apart, weighted down against the mattress with grief. Then, about a year after Joe died, we had a period of really frantic sex, I don't know why or where it came from. Possibly we were trying for another baby; I left my cap out once or twice but I never conceived. Just as well. I'm not sure I could have opened myself up to all that potential heartbreak again. Now the sex we have is, what, desperate; Tom holds me tight as he can, pushes so far into me I can feel him in my guts, like a faint labour-twinge. Once he burst into tears afterwards, but when I tried to talk to him about it he threw the covers back angrily and took himself off to the bathroom, locking the door.

I often find myself wishing someone would tell me what the rules are for bereavement.

So we had sex, then Tom turned the light out, and then he suddenly asked about Kim. 'How did your lunch thing go?'

I hadn't reported it in any detail because I thought it would make him cross. 'All right,' I said cautiously into the darkness. 'I told you, she seems OK.'

'Really?'

'She comes over as quite warm.' I hesitated, remembering her smile, her hair flick. 'A no-nonsense sort, that's how she likes to present herself. But I get this feeling about her, that there's more going on. I felt slightly . . . probed. Manipulated. No, that's too strong a word. I wasn't there long enough to tell. You can't know someone in an hour, can you? And yet. I'd say there was a hardness under all the friendly chat. I think she's putting on a front.'

'Don't we all.'

Next door's outside light lit up the edge of our curtains and I thought, I bet that's Kim having a fag on the doorstep.

'Let's face it,' said Tom, 'you were never going to clasp her to your bosom.'

Mov, I thought. What was Mov? I said, 'I just hope she's not going to upset Juno when she gets back.'

'Bit late to think of that now, isn't it?' said Tom.

*   *   *

Juno—I only asked if we could have the TV off while we ate. I'm not a snob, I just think too much TV makes you passive, that's all.

*   *   *

I'd only just got back in from work when the phone rang. I'd made myself a drink and was pulling wet sheets out of the washing machine, so I wasn't best pleased.

'Yes?'

'It's Mr Tate here.'

Ben's headmaster. My breath caught in my throat.

'Am I speaking to Mrs Weaver? Ben Weaver's mother?'

78

'Yes.'

'I wonder if you could come along now to the school and have a word.'

'Is he all right?'

'I'd say he was, although he'll have a few bruises. I'm afraid he's been fighting.'

Fighting? Ben? 'But is he hurt?'

'Only superficially. We stopped them before it got too serious. He has bitten another boy, though, and I'm concerned that it might be a nasty wound; the lad's been run up to A and E, in fact. So it's quite important that you get here as soon as you can and we talk this through. Ben's waiting in reception.'

This time I did call Tom. More than my life was worth not to. 'Fuck,' he said. Then: 'Don't go overreacting, will you? Get there and just hear the story. I'll be with you as soon as I can.'

I quite liked Mr Tate. He brought Ben into his office straight away and sat him down opposite me, so we were all three in a triangle. Mr Tate had the advantage of a desk, mind.

'Do you want to tell your mum what happened, Ben?'

I'll say this for Ben, he doesn't usually lie. He doesn't say much, but what comes out tends to be the truth.

'Patrick Neale's been calling me names,' he said without looking up. 'He's been hassling me for weeks. He's been leaving notes in my locker. Today he left some rubbish.'

'What do you mean, rubbish?'

Mr Tate said, 'Patrick hung a tampon from Ben's locker handle.'

'Oh, God.' No wonder Ben bit him, I wanted to

79

say. Christ! Little git. 'That's horrible.'

'A clean one, I should add. But yes, it is a horrible thing to do.'

Ben drooped in his chair.

'Why would he do that? What's his quarrel with you?'

Ben shook his head. 'I don't know. It was someone else last year. This year it's me. I'm the victim of choice.'

'Not such a victim,' said Mr Tate. 'That was a nasty injury you gave Patrick. We take that kind of violence very seriously in this school.'

'What's he been calling you? Have you kept any of these notes?'

Ben sighed. 'No, Mum.'

'Why not? You could have shown them to Mr Tate.' I turned to the head, wishing Tom would hurry up and make an appearance. 'Because, look, if Ben's been provoked, I mean he's not the sort to lash out on a whim; if he's been *subjected*'—this was the right tone, I'd got it now—'to repeated bullying, to systematic abuse from a boy who's *known* to have picked on others, I'd say he was probably acting in self-defence. In fact, what anti-bullying procedures do you have in place here? It's all very well saying he should have gone to a member of staff, that's what teachers always say, but we both know that isn't always practical.' I'd run out of steam. I sat back in my chair, heart racing.

Mr Tate leaned forward as if he were imparting a confidence. 'Mrs Weaver, let me tell you now I do believe Ben, even in the absence of the notes. He says they were abusive and I'm sure he was right.'

'But what did they say?'

Mr Tate stood up. 'Ben, can I ask you to wait outside for a minute?'

Ben stood up at once and made swiftly for the door. As soon as we were on our own, Mr Tate said, 'When boys get to a certain age, they can become very fearful. Very insecure. You think what society throws at them, some of the images they see in the media.'

I was nodding, but I didn't get it.

'And one of the ways in which this general fear can manifest itself is, I regret to say, homophobia. Which is what's been going on here. Patrick's been calling Ben gay, and putting notes to that effect in his bag and under his locker door, and he wrote something in the boys' toilets too which I saw and I've had cleaned off.'

'But a tampon? Why would they think gay men used tampons?'

'There's no logic in it,' sighed the head. 'It's fear, ignorance. And confusion about themselves, their own sexuality. Calling someone gay is the stock insult of the adolescent boy.'

'Ben isn't even effeminate. There's nothing about him that would suggest—' I stopped short.

'Mrs Weaver, it makes no odds. I'm sure Patrick doesn't believe his own accusations, it's just something he knows will wound. Look, I heard one of the Year Eights say a Play-Station game was gay. It's becoming almost a meaningless adjective.'

Not meaningless to me.

Do you think he is? I wanted to ask Mr Tate. What can I do about it? Is it my fault? Mr Tate, I was on the computer the other night and I found—

There was a knock on the door and Tom walked

in. I could have run up and hugged him.

'Ben's being bullied and he's bitten a boy in self-defence,' I gabbled as the head leaned over to shake Tom's hand. Tom pulled the other chair next to me and sat down. He reached across and touched my forearm. 'It's OK, I'll take it from here,' he said.

*   *   *

I ached to phone Juno. 'He's been suspended,' I'd say. 'Can you believe it, our mild-mannered Ben. One more incident and he'll be in a serious mess. I don't know what's going wrong.' Juno would say something like, 'Don't worry so much. He's got an excellent track record so far. His teachers'll understand these are only blips. Anyway, that bully sounds as if he got what he deserved. They probably want to give him a Merit Mark for it but they can't for fear of setting a precedent—you know, Speech Day, visiting dignitary awarding the Silver Molars Cup for Biting Wrongdoers—it wouldn't look good.'

Tom was brilliant with the head. I went outside and sat in reception with Ben, the secretary ignoring both of us. I don't suppose she can get involved. I bought Ben a Twix from the machine by the door because I didn't know what to say that wouldn't make it worse. 'Thanks,' he said, but he didn't eat it.

Then we drove home. Ben disappeared upstairs and Tom poured us a glass of brandy each which we drank in the kitchen. I waited for him to ask whether I thought Ben was gay, but he didn't. He seemed somehow pleased.

82

'What are you going to say to him?' I asked eventually.

'I thought you could go and have a talk with him. You're good at that sort of thing. I sorted out Tate for you.'

'Are you cross?'

'Who with?'

'Ben.'

Tom finished his brandy at a gulp. 'No way. I thought the boy done good. This Patrick'll think twice before he picks on Ben again, won't he? Tate thinks the same, although he'd never admit it. The trouble with schools is that, when you get right down to it, the kids are animals. You can lay down every rule you like but, at a basic level, it's the law of the jungle. I think what Ben did was exactly right. Let's hope the little bastard's hand goes septic and drops off.'

'What did you think of the notes?'

'I think it's a bloody good job Tate believed Ben. That's a decent man, actually.'

I don't know why I didn't tell him about the website.

Yes I do.

*   *   *

Chris—You can't do that! You can't! That's going the wrong way!

Marco—So?

Chris—Because it's not in the rules! You can't just decide to go backwards.

Juno—Marco, put your counter back where it was and throw again.

Chris—Yeah, and he'll chuck it under the table

83

where we can't see, and say it was a six, like he did last time. You're such a cheating git, Marco.

Lee—Now, lads.

Juno—Come on, boys. It's only a game. Marco, throw the die on the table.

Chris—See? See? He's done it again.

Marco—Six. Fancy that.

Marco—Why can't we have Club Reps on? They bleep out the swearing.

Juno—Because we agreed it would be nice to have the TV off tonight and spend some time together.

Marco—Like bollocks it would.

Lee—Watch yourself.

Chris—It's pants, this. I hate board games.

Juno—Do you really think you've given it a chance? Do you think you've given me a chance?

Lee—Thing is, Juno, they're too old for this stuff. Let them watch their programme.

Juno—I said they could tape it.

Lee—Oh, go on, switch it on, Chris. Yeah, go on. I've had enough of Ludo too. I never liked it as a kid.

Juno—So you're just walking away.

Lee—Looks like it.

Juno [To camera]—Do you see what I'm up against?

*   *   *

Ben was on the PlayStation when I went up, killing Rhinocs.

I sat near him and watched for a while until he got clumsy and fell into a volcano. He put the

84

console on the desk and turned round.

'Did you draw the short straw?' he asked.

'How do you mean?'

'You get to deliver the pep talk.' He didn't say it cheekily; his voice sounded tired.

'Spot on.'

'OK, then.' He settled back and looked straight at me. His lovely eyes were Joe's, mine. 'Fire away.' Let's get it over with, he meant.

I said, 'Are you in any kind of trouble? Apart from this incident with the bully.'

'No.'

'Have you any idea why he targeted you?'

'Wrong place at the wrong time, that's all.'

'What do your friends think?'

'What of?'

'Well, the notes.'

Ben shrugged. 'Not a lot. Shit happens. If it wasn't me it would be one of them. People are posting weird stuff in lockers all day. You just chuck it in the bin. Usually.'

'So why did you bite Patrick this time?'

Ben frowned as though he were considering deeply. 'Don't know,' he said at last. 'Bad day, I guess. He smirked at me and I was like, That's it, I've had enough. And all I wanted to do was knock him over, but he put up more of a struggle . . . Then the dickhead put his hand actually in my mouth. We were on the floor—I've been through all this with Mr Tate.'

'OK.'

'You'd have done the same. Dad would, anyway.' I swallowed, because we were getting nearer to the question I had to ask. 'Do you understand why it's so important for you to keep out of trouble for the next, for the rest of the year?'

'Yeah. Tate told me that two conduct interviews so close together was major bad news. He goes, *Theoretically it could be expulsion next time.* Although I don't believe that; I mean, there are kids loads worse than me.'

'I shouldn't bank on it.' I reached over and stroked his hair. He stiffened slightly, but bore it. 'Seriously, keep your nose clean. It's not like you to get hauled up in front of teachers. You've always had good reports.'

'I'll try, Mum.'

'You're not made for crime.'

He smiled. 'That's true. It was something, though, flooring Patrick; you know, a buzz. I can see the appeal of being a sadistic thug.' He saw my face. 'Only joking.'

But I was scared because I knew what was coming. 'I have to ask—Ben—'

'What?'

'Are you gay?' The words stuck like needles. My heart was hammering.

'*What?*'

'Because it wouldn't matter, it would be OK if you were.'

'Jesus, Mum!'

'We'd still love you. Nobody would—I wouldn't—'

'I'm not.'

'We wouldn't get angry with you. But it's a hard road to travel on your own—'

'*I'm not!*' He half-rose from his chair and I wondered for one mad moment whether he was going to hit me.

'All right, all right,' I said soothingly. 'Only, I

wanted to ask, because it must be very difficult telling people—'

'I'm not gay. Now, can you leave it, Mum? Please?'

He swung back round in his chair and started up the game again. There could be no mention of the website this time.

*   *   *

Tom came out to see what I was doing in the flowerbed.

'Are you more or less ready for your tea?' he asked, before he spotted my tears. 'Oh.'

'I was getting some polys in,' I sniffed. I needed to wipe my nose but I had soily gloves on. Tom fished in his trouser pocket and pulled a hanky out for me, held it to my nose.

'Blow.'

I did as I was told, then ran my forearm across my cheeks.

'Anything specially the matter?'

I showed him the Early Learning Centre plastic trowel that I'd dug up.

He nodded. 'There were a load of little cars down the back of the bookcase when I shifted it to do the painting last summer.'

'You never mentioned it.'

'No. I didn't want to upset you.'

I stood up and took him in my arms. After a while, he said, 'I'd best go in and turn the potatoes down.'

Four days till Juno came home.

*   *   *

Gill—We think she's lovely. We do. She's coping really well.

Kim—Get away, it's only being pleasant with people.

Gill—There's not everybody can do that. But you should see that stack of clothes she's ironed in the back. And we've had hundreds of customers in this morning.

Mary—They all want to see the TV star.

Gill—I like this music Kim's brought in. We normally have the radio on, but she's brought in this CD of summer hits and we've all been having a boogie, haven't we, girls?

Kim—Get that blood pumping.

Mary—She's brought a flush to my cheeks, that's for sure.

Gill—We've had a laugh this last two weeks. I shall be sad to see her go. I don't know, she's sort of . . . brightened the atmosphere, wouldn't you say, Mary?

Kim—Aw, y' are sweet.

*   *   *

I tried to think what Juno would do. *Get advice*, I could hear her saying. *Don't try to go it alone.* So I trawled through the phone book and wrote down every advice-line number I thought would help, then hid the sheet of paper in my jewellery box. I wasn't ready to phone anyone yet. On the Thursday afternoon I went straight from nursery to the library and took out the video of *Queer as Folk*. I watched it till 3 p.m., then scooted back to the library and returned it. What I'd been hoping for

88

was to be let in on some gay code, some telltale sign that I could check against Ben, but there wasn't anything. With drugs you look for blackened tinfoil, I know, and little tablets with pictures on; we had a leaflet on it from his school.

I died a thousand deaths when Tom came back in from surfing the Net that evening and casually announced, 'We don't half get some weird spam these days.' Ben was upstairs, thank God.

'Like what?'

'Hot Nude Teens Roll in Fur.'

I frowned. 'Pardon?'

'You heard. Don't ask me for details because I deleted it. Have you been posting our email address on your self-help forums again?'

'I might have,' I lied.

'Do you think you could un-post it, ASAP? Only it'll be donkeys next, or worse. I'm utterly sick of loan offers too.'

'Will do,' I said, my voice high and scared-sounding.

I don't think Tom noticed.

*　　　*　　　*

Kim [To camera]—The little beggars have hidden my cigs.

Sophie [To camera]—Yeah, we've taken her cigarettes because we're trying to help her. We know she doesn't want to smoke, she told us she was trying to give up. So we're helping, aren't we, Paxo?

Pascale—Yep.

Kim—I know you've got them. If you don't give them me back, I'll only go out and buy some more. You're just making yourselves look stupid.

Pascale—Don't say that. We're trying to make it easier for you—

Sophie—Because we like you—

Pascale—Have you any idea what smoking does to you? Mum said, when we went up to secondary school, we could completely make up out own minds about it but we had to research it first.

Sophie—Did you know it can give you oral cancer? Like, make your tongue rot in your mouth, or your lip fall off?

Pascale—And it can make you lay down fat round your waist, and shrivel your skin up, and cause osteoporosis and heart disease and emphysema—

Sophie—And when you inhale, you take over five hundred chemicals into your lungs, with the tar, a whole cupful a year, and nicotine, and carbon monoxide which is what comes out of your car exhaust and people use to commit suicide.

Pascale—So you don't want to end up a wheezing barrel-shaped wrinkly with no lips, do you?

Sophie—And possibly dead too.

Kim—Back off, girls. Bloody hell.

Sophie—We're only trying to save you from yourself.

Kim—OK, right; what if I don't want saving? What about freedom of choice? I'm an adult, I can decide what I want to do with my body. It's my life.

Pascale—You haven't got freedom of choice. You're in thrall to the weed.

Kim—Look, just give me my bloody cigarettes, will you?

Pascale—No way.

Sophie—You'll thank us in the end.

Kim [To camera]—Bloody stuck-up pair of know-it-alls. Who do the hell do they think they are?

Kim—Tell you what.

Pascale—What?

Kim—I've got an idea. I'll do a deal with you.

Pascale—What sort of a deal?

Kim—I know something you want.

Pascale—Huh?

Kim—Something that we'd have to do in town. At the beautician.

Sophie—Do you mean more piercings? Yeah? Oh, fantastic! Really?

Pascale—Are you saying Soph can get her navel done?

Kim—I'm in loco parentis. It's no big deal, anyway, loads of women have them. We'll do it at a proper clean place. My treat. And if your mother dun't like it when she gets back—

Pascale—I can tell you, she won't.

Kim—You can just take it straight out again, no harm done.

Pascale—What do you think, Soph?

Sophie—I think you should get your ears re-done.

Pascale—Oh God. Yeah. Let's do it.

Kim—And?

Pascale—Oops; they're in Sophie's violin case, in the hall. Hope they're not bent.

Kim—So do I, love, so do I.

I was closing the upstairs curtains in the front bedroom when I saw Manny's car draw up; that would have been the Thursday evening. I stood and watched as the doors opened and Manny, Kim and the girls piled out. They were laughing about something; Sophie had a stick of yellow rock and was poking Pascale in the back with it. Kim was wearing a headband with white furry ears that stuck up like a rabbit. Manny had on a coat I'd never seen before. I waved but they didn't see me.

'What's that row coming from Juno's house?' asked Tom later. We could hear the beat even across the space between the walls.

'I don't know. It sounds like . . . it's Wham! Listen: "Baby, I'm your man". Do you think they're having a party or something?'

'If they are, we haven't been invited,' he said crisply.

CHAPTER SEVEN

Juno—So is this your local?

Lee—Yeah.

Juno—Lovely.

Lee—What are you having?

Juno—Dry white wine, please. Thanks.

[To camera] This is very pleasant. A little loud,
   maybe, but—

Lee—There you go.

Juno—Do you know, I can never understand how
   those fruit machines work. The lights alone
   make me dizzy. Have you seen, it's like a
   control panel at NASA. Which buttons are you
   supposed to push? They seem terrifically
   complicated to me.

Lee—Do they, love? Right.

Juno—What sort of beer is that?

Lee—Boddington's.

Juno—I ask because Manny's quite interested in
   beers, he's got quite a collection. Fascinating
   names, Bishop's Toe and Sheep Waggler and all
   that.

Lee—Oh aye.

Juno—Do you like those sort of beers?

Lee—Never had them.

Juno—This wine's very nice—

Lee—What? Were you going to say, 'considering'?

Juno—No. I was going to say I wondered if it was
   French or New World. Don't be so touchy. Let's
   enjoy the evening out. It's the first one I've had

since I've been here.

Lee—You're unlucky Mandy Flatters is away, or you could have gone round there. Kim's always round her house yakking, they were at school together. Mind you, if you think our dog's bad you should see theirs.

Juno—Don't you and Kim go out together?

Lee—Yeah, we do. A bit. Depends how tired I am after work. More often than not I flop down in front of the TV and that's it, I'm gone. It's hard making the effort sometimes. Building's so physical, it takes it out of you.

Juno—What sort of places do you go to?

Lee—Here, for a start. It varies. Anywhere. The pictures. Sometimes Kim books a meal. Why all the questions? Where do you and Manny go, then?

Juno—I don't know why you're so touchy tonight. Have I said something wrong?

Lee—Hang on a minute.

Juno [To camera]—I assume he's just gone to the gents', not done a runner. What is the matter with the man? Kim told me he was laid back.

Lee—That's better. Look, love, I'm not really in the mood for it tonight.

Juno—Why, what's bothering you? Is it me? Can I do anything to help?

Lee—Just missing my wife, if you want to know. So no, not really.

Juno—Oh.

Lee [To camera]—I can see she's trying. God, though, in't she skinny? I'd never really noticed before tonight. She's nothing—you know. At the front. I reckon Manny should invest in one of them Wonderbras next birthday.

*   *   *

I kept humming to myself all morning, although I never especially liked that song. *If you're gonna do it, do it right.* The tune was still going through my head when there was a tremendous knocking at the back door. I could make out through the glass Kim, and the black bulk of a camera behind her. For two pins I'd have pretended I wasn't in but it was too late, they'd seen me.

'Hi,' I said awkwardly. If only I'd had time to run a brush through my hair.

'Look,' said Kim, holding out her hands like Oliver Twist. Her face was grim. 'Can you help?'

I stepped back and she followed me in. 'Look,' she said. 'Look.'

In her cupped palms, on a folded pad of kitchen towel, was a great tit. It lay on its back with its claws curled against its body and one wing splayed out slightly. Its breast heaved.

'Bloody cat,' said Kim. 'I had to chase it all round the garden before I caught it. Then I couldn't get the damn bird out of its mouth. I think it might be injured.'

I could see it was dying. 'Yes,' I said.

'I didn't know what to do with it. I thought you could help me.'

'Help you?'

'Can you phone a vet?'

The bird's beak opened and its tongue stuck out like a leathery worm. It looked as if it was

95

screaming.

'It's going to die, Kim.'

We leant over as she laid the bird carefully on the table.

'I can't see any blood.'

'No. It might have internal injuries, though, it might be bleeding inside. Sometimes they die of fright, too.'

'Uh.' She pulled a face. 'Shall I put it back outside, under a bush or summat? Let it die in peace?'

I shook my head. 'Fing'll get it for sure.' I watched its tiny chest strain up and down. When the yellow feathers ruffled from my breath, there was grey skin underneath. Why did she have to bring it round to me? 'Leave it here. I'll keep it quiet till it goes.'

'There's no one in next door. I thought you'd know what to do,' she said. 'You look so capable.'

My head whipped up to see whether she was joking, but she didn't seem to be. 'I'm terrible with suffering,' I said.

'Do you think we should put it out of its misery, then?'

'You mean, will *I* put it out of its misery?'

Kim looked away.

I've never done anything like that, killed a living animal. I even shoo woodlice out of the door (Tom steps on them). But the little thing was in pain, you could see that. 'I think you have to do it quickly, a sharp tug. Juno killed a chicken, once.'

We leaned over the bird together.

'You want to stroke it, don't you?' said Kim. 'Soothe it. Or do you think that would give it more stress?' Her index finger straightened but in the

96

instant before she could touch the quivering down, we saw the eyes glass over and the bird was dead. 'Oh! Like a candle going out,' she said wonderingly.

I might have cried if it hadn't been for the cameras. I wanted her to go, but at the same time I didn't want to be on my own.

'Do you fancy coming round for a drink?' she said. 'I could just do with a cider.'

'I don't know.'

'Come on,' she said, taking me by the arm. 'I need one. After that.'

'What about the bird?'

'Give it here,' she said, and wrapped the kitchen towel over the top of the body.

We went out together.

'I hate cats, me,' said Kim as she levered the tops off the bottles. 'Give me a dog any day. They're more honest.'

I said, 'Did you have a nice time yesterday?'

She looked puzzled for a second, then her face broke into a wide smile. 'I'll say.' She took a long swig, stretching her neck brazenly. Her smooth hair fell round her shoulders. You could tell she thought she was sexy. 'We had a day in Blackpool. It was brilliant. Have you been?'

'Lots of times. I used to live in Bolton, and it's not so far.'

'Do you know, I thought that was a Bolton accent. A very faint one.'

'You should hear my husband.'

'So whereabouts did you live?'

'Just on the outskirts. Eastern Road, Breightmet.'

'I get you.' She looked me up and down. 'You've

97

come a long way, then.'

'Chester's not so far,' I said, choosing to misunderstand.

'D'you ever go back?'

'We pop up there every month or so to see Mum.'

She sipped her cider thoughtfully. 'Yeah, anyway, it was a good day out. Manny'd never been, nor the girls. But I said I wanted to treat them to a special day, so Manny booked the afternoon off work and we took the girls out of school.'

Juno'll go berserk at that, I thought.

'And did they like it?'

'Loved it. It's what I said, the whole family needs loosening up. It did them all good.'

'And you're getting on better with Manny?'

'How do you mean?'

'You didn't seem so sure at first.'

She shifted in her seat, recrossed her legs. 'I think he's one of those people you have to get to know. Break their defences. I'm good at that. There's a fun person inside Manny, struggling to get out.'

The clock above us began to strike; it was as if I'd never heard it before. The mellow note sounded right through me, through the moment, and I was looking round the kitchen and seeing it with Kim's eyes: the old tin advertising signs, the striped French jars, the framed posters for plays Manny had helped fund.

'You go home tomorrow,' I said.

'Yep.'

'That'll be a relief, I should think.'

'Back to the brood. Oh aye; it's chaos at ours.

But I've missed it, you know. It's been way too quiet here.'

'It didn't sound quiet last night.' I made sure I was smiling.

'Oh, yeah. Oops. Did we keep you awake? We went on longer than we meant.'

'What was it?'

'Karaoke. We got a machine from Argos on the way back, impulse buy. I tell you what, the girls are really good! They did that "Mad World", really sad, and Pascale's a dead ringer for Norah Jones; looks like her and sounds like her. Fantastic. She should be on TV. Hey, what am I saying?'

We laughed. 'They are lovely. They get that hair from their mum.'

'Are they mixed race?'

'Manny's grandmother was Algerian. So their colouring's from Manny's side. But those Pre-Raphaelite waves are Juno's.'

'I always wanted a girl. Them little frilly socks they have; someone to go shopping with later on. They don't care so much, lads, do they?' I could have said, as long as you have them and they're safe and alive, it doesn't matter what damn sex they are. You should be down on your knees saying thank you. Instead I said, 'It depends on the individual.'

'Yeah,' said Kim, tugging at the neck label on her cider bottle. 'Suppose so. Anyway, Pascale should get her name down for *Stars in their Eyes*. Never mind mucking about with that violin, she wants to train her voice up.'

'I think she is in the choir at school.'

'You know what I mean. Proper singing.'

Before I went she said, 'It's been nice to chat to

you. I wish we'd seen more of each other.'

I was taken aback, and touched. 'I've not done anything.'

'You've helped today. Calmed me down. I'm a bag of nerves, what with going back to God-knows-what tomorrow, and trying to give up smoking on top.'

'You've given up smoking?'

'Thinking about it. I've only had two today; normally I'd have had about ten by this time.'

'That's brilliant.'

'Actually, though, I do need another now, if you'll excuse me.' She went into the hall and came back with a packet of JPS. 'Only three left. I might stop altogether when I run out.' I watched her concentrate as she lit up the tip, then she took herself over to the door and assumed the position. 'Manny was saying,' she breathed, 'how you could get away with smoking when you were younger, but it took away your quality of life as you got older. His granddad died of lung cancer, didn't he? I suppose he smoked a lot, being French. We had a long chat about it the other night. Family, and stuff. Didn't get to bed till two.'

As she was speaking, Kim reached over for the bird-parcel and dropped it neatly into the steel bin. I did a double take.

'Oh!'

'What?'

'I thought you were going to bury it.'

She shrugged. 'What's the point?' she said.

*   *   *

I told Tom about the bird later.

'So?' was his response.

'It shocked me. I'm probably being silly but it seemed callous.'

'It would have been callous if the thing had been alive.'

'Well, yes. But it's . . . I don't feel as though I can get a handle on Kim. You think she's pretty straightforward at first, but there are—cogs—going round inside.'

'Do you need to Get a Handle on the woman? She'll be out of our lives in twenty-four hours.'

'Let's hope. I want normal service resuming as soon as possible. Juno in her kitchen, and the faint screech of violins through the French windows.'

Tom looked at me thoughtfully. 'I'll tell you something.'

'What?' I thought for a second he might have an answer.

'Whatever you say about Kim, she's rubbed off on you.'

'What do you mean?' He reached across and pinched my cheek. 'You sound ever so *northern* tonight, my love.'

*　　　*　　　*

Kim—What's this? Champagne? You celebrating my departure, have I been that bad?

Manny—You've been great. And congratulations on the cigarettes. What's it been now?

Kim—Four hours.

Manny—That's excellent.

Kim—If you say so. I'm always giving up, it means nowt.

Manny—You must be looking forward to going

101

back.

Kim—Yeah, I am. It's what you were saying, yesterday, about everyone needing a sense of place. A place you know's home. Oh, cheers.

Manny—Cheers. To a successful Queen Mum, whoever it turns out to be. Yes; I believe everyone has a particular landscape that strikes some mental sympathy, whether it's urban or rural. And it's not necessarily anything to do with where you were born.

Kim—If I won the lottery tomorrow, I wouldn't move, I wouldn't, honest. I love the moors, they're so . . . free. I even love the streets and the chimneys. It's what I grew up with. Mind you, it is nice round here.

Manny—Mmm. It's probably the first time I've ever felt properly settled, living in Chester. We were always moving around because of my father's job, when I was young. Although it was fun, in many ways. Travelling's an education, and I am a bit of a gypsy by nature. But if I had to settle anywhere, this is probably the right place. Juno's made this house home.

Kim—You'll be glad to have her back, then.

Manny—And sorry to see you go. Top-up?

Kim—Get away. You'll be putting the flags out.

Manny—Mrs Beale will miss you. You scored quite a hit there, she was telling me.

Kim—We were driving right past Superbowl anyway. I said to her, you do crown-green bowling, it's the same action. And she wasn't so sure, but she turned out to be dead good at it. She's small but she's strong. I tell you what, she sent some skittles flying that afternoon. Reckoned she was imagining aiming at that consultant last year who told her to forget she had a husband.

Manny—I remember Juno telling me about that. Disgraceful.

Kim—Yeah. And I don't think Mr Beale was on top form that afternoon we saw him. Not that I hung around; I thought she'd want to be on her own with him. I had a walk down the road and looked at house prices.

Manny—You probably did her a lot of good.

Kim—She's going back to Superbowl with her friend, she said. I wonder if she meant Juno?

Manny—And the girls'll miss you.

Kim—Aw, that's nice. The lads won't have.

Manny—Don't say that. They will have done; their mother.

Kim—You don't know them. Rabble. It's a nice drop of stuff, this.

Manny—Oh, can I—

Kim—Cheers. I wonder how Lee and Juno got on, in the end? He's so easy-going it's not true, so she'll probably have been all right.

Manny—She'll see a few changes when she gets back here.

Kim [To camera]—I envy Juno. I do. Those girls, she's so lucky. And being needed; I'm too old for anyone in our house to need me. I mean, we've talked about another baby, but we never did anything. That's what always happens, talk talk talk and never act. If I want anything doing, I have to sort it out myself. You know, going out and that, I have to ring up, get tickets, arrange transport. No bugger else'll bother. Sometimes I get fed up of instigating all the time. Lee's so

103

passive. It's been great this week to have people saying thank you. 'Cause it's not too much to ask, is it?

Lee [To camera]—I don't rile easily, but, by God. She's altered all the pre-sets on my radios, and she's changed my daily paper order at the newsagent's. All I can say is, I'm counting the hours; no, the minutes. It's not that she's a nasty woman, just, she's no idea. I reckon the root of the problem is, she's come in this house thinking, I'm better than them, I'll show them how to do it right. She's tried to hide it, but I know that's what's going through her mind.

Juno [To camera]—Call me Sisyphus. *[Laughs]* It's been a fortnight of tremendous effort and I don't honestly know if I've made any kind of positive impact at all. No one's fallen out with me, as such, but I get the impression I've been being smirked at behind my back all this week. Lee's been absolutely zero support; I don't know if he's like that with Kim. At this exact moment I couldn't feel less like a Queen Mum, which is probably something I shouldn't be admitting on camera because it's shooting myself in the foot as far as the voting goes, I know that, but I don't care because I'm going home and anyway, Manny's promised to take me for a weekend in London whatever happens. *[Blows nose]* I have so missed him. I want to get home now.

Kim—Do you ever feel like, I don't know, like you've taken a wrong turning in your life? Or looked around and thought, How did I get here? I mean, if you had your time again, would you have done anything different?

Manny—That's difficult to say. I—

Kim—You see, most of the time I jog along, and it's all fine, lah lah, and then every so often it hits you. You're not young any more, and you're looking on the Internet at what your school friends have been doing, and I always meant to go to America—

Manny—You could still do that—

Kim—On my own, I meant. It wouldn't be the same if I went now, everyone in tow, dragging along, complaining. And anyway, I'd never be able to prise Lee out of his chair long enough. I was watching that film, *Shirley Valentine*, a couple of weeks ago and I got to thinking, I've felt like that sometimes. You know, submerged. I don't know how to explain it; a feeling, some days—*[Kim starts to cry]* I'm not usually so soft. I'm, I don't know what's up with me.

Manny—Come here, give me your glass before you tip it over. That's right. Now, come on. You're all right. I expect you're excited about going home tomorrow. I can imagine it must be very emotional, very unsettling, everything upside down for a fortnight. No wonder you're . . . But you'll be home in less than twenty-four hours. It'll be fine. It will. *[To camera]* Look, can you switch off, please. Switch *off*.

*　　　*　　　*

There are times when, if I lie very still in bed with my eyes closed, Joe comes, as he used to. I hear

105

the creak of a floorboard along the landing, the tiny shush of the bedroom door. My mind's eye sees him standing in the light. Then he pads over to the bed. I keep my lids tight shut, but I feel him standing there, breathing through his mouth, waiting for me to acknowledge him.

I once tried to tell Tom about this but he just looked alarmed, so I turned it into a dream I'd had. 'I dream too,' he said, unexpectedly. 'You never tell me about it,' I said. 'No; it wouldn't be helpful for me,' he muttered, and turned the TV on.

I was lying here now, on top of the duvet, waiting for Joe. Tom was downstairs watching *Newsnight*; Ben was up to God-knows-what in his room.

The bedside clock ticked quietly next to my ear. I put my hands on my belly as I used to when I was pregnant, when the skin was tight and full. It was soft there now, squashy. I squeezed a roll of flesh.

Joe came into my head, waving two toilet rolls. 'Stick these together,' he commanded, holding them to his eyes like field glasses. 'Make a telescope.'

'Do you mean binoculars?'

He pointed to his knee. 'Look at my bruise.'

'I can't see.'

He pushed his trouser leg up. 'Oh dear. Was that when you fell at nursery?'

He nodded. 'And Eden hurt her head, and she cried. I didn't cry.' A memory of wrapping masking tape round the toilet rolls while Joe watched intently. 'There.' I held them out, pleased with myself.

'No!' He howled with impatience and pulled the tubes apart.

'Well, how did you want them? What was I supposed to do with them?' I asked him now.

'God Almighty, they must think the electorate are a bunch of dunces!' said Tom loudly. The bedroom door banged against the linen basket. 'It's a good trick if you can do it: every single bloody party's going to cut taxes and yet somehow spend loads more on services. If it was that easy, wouldn't they be doing it now? They wonder why no one's voting and yet there isn't anything to tell them apart; just suits, talking.'

Joe vanished.

'The country's run by fools.'

I kept my eyes closed.

'But the trouble is, there's no one smart enough to provide any real opposition. Oh, and your mum phoned, did you hear it go? But I let the answerphone pick up. She'll only want to go on about that mudslide in Russia. Where are the nail scissors, Ally?'

'On the chest of drawers. In one of my boxes.'

'I've a nail catching on my sock—do you mean the black and gold casket?—been driving me mad all evening—I can't see it, Ally; which box?—got them.'

I felt the end of the mattress fall away by my feet, then lurch back up thirty seconds later, and the clink of the scissors being dropped back.

There was a pause, which made me open my eyes.

'What are these?'

Tom was holding the scrap of paper with my gay phone numbers scribbled on it. I'd forgotten they were in there. I rolled my eyes up to the ceiling and exhaled slowly. Thank God I hadn't written the names of the organizations down.

'It's not more of your bloody bereavement helplines, is it?'

'No,' I snapped. 'It's a list of all the lovers I've got on the go at the moment. Will you put it back, please?'

It says something about our marriage—I'm not sure what—that not for one second did Tom believe I was having an affair.

'Keep the damn things, then,' he said, screwing the paper up in his fist and pushing the crumpled ball back in my jewellery box. 'It would be a hell of a lot healthier if I put them in the bin for you.'

'*What's* unhealthy?'

I sat up then, angry as well as shaken.

'Oh, you know; spilling the beans to people you've never even met,' he said testily. 'It's been four years now, Ally. Sorry, but it has. You shouldn't be—You don't get me calling up total strangers and telling them personal information.'

'You don't talk to anyone at all.'

He shrugged. That's the way I am, his body said.

'I talk to strangers,' I hissed, 'because I can't bloody get through to my own husband!'

That made him flinch. I could have stopped and calmed down then, softened, so he could find a way in. But I didn't.

'You're so closed up, Tom. It's like you have a separate *life* from me. I can't tell you anything emotional because you make me feel as if I'm just wallowing in self-indulgence. That's not right. I'm fed up of trying to keep everything inside.'

He stood with his feet apart, staring at me. After a moment, he said, 'You don't, though, do you? You give it all up to St Juno next door. I'm redundant.'

But look at what Juno did. Taking care of Ben while I went to hospital, sitting in our house all evening so he could be in his own bed; all those self-help books and website addresses she gave me afterwards. And while the rest of the road was avoiding me and my radioactive grief, Juno let me sit in her kitchen and weep for hours because I didn't want to do it in front of Ben. Don't you remember, I could have said, when you walked to the post box and it emptied the street, and you came back and threw a box of nails at the wall? Juno's never hidden from us. She's the best friend we've got.

He knew all this, though. I said: 'It's the other way round. I talk to her because you don't want to listen.'

He turned away from me and strode towards the door. 'Never mind, eh, she's back tomorrow.' And there was such an edge to his voice. 'Thank Christ.'

*   *   *

'It was *The Merchant of Venice*. MOV, Act 2, scene 3, line 2; "Our house is hell." Just a silly joke. I shouldn't have even been sending emails; I'd have been in trouble if they'd found out, but I thought a coded message would be all right.' Juno looked done in. I'd never seen her hair so flat; it needed a wash. She looked thinner, too. 'Anyway, you couldn't have sent one back, could you? So it doesn't matter.'

'I still feel like I let you down.'

'Don't be daft,' she said brightly, pushing a cup of coffee across the kitchen table at me. 'I was only

109

letting off steam. I felt loads better after I'd sent it.'

'So, was it?'

'What?'

'Hell?'

'Good Lord, no. I was joking, like I said. Although I could have done without that *awful* dog.'

'Why, what did it do?'

She grinned. 'I think it must have been on Viagra. It was humping every damn thing in sight. I spent half the time pulling its nose out of my crotch.'

'Eugh.'

'Absolutely. I never want to see another dog's penis as long as I live.'

We laughed for a long time; I think we were both quite high. I'd made myself wait till the Monday afternoon before going round, partly because the TV vans were still there and partly because I thought she'd want some time with Manny and the girls. Also, I didn't want to prove Tom right by panting on the doorstep as the car pulled up.

'Is it weird to be back?'

'I'll say. Do you know what I came home to on the Saturday morning? You won't believe this; the girls, in their pyjamas—this is ten thirty, mind—sitting watching *The Powerpuff Girls* and eating foam bananas. Foam bananas! And Pascale wearing one of those necklaces made of coloured sweets round her neck. How old are you, exactly, I said to them. You'd never think GCSEs were on the horizon. And then, did you know about Sophie having her navel pierced?'

'No! Did Kim—? Oh, Juno, that's bad.'

'You're telling me. I was bloody furious about it. The girls knew how I felt about extra piercings. I've said; when they turn eighteen it'll be up to them, but in the meantime—Anyway, Soph took it straight out so it should heal up in a week or two. I think she was quite relieved to be told. It looked terrible. And school wouldn't have allowed it, so . . . ' Juno yawned. 'Oops. Still catching up.'

'Do you want me to go?' I said immediately. What I really wanted to ask was, Do I lean too much on you? Am I too needy?

'Don't you dare,' she said, mock-stern. 'I've been *dying* to talk it through with you. You have to hear all the gory details.'

'OK. Go on.'

'So I got the girls to go upstairs and sort themselves out and then I found, it was so nice, a cake they'd made for me, well, bought. But they'd iced it themselves; *Welcome Home Mum*. I asked them if Kim had got them to do it, but they said no; wasn't that sweet? And after I'd shouted at them, too. Then Manny came in—he'd been down to the garage to get some flowers for me—and we had some time together. He looks as if he's had a time of it, poor man. He apologized about Soph's navel but Kim took her to have it done while he was out. Although he could still have got her to take the stud out. He says he did but she mustn't have heard him. Then I set to tidying up and stripping the beds, because frankly it smelt of cigarettes in the spare bedroom, even though Manny says Kim only smoked outside, and there was a little pile of tab-ends under the flowering currant bush; I assume that's her. Honestly! And another thing; when I went to have a soak later on, she'd used nearly all my Freesia bath oil. You're only supposed to put a couple of drops in.'

I wanted to hug her. 'I'm glad you're home,' I said. 'I've missed our chats.'

'What was Kim like with you?'

'OK. Quite a pleasant manner, on the surface. I think she was perfectly nice to the girls, in case you were worrying. But I didn't feel much of a connection with her.'

That seemed to please Juno. 'That's more or less what Manny said; isn't it strange?'

'And what was it like being with Kim's family? Apart from the randy dog.'

Juno stretched and smiled. 'In a nutshell? Fine,' she said. 'I'd say it went very well.'

*   *   *

Juno—What have I learnt from this fortnight? The value of family life. The importance of pulling together. I'm not sure Lee's learnt that, though.

Lee—I'm hoping she'll have learnt to chill. She makes a right meal out of everything. Must drive her husband up the wall.

Chris—She should stop trying to control everything, yeah? She'd have more fun if she loosened up, went with it.

*   *   *

Manny—I'd say we've all learnt quite a lot, really. I've learnt the words to several Wham! songs.

Kim—God, loads. How to operate an espresso

112

machine, how local funding for the arts works, about the role of the Free French during World War Two. He's a mine of information, that Manny.

Pascale—She's brilliant at braiding hair, she's
   shown me how to do all different styles.
Sophie—And make-up too. I reckon she could
   have been a beautician if she'd wanted.

*   *   *

That first afternoon I held back from telling Juno about the Ben-thing; it felt too big to talk about yet. Instead I confided in her about my row with Tom.

'Just, every so often I feel *bleak* about my marriage,' I said, swirling my coffee grounds in the bottom of the mug.

Juno frowned. 'But you're so good together.'

'Are we?'

'Yes. When you think what you've been through.'

No one but Juno could have got away with those words. I said carefully, 'I think part of the problem is that we sort of—remind each other to be sad. He's still so angry about Joe. Sometimes I want to run away from his anger.'

'But you can't run away from your own feelings.'

'No.' I imagined myself for a moment sitting on a seafront, watching the spray, alone. It would be worse on my own. 'And Tom's the only person who can really understand.'

'Of course he is,' she said.

When I got in Tom had come home early from work and there was wet washing on all the

113

radiators; an apology. Tom's magic ear can detect the finest of tuning changes in a car engine but is ordinarily deaf to the end of the spin cycle.

'Thanks for sorting out the clothes,' I said.

'I vacuumed too.'

'Yes, thank you.'

'Juno all right?'

'Great. Sends her love.'

Ben was at a friend's for tea so we ate our shepherd's pie on our laps in front of the TV news.

After we'd finished, I stood up to take the plates. Tom raised his face to me and said, 'You see, I'm no good at talking. It stirs everything up, for me.'

'I know.' I took the plates through to the kitchen and brought back some wine. On television, Rick Stein was unpacking a lobster.

Before he went to pick Ben up, Tom pulled me to him and mumbled into my hair: 'I want to make things better for you, and I can't. Do you understand what that's like for me? There's nothing, nothing I can do. I feel completely inadequate.'

I nodded against him, and he left.

CHAPTER EIGHT

Joe died on a beautiful March day. He was knocked down by a car.

This is how it happened: Ben, Joe and I walked out of the house together, on the last minute as usual because Joe hadn't wanted any breakfast and had dawdled over his toast as only a four-year-old can. He'd been playing with shells, lining them up on the arm of the sofa, rearranging their order between every bite of toast. Even with my nagging, he'd only managed half a slice.

Ben was keen to get to school on time because he'd made a model pyramid as part of an Egyptian project, and he wanted to show it off. I'd shouted at him for showering sand on the hall carpet and he was sulking at me, and also sulking at Joe for holding us all up.

I parked on the road that day because the front garden was being landscaped and the drive was just a trench. We were half-running along when a gust of wind buffeted Ben's pyramid and tore up one cardboard edge from its base. Ben howled and I stopped to help. I tried to shield the model with my coat but the wind was strong and the whole pyramid lifted up and tore along another of its edges. Ben began to squeal with frustration.

I took the bulky structure out of his hands and turned towards our car just as the Maestro hit Joe.

At first I couldn't work out what had happened. I called for Joe when I couldn't see him; I thought he might have been hiding, or gone back to the house. But I didn't get any reply, and there was this silver Maestro stopped in the middle of the road, a door opening and an old man getting out. Ben was still wailing about his pyramid. I handed it back to him and stepped out into the road.

Joe's navy coat sleeve was sticking out from under the Maestro's body. I started to scream his name. Then I threw myself flat onto the road and put my cheek to the tarmac so I could see what state he was in, but it was dark between the wheels. All I could make out was that he was lying completely still.

The old man was babbling, telling me not to move him, and I turned and yelled something like, 'Do you expect me to leave him there, then?' Ben had cottoned on that something was wrong and he was shouting 'Mum! Mum!' over and over again. As gently as I could, I dragged Joe out into the light.

I could see at once that the car tyres had passed over his body because his pale blue sweatshirt had black marks across it and the material was rucked up and pleated flat. I couldn't see the skin of his stomach because he had a vest on. He was limp and I couldn't get any response when I patted his cheek or called his name. His face looked untouched, but dead. I felt for a pulse by kneading his neck because I knew I ought to do something like that, and I thought I could feel a faint one. All the time I was saying his name in case he could hear me. I heard the driver calling for an ambulance on his mobile.

'He ran out,' I heard him say, his voice cracking. 'I don't know. I don't know. Yes. Cestrian Park. C-e-s-t-r-i-a-n. Yes. I'm not sure.'

He tried to hand the phone to me but I wouldn't

let go of Joe. I was trying to work out whether he was breathing or not. Then I heard Juno's voice saying, 'Manny, take Ben inside. Give me the phone.'

I slipped my coat off and laid it over Joe to try and keep him warm because it was freezing down there on the tarmac. I stroked his hair and forehead till the ambulance came. 'I didn't dare do any chest compressions because I thought he might have internal injuries,' I told the paramedic, quite rationally. He was nice with me, nodded, but I think he must have known Joe was dead then. 'Should I have done chest compressions?' 'You did the right thing,' he said.

I didn't ask, 'Will Joe be all right?' Afterwards I thought maybe I'd given up too easily; if I'd expected him to pull through, then he would have done. I expected him to die, and he did. Tom's never once said, 'What were you doing? Why weren't you watching him?' But I still think it was my fault, when you get down to it; if not for failing to hold his hand, then for letting Fate take over.

*   *   *

Juno was wearing a grey devoré skirt suit and a tiara. The tiara was from Manny.

'He says I'm Queen Mum, whatever happens,' she laughed. 'Let me top your glasses up.'

Tom was smiling because he was mildly drunk and it was late, but I couldn't tell whether it was an ironic smile or a genuine one. I followed his gaze across Juno's living room and saw Sophie draping her arm across the back of Ben's chair. Ben was doing his best not to notice.

'It's so wonderful to be back,' Juno was saying. 'You don't realize how many little domestic things you rely on to get you through the day.'

'Such as?' I held my glass up for Manny.

'My cookbooks. My herbs. The Gaggia.'

'It's all food-related, notice,' said Manny. 'She hasn't said anything about missing the family.'

'But I *did*! How can you doubt it?'

She was glittering this evening. The sleeveless tunic top draped beautifully across her hips and the skirt kind of swirled round her ankles every time she stood up. I'd have liked one of those skirts but it wouldn't have looked the same on me. I'm not as willowy as Juno, and my complexion's too fair for grey, I look washed out. I'd have looked an absolute twit in a tiara.

Even Tom had seemed impressed by how lovely she looked. 'Goodness, we must have the wrong house, Ma'am,' he'd said when she first opened the door to us. He'd done a little bow. 'You're very regal tonight, Mrs Kingston.' While Juno was taking our coats, I took the opportunity to kiss him on the lips. He squeezed my hand; not angry tonight.

'And you should see the way Lee eats pizza,' Juno was saying now. 'He folds it up and *stuffs* it in. Then his mouth's so full he can hardly chew.' She mimed it for us, and it was funny. 'Of course, the boys just copy him, and the whole lot talk with their mouths full, so there's all this mashed-up food on display.'

'Charming,' said Tom. 'You've put me right off my cashews.'

'I don't know why Kim hasn't said anything to them. What were her table manners like, Manny?'

He shrugged. 'I didn't notice.'

'But you reckoned her cooking wasn't up to much.'

'It was mostly ready meals.'

Juno pulled a face. I thought, We had Tesco's lasagne last night, but I didn't say anything.

'The horror, the horror,' said Tom. 'You'll all have gone down with scurvy by the end of the week.'

'We did have vegetables,' said Manny. 'We weren't fed entirely on E numbers and preservatives.'

'And she's a real chain-smoker, isn't she?'

'She's giving up,' chimed Sophie from the arm of the sofa where she was now perched. If she got any closer to Ben, she'd be in his lap. 'We persuaded her, didn't we, Paxo?'

Pascale, sitting on the floor at Ben's feet with her back against the sofa, nodded seriously. 'We gave her all the facts, and told her it was her choice.'

Juno smiled sadly. 'I'm sure that's what she intends to do, Soph, but I wouldn't pin my hopes on her sticking to her resolution.'

'Her sort never do,' I heard Tom whisper, but luckily nobody heard him except me.

I said: 'Do you think they will change their lifestyle in any way as a result of your visit? What kind of an impact do you think you made, overall?'

'They didn't appreciate you, did they, my love?' said Manny.

Juno laughed. 'Oh, I wouldn't say that.'

'You did say it. When you first got home.'

'I was tired and emotional, that's all. No, there was a little friction, it's true, especially at the end

119

of the first week, but that's only natural when you come into someone else's household and disrupt their rhythm. Everyone's feelings had settled down by the start of the second week, though. Lee's so passive it's not true; I think you couldn't have a good row with him if you tried. And the boys were hardly there. I've never seen such a fragmented family. Lee kept saying, "It's the modern way," and I kept pointing out that my family weren't like that. It's not parenting what Kim and Lee do, it's Bed-and-Breakfasting. I swear they don't know where the boys are half the time. See, I *always* know where Soph and Pascale are.'

'That's true,' said Sophie.

'No, but that's because I'm being a responsible mother. And you're only thirteen.'

'And the minute we turn, what, sixteen, seventeen, you'll be off our case?'

'Don't be ridiculous,' said Juno.

'Actually,' said Manny, 'I'm sure Kim does know where her boys are even when they're out. She didn't strike me as blatantly irresponsible. Even if her cooking wasn't up to much.'

While her dad was talking, Sophie murmured something in Ben's ear. He looked shifty, then turned to Pascale and spoke to her. She nodded and got up. 'We're going to leave you sad oldies down here,' she announced, 'and go listen to some decent CDs. If that's OK?'

'Us oldies'll manage to stagger on without you, yes,' said Manny. 'You may be excused. But if your so-called music gets too loud, it's a boat trip up the River Dee, remember?'

Pascale grinned and held out a hand to Ben. He took it awkwardly, then Sophie grabbed his other arm and they more or less frog-marched him out. I couldn't read his expression.

'I do believe, though,' Juno was saying, 'that I gave them something to think about in some areas. I'm sure Kim will find Chris and Marco behaving much more responsibly when she comes back. I did get them to make a meal from scratch, in the end, by standing over them. They promised me they'd do her my roasted vegetable and bacon sauce when she came back. In fact, Chris said he couldn't believe it was so easy.'

*   *   *

Juno—It is easy, isn't it? And full of fresh ingredients. You could make this for your girlfriend sometime.
Marco—He dun't have a girlfriend, he's a homo.
Chris—Piss off, Marco.
Marco—A big bender.
Chris—Shut up, will you?
Marco—Homo, homo.
Juno—People's individual sexuality—
Marco—Put that tomato down now, it's loaded.
Juno—Yes, Chris, take no—
Marco—Fuck! Oi, you've done it now.
Juno—Chris! Oh, honestly! Have you seen this? Have you seen? It's all down the cupboard.
Marco—Uh-oh.
Juno—Get a towel.
Marco—Yeah, get a towel, bum-boy. Ow! He hit me!
Chris—Serves you right, you git. You mop it up, it's your fault.
Marco—Come back! I'm gonna have you, you little

121

shit—

Juno—Lee? Lee! Lee! Oh, I give up. It's easier to do it myself. *[To camera]* Is this what you do, Kim? Is this how you end up running your household? Because if it is, you have my sympathy. You're welcome to it. You are.

*   *   **

'Do you think Juno was drunk?' I asked Tom when we'd got back home.

'Drunk on something.'

'Rioja.'

'Relief, I'd say,' he smiled.

CHAPTER NINE

When I told Tom that Juno would be joining us in Cadgwith for the day, he groaned, but not with any real conviction.

'It's only for the day. Not even a day; lunch.'

He looked out of the hotel window at the narrow line of sea. 'If they're not still here for the evening meal, I'll eat my suitcase.'

'I had to invite them.'

'Why? It's our holiday. Emphasis on *our*.'

When I hung my head and sighed, he turned round and ruffled my hair, saying, 'Oh, I don't mind, really. So long as they don't end up staying over, booking into the hotel next door on one of Juno's mad whims. I take it they're all coming.'

'Manny's down to see a gallery in the area, an exhibition by someone he helped fund a few years ago, I think Juno said. So they were kind of going right past us.'

He nodded over at Ben, who was sitting on the opposite window seat, wearing his headphones. 'If it's a windy day, I still want to fly the kites.'

Ben had spotted a stunt kite on the second day and bought it immediately with his pocket money. Of course, Tom had to show him how to fly it— lucky we were holidaying on a cliff—and from then on, they'd both been hooked. Tom had bought two more kites since, and was seeing if they could be modified to make them fly even better. Father and son hadn't got on so well in ages. Boring old Mum sat and watched them from far away, with an unread paperback in her hand.

When you lose someone you love intensely, you have to learn again how to sit alone and think. Time makes the memories manageable. Still painful; you never get over the pain, but you learn to live around it. People talk about different shades of grief, but I'd say there's a whole spectrum of colours, not all of them ugly. Four summers later, I could recline on the grass and observe Ben and Tom together, and think: Joe would have loved this. What would he have been doing? We'd have bought him his own kite, and he'd be crashing it repeatedly and laughing, or getting cross. He'd be bringing it over to me all the time to help him untangle it. Ben might be teasing him; Tom would be grumbling about the way he should look after toys more, the way dads do in normal families. We probably looked normal from the outside.

Do you regard us as normal? I could have asked Juno, now, as she sat next to me making the world's longest daisy chain: Does Manny?

She squinted sideways at me, shading her eyes with her hand. 'I've never seen the sky so blue. Fantastic. We could be in France.'

It was still cold, sitting on the cliff top, watching kites. 'If we were in France, we wouldn't have to wear our cardigans.'

'True.'

A brown butterfly landed on her handbag, fanning its wings gently up and down. 'Oh, look,' I said, in the voice I use at the nursery.

'It's a small copper,' said Juno, amused, 'and I'm not three any more.'

'How come you know everything? Does it not get boring?'

124

The butterfly took off again and Juno began draping daisies over my hair. 'Unimaginably.'

In the distance, Ben crashed his kite at Pascale's feet. She jumped and laughed, and Sophie took the opportunity to mock-hit him. Manny strode over to pick it up and Tom came and stood next to him, holding one edge and flexing one of the struts.

I said, 'I think Sophie fancies Ben. Don't you?'

She turned her head to where Sophie was pointing up into the sky, stretching on tiptoe in a pose that showed off her bare stomach and slender waist. What teenage boy could resist that? Ben apparently; he was studiously knotting a piece of new line to the centre of the smallest kite.

'Soph fancies everybody at the moment. She's a raging inferno of hormones.'

'You are at that age.'

'Pascale isn't. Still. Ben doesn't seem to be too much in thrall to his testosterone yet, does he?'

I caught my breath. Did she know? Was she trying to tell me?

'He's managed to stay out of trouble at school for the last term, so that's something. No more fisticuffs.'

'Has he got a girlfriend?'

Ben threw his kite into the air and the wind took it, pulling it up out of his control. He tipped his head back and the breeze blew his fringe to one side. He looked so handsome.

'No,' I said.

My daisy chains fell off into the grass.

'We still can't get Soph's navel to heal up,' said Juno. 'You'd have thought, a tiny hole like that, it would have skinned over pretty quickly.'

'Do you think Ben's gay?' I heard myself say in

125

my head.

'I can't forgive Kim for doing that,' she went on. 'It was a *violation*. There should be something in the rules about it. I've written to Kieran. What if it had gone wrong and she'd got septicaemia, or been scarred for life?'

I pulled a sympathetic face.

'As it is, getting her navel pierced seems to have opened the floodgates on all sorts of unreasonable demands. She wanted boys at her fourteenth-birthday sleepover. Boys! I said to her, "You know what people are going to start saying about you, don't you?" Then, of course, we had a huge strop over it, doors banging, not eating, the works. And you know how liberal I am in most things. Between you and me—' Juno lowered her voice, even though the others were out of earshot—'I think she looks a bit of a tart right now. But Soph assures me that's what *all* the girls are wearing, from eight years up. It's, I don't know, as if having Kim in the house unsettled everyone. Even Pascale had a row with me the other day because I wouldn't let her skip music practice to go out with her friends. Even though I *said* I'd drive her to the restaurant afterwards, at great personal inconvenience, half an hour later: no, that wasn't good enough, she wanted to go in the car with them all together. But if she misses one day's practice here, then it'll be another there, and then she'll get out of the habit and all that work she's put in over the years'll go down the drain. She can't see it.'

'No,' I said.

'And, to be honest, I'm not sure we should be keeping in touch with Kim and Lee. I know it's the mature thing to do, but I didn't especially get on

126

with them. I had thought we might be able to help Marco out with his work experience, although he doesn't seem that interested so I'm not going to push it. Kim does want Manny to advise her on summer schools, though.'

I was surprised. 'What's she want to study?'

'Art history was one suggestion. Then it was crystal healing.' She laughed briefly. 'Not much difference. So I don't know what she ended up with, but I know Manny went all over getting her booklets on all the different courses that were running.'

'That was kind of him.'

'You know Manny. Anything to do with the arts and education.' She closed her eyes and let her head fall back against her shoulders. The posture should have looked relaxed, but somehow it seemed self-conscious and uncomfortable. Last month she'd said to me, out of the blue, 'I feel as though the cameras never went away, like I'm still being observed.' I'd thought to myself, It's going to get worse before it gets better. Now *Queen Mum* was twenty days away from airing and Juno was tight and brittle under the banter. I wanted to reassure her that the nation would love her, but that would have implied she ought to be worried. I'd banned Tom and Ben from doing a countdown every time they saw her. 'It's like when you're pregnant,' I'd told them. 'You don't need anyone telling you, "Only four weeks to go," or whatever. Trust me.' Ben had shrugged obediently, but Tom said, 'She got herself into it.'

Tom was coming over now with Manny, both of them holding an edge of the biggest kite. No change in Manny, I thought; nothing on his mind.

127

'We're going to have to take this one back to the hotel,' said Tom. His cheeks were flushed and his hair on end where the wind had blown it about. 'It's jiggered. It needs to go to the kite hospital.'

'Not the kite graveyard?' asked Manny.

'It can be redeemed with a new central strut, I reckon.' Tom laid it on the grass gently, as if it were alive and wounded. 'What I was thinking was, shall we go down for lunch now? It's early, but we could have drinks while we were waiting.'

Juno was about to get to her feet when her Scarlatti ringtone went off. Kneeling, she pulled the phone out of her bag and held it to her ear. 'Hi!'

'Have you booked?' Manny was saying.

'Oh, yeah, you have to; the Cove's a really popular place,' said Tom, touching the kite with the toe of his shoe.

'Great, that's great; only, next time, there's this fantastic little restaurant about two miles down the road, seventeenth century, originally a smugglers' meet—'

Manny stopped speaking as Juno crumpled before him. Her shoulders drooped, the phone rolled down her skirt onto the ground and she buried her face in her hands.

'It's fine, fine,' I heard her say through her fingers. 'Give me a minute.' She let out a long, ragged breath. 'Oh, God.'

Manny got down beside her and took her wrists. 'Juno?'

The children were coming up now, laughing and throwing handfuls of grass.

'SHHH!' I hissed at them.

The girls' faces fell and Pascale ran forward.

128

'Mum?'

Juno lifted her head and quickly wiped her eyes with the balls of her thumbs. 'It's OK. I've had a shock. That was the hospital in Bradford to say my mum's collapsed. They think it might be a brain tumour. They're doing tests—'

Manny put his arms round her and I felt my eyes pricking, willed the tears not to come. Pascale stroked her mum's arm and Sophie buried her face against Ben's chest. I stared into the sky and counted seagulls.

'Is there anything I can do?' asked Tom. 'Help you pack or . . . ?'

Manny got to his feet. 'No, it's all still in the boot. There are a couple of people you could ring, let them know I won't be coming—on second thoughts, I'll do it, probably easier. I think we should get going, really. Juno?'

He helped her to her feet and she started to apologize.

'Come on, now,' said Manny, 'enough of that. Let's get to the car. Do you want me to call the hospital back, ask for more details?'

'I don't know,' sniffed Juno. 'I'll call—'

'We'll be in touch,' said Manny, over his shoulder. 'Girls.'

I stepped across and hugged Juno briefly, then they walked away from us across the cliff top. We watched them get down to the car park, saw Manny lean against the bonnet and talk into his mobile, then pass it to Juno. At last they got in the car and drove away, by which time I was crying.

Tom looked at me. 'That's that, then. Let's go and have a bloody big drink.'

129

I knew I'd never settle that night. I waited till Tom was asleep, then I crept across the room and peered round the door to the annexe where Ben was. He was lying at an angle with the duvet down by his waist in a *Death of Chatterton* sort of pose. His smooth chest rose and fell, hypnotically. I almost went across and kissed him, but I didn't want him waking up and making a fuss.

I tiptoed to the coat hook and took down my mac, slipped Tom's trainers over my feet, and turned the key in the door. Before I closed it behind me I looked back longingly. It must be a wonderful thing to lie down and just go to sleep.

The yard outside seemed pitch-black at first, but as I struggled to get my arm through my mac, a security light clicked on and showed me the gate with the single-track road outside. I checked my watch and saw that it was 1.50 a.m. I hoped the main street would be empty.

It was difficult to see where I was going once I was out of the range of the floodlight. Thick rhododendron bushes rose up at each side. There was a lot of rustling, and you could hear the sound of the sea too. I kept going and came to a thick white wall on the left-hand side which stood out of the gloom. I put my hand against it and it led me down a steep hill in the direction of the beach.

There were more lights on outside the pub, and the cloud had thinned a little to let some moon show through. I could see the boats pulled up on the shingle, a tractor, coils of rope, plastic drums, lobster pots, and the wave-edges further off. There were people up on the cliff but the beach itself was empty. I threaded my way between the wooden hulls and down across the clacking pebbles to the water's edge.

Juno's mother had been frail for a long time. She'd gone in last year for a hip replacement, then she'd caught bronchitis. I'd offered to help with the girls so Juno could go to Bradford for a few days and supervise her mum's discharge from hospital. But Juno had got on the phone and hired an agency nurse.

'Don't you think it's strange Juno does all this local charity work but leaves her widowed mother to fend for herself?' Tom had asked late in the afternoon, when he judged my tears had dried up, and while Ben was off skimming stones some distance away.

I'd thought the same myself, but didn't want to admit it. 'They never see Manny's parents either.'

'His mum and dad are at opposite ends of France.'

'OK, granted. But you don't know what the background is with Juno's family.'

'Do you?'

'No. Not in any detail, but I get the impression there was some sort of big bust-up years ago, even before her dad died.'

'Did she say that?'

I ignored him. 'I think modern society encourages people to drift away from their roots. We don't see much of our parents, do we?'

'We trail up to see your mum often enough. I'd see mine more if they didn't live in the back of beyond and I didn't have a full-time job. Juno's mum's only in Yorkshire, you could do it in a couple of hours.'

131

I knew what we were working up to. His theory is that Juno's turned her back on her past because it doesn't fit with her present life—that her parents weren't posh enough. I don't know where he's got this idea from, because Juno never talks about her childhood and has never shown us any old photos. I say there's no reason why she shouldn't have grown up in a grand stone house like the ones in Harrogate, and Tom says you've only got to listen to the way she talks—not a trace of Yorkshire in there. That's deliberate, that is. Wiping out her roots.

'You don't know any more about it than me, so don't judge.'

Tom shrugged.

'You're really weird with Juno, you know that?' I snapped. 'One minute you like her, the next she's a selfish bitch.'

'I never said she was a bitch.'

'You implied—'

Tom put his head in his hands for a moment. 'Right, listen; I like Juno, more or less. She's all right, bossy, but OK. I know she's been kind to you, to us. I *don't* worship the ground she walks on. See?'

Meaning I did. He took my arm and moved against me, leaning his face against my hair. 'Let's not fall out. We're on holiday.'

I'd let him hold me and we'd sat like that till Ben had come back to show us his giant crab shell.

Are all marriages like this, coming together and drifting away again? Or only the damaged ones?

The phone in my pocket bleeped suddenly, making me jump. I pulled it out and saw in the glowing screen that I'd got a text message. From

Juno. I opened it up, heart thumping.

Mum v poorly. Grim here.

I phoned her back straight away. 'Juno? Are you OK to talk? Where are you?'

'Hospital,' she said wearily. 'Outside the front doors because they won't let you use your phone inside in case it sends all the machines haywire. Where are you? God, did I wake you up? I must have woken you.'

'I'm on the beach.'

'What, at two in the morning?'

'Yeah. It smells of fish.'

'Better than cigarettes. I'm in the smokers' shelter because it's raining. What are you doing on the beach?'

'The usual, couldn't sleep.' I took a deep breath. 'I'm sorry about your mum.'

'Yeah. Well. These things.' After a moment she said, 'She was with the next-door neighbour at the time looking at some plants, or something, so it's not like she was lying on the floor alone for ages. They had an ambulance there in twenty minutes.'

At my feet the stones shifted and I felt the slime of seaweed under the sole of the trainer. The sea shushed on. Was it going out or coming in?

'Is she conscious, does she know what's going on?'

'She has been told, but I don't know whether it's gone in or not. I've been sitting by her bed but she's fairly drugged up. I'm not getting a lot of response. We're waiting on the biopsy results.'

'Oh, hell, Juno. That's awful.'

Clouds broke apart above me and a piratey sort of sickle moon shone through. You could taste the salt in the night air. Still I could picture the ward,

133

and her mum, like Juno but with white hair, and Juno at the bedside, holding her hand and talking softly. 'So you'll stay up there for a while?'

'Yeah. Although I don't think Mum's coming home. There's a lot needs sorting out, it all keeps going round in my head. I need to speak to the consultant in the morning. They don't know anything for certain yet.' She paused and the phone crackled. 'I'm so glad you were awake, Ally.'

I felt a rush of guilty pleasure. 'No problem.'

'Better go.'

'Yeah.'

'Juno?'

'Huh?'

'I wish you were here.'

It was a stupid thing to come out with, but she just said, 'So do I, Ally. So do I.'

I put the phone back in my pocket and all at once I had so much energy I wanted to run up the beach and sprint up the cliff path, singing. Isn't that awful? My best friend in such distress. I don't know what got into me.

I didn't run anywhere. I threw smooth stones hard into the water until my arm ached, then I made my uncertain way back across the shingle, through the boats, to the road, and walked up the hill to the hotel. Another hour and it would be dawn. This time I could make out clumps of orange montbretia at the bottom of the white wall that led me back. The night felt charged. My body buzzed as if I'd been out meeting a lover.

*   *   *

Kim [Reading to camera]—Dear Juno, I think you

134

are a very lucky woman. You have a beautiful house, two lovely girls and a good-looking husband. From my experience this week, though, I'd say you need to step back and let everyone have more space. Stop trying to run your family's lives for them. No one likes a boss. Teenage girls need freedom and if they don't get it, you'll soon find they can make the house very unpleasant. I know the devil makes work for idle hands, but you can't fill every minute for them. Chill out, girl, and get on that karaoke machine! Your friend, Kim.

Juno [Reading to camera]—Dear Kim, It's been an interesting week for me, seeing how a very different sort of household is run. I think my main concerns here are that the boys are rather spoilt, and need to take on more responsibility, and that you and Lee need to pull together more. Frankly, Kim, he needs a rocket under him. It seems as if he's spent his life taking the path of least resistance. Those boys are crying out for a firm hand. I believe your family will drift apart unless you make real efforts to do more as a unit. I don't blame you personally, I know it's part of the modern social trend. But doing things together can be so rewarding, even if at first everyone else seems reluctant to join in. Trust me. Good luck! Juno.

*   *   *

In the fortnight leading up to the airing of *Queen Mum* Juno was away a lot. I had a pregnancy scare that sent me wild with fear for a few days and

135

made me nearly smack a pre-schooler for smearing potato on the tabletop. When I confessed to Tom—after I'd got the all-clear—he'd been quiet for an hour or so, then blurted, 'Would it have been such a disaster?'

'What?' We were gathering up hedge clippings at the time, me holding the green sack open for him.

'A baby.'

'That shows how much you don't understand me at the moment!' I'd shouted, and burst into tears.

He'd hesitated, taken the sack out of my hands, then propped it against the wall and carried on sweeping up sadly.

I'd gone and sat in Ben's room and looked out of the window at Juno's lovely back garden. Fing was sleeping on the shed roof, Pascale and Sophie were sunbathing on the lawn. They were stretched out on a travel rug, Sophie with her face to the sky, and Pascale on her front so she could read a book. Even from this distance you could see how perfect their skin was. There was a photo of them both, with Ben, on the pinboard, above his PlayStation; Tom took it last summer when we all went to Cholmondeley Castle together. They're on a stone bench in the gardens and Sophie's larking about, falling backwards so you can't see her face properly. Pascale, though, is looking directly at the camera as if she's about to say something. And Ben's sitting in the middle, his back very straight, his arms to himself. Pascale's long hair lies against his shoulder.

Without thinking, I climbed into Ben's bed and curled up around the period pain. The pillow smelt of his hair gel. Joe came and stood by the bed again. The wristwatch by my ear ticked softly.

'Mum?' Ben was leaning over me with a puzzled expression on his face. His hair was still damp and spiky round the front. 'If it's not a daft question, what are you doing in my bed?'

I groaned and unpeeled the watch face away from my cheek. 'What time is it? Oh, God, I've been asleep for nearly two hours.'

'Are you all right?'

'I'm fine. I just lay down for a moment . . . Where's your dad?'

'Downstairs watching the bike racing on TV. Have you had a row?'

I sat up, rubbing my skin back to life. 'Of course not. Whatever makes you think that?'

'Dad said you had.' Ben swung his swimming bag off his shoulder onto the floor and went over to the mirror to comb his hair into shape. He spoke through his reflection: 'Was it about me?'

That made me look up sharply. 'No.'

'Oh. That's OK, then.'

I got to my feet and pulled the bed covers back into place, glancing through the window as I straightened up, but the girls had gone. Ben was absorbed in combing on gel.

'Everyone has rows, Ben,' I said, attempting cheerful. 'Especially people who live closely together. It doesn't mean they don't love each other.'

'Yeah yeah,' he sneered.

I pulled the damp towel out of his bag and flicked at him with it. 'Less of your lip.'

He grinned and turned back round to face me. 'So they must love each other a hell of a lot next door at the moment, then.'

'How do you mean?'

137

'Juno's back—'

'Have you been round there? How's her mum?'

'Dunno, I didn't get chance to ask—no, don't start, I really didn't, 'cause they were having a major ding-dong, her and the girls. A Jerry Springer-type shouting match. I nipped in to borrow this off Soph.' He held up a PlayStation game. 'It's a new "Broken Sword", I've never seen this one before, the original one's fantastic. Soph said her mate was getting it for her, and when it came I could borrow it and keep it as long as I wanted. Then she texted me it had arrived, so I thought I'd pick it up on my way past, only I didn't ring the bell 'cause sometimes Manny's in the middle of something and he doesn't like being disturbed, so I went round the back to knock-as-I-let-myself-in.' He flushed slightly. 'Won't be doing that any more.'

'Why?'

'Like I said, they were having this barney. They were in the lounge and they didn't know I'd come in. I didn't stay long.' Ben leant down to switch on the console. 'I'd heard enough.'

'What did you hear? Is Juno all right?'

'You sure you want to know? OK, then, it was something like, *Just because I'm not in the house doesn't mean my rules don't still apply!* And then—' he drew out his chair from under the desk and sat down, took out his new disc and slid it into the machine—'Sophie comes in with, *But we asked Dad. It's not fair.* So then Juno goes, *That's not the point. You knew how I'd react. That's playing one of us off against the other. I've always made it clear that that sort of ruse might go on in other people's households, but it's never going to happen in ours!*

138

'What had Sophie done, do you know?'

'It started as something to do with the TV, I think. Because then Juno goes, *I never stop you from watching television*, and Soph goes, *Yes you do!* and Juno goes, *Only when it gets in the way of other, more important things*, and Soph shouts, *Important to who, Mum?* That's when I knocked into the kitchen chair and they realized I was in the house. Juno came storming through the door, then she tried to put on a smile because it was me, but really she was livid. Soph shouted, "Who is it?" and came through, and when she saw it was me she goes, "I'll get that game," and runs off upstairs. Juno turns to me and says, and this was dead embarrassing, Mum; she goes—*She reads trash, she watches trash, she looks like trash!*'

I could see he was buzzing with nerves.

'Was Pascale there?'

'Dunno, don't think so. Manny wasn't, because Juno used that line about waiting till your father gets home.'

The game loaded, he began to flick between screens.

'What happened next?'

'I came home to get some peace and quiet. Except you've been at it too.'

I touched his neck. 'Not like that, we haven't. I'll go down now and make up, OK?'

He grunted.

I said, 'What's the matter with Sophie, do you think?'

'Search me.'

'I thought she might have told you. You seem very close.'

'Nah, not really. Tell you what, though; that hole

in Soph's navel Juno's always going on about, no wonder it won't heal up.'

'Does she keep putting the stud back?'

'She's got about ten different ones. Juno made her throw the original one away. But Soph just waits till her mum's off the scene and sticks one back in. You knew that, did you?'

'I guessed.'

'There's not a lot gets past you, is there?' he said, shifting forward in his chair to watch some men in robes waving their arms about. Then the action cut to the interior of an aeroplane flying over a jungle.

'You'll want these washing, I take it?' I asked, holding up the towel and the bag containing his swimming trunks.

'Mmm.' Lightning was playing about the aircraft.

I watched him for another twenty seconds, then I said, 'Did you realize that Sophie's got a crush on you?'

The aeroplane was now hurtling towards the ground.

'Ben?'

'I know,' was all he said, but his back was rigid.

I went out before he crashed.

CHAPTER TEN

When the whole thing first kicked off, there'd been much debate at about where and how *Queen Mum* was going to be watched. Juno was supposed to be in London, at a TV studio, with Kim, to absorb the poll results when they came through. But she'd still had this idea that we could be having some kind of party back at the house, in her absence. 'You can all watch me on TV in my posh togs,' she'd said. 'I'll keep waving to you. It'll be fun.'

But that was then. Now, with her mother so poorly, dying as far as I could understand, Juno wasn't even sure where she'd be when the programme aired.

I managed to catch her as she packed her overnight bag again.

'It must be awful, having to sort everything out on your own,' I said. 'Are you staying in your mum's house?'

'Yes.'

There was something very taut about her. I wanted her to talk to me about how she was coping. But the thing about bereavement is, it takes everyone differently. I wanted Juno to cry into my arms so I could give her back a little of what she'd given me in the past. Instead she was getting through by being busy and snappy. Well, that was OK. You have to go with it, I'm telling you.

So I thought about my dad instead. How he left us when I was thirteen, for another woman. How furious I was. How upset Mum had been, and how she'd never even dated anyone else, then how pleased she'd been when I found Tom. 'He's a good 'un,' she'd said after their first meeting. 'He'll see you right.' She hadn't wanted us to get married so quickly, so young, but I couldn't see any reason not to. Dad hadn't come to the wedding, but he had sent a big cheque, which I felt honour-bound to offer to Mum. She didn't want it, though, so Tom and I used it to buy a washing machine. We weren't in a position to go ripping up money.

The last time I heard from Dad was after Joe was killed. Mum must have told him, and he came down, actually came to the house, to see what he could do. 'Nothing!' I'd shouted in his face. 'You can't do anything in this situation—no one can— go away!' I think he'd been glad to get straight back in his car.

After Mr Peterson died, he became the man I hated most in the world.

All this Juno knew, because she'd let me tell her, over years' worth of coffee.

'Can I do any washing for you while you're away?' I asked, as she folded a cerise sweater and laid it neatly in her case.

'Mmm, no. Thanks for the offer. It's enough that you're taking the girls to school and looking after them when they get home.'

'I could get Tom to trim your lawn, if you want, next time he's got the mower out. I know Manny's got a lot on his plate too.'

She smiled. 'That would be good. Thanks.' She shut the lid of the case and sat down on the bed. 'You know, Kieran was all right about my not going down for the results. I thought he'd be furious.'

'What did he say?'

'I've to keep them up to speed, and they'll set up a phone link if necessary, so I can be kind of present in the studio when they announce the winner. I'm going to pull out all the stops to be back here, if I can. Don't fancy doing it live from Bradford.'

'I wish I could be more help.'

'You're being great. You and Tom'll come and watch with us, though?'

I could imagine Tom's face when I gave him the invitation. 'Yes, of course. Do you want me to bring some nibbles?'

'You're so sweet. I should be able to manage.' She looked at her watch. 'Now, have I time for a bath before I set off? Oh, sod it, I'll have a shower tonight at Mum's, after I've visited. It's such a pain, Mum had her bath taken out because she couldn't get in and out on her own. I hate that most about going over there, not being able to unwind in a long hot bath.'

I said, 'Does it seem weird, going back to the house you grew up in?' I had a picture in my mind of girl Juno sitting, like a Mini Boden model, on a window seat overlooking the Yorkshire moors.

'I don't believe I ever was there,' she said. 'My childhood feels like a programme I watched on TV once, a long time ago. It's about *that* relevant to my life now.'

She held her thumb and forefinger a fraction apart as she spoke, and I thought about my own childhood, how the memories of my Good Dad, and the way we'd all been before he left, were now like leafing through someone else's photo album. Foreign, unconnected.

'Did you never get on with your parents?

'No. *Never*. You know I didn't!'

Her tone was so unexpectedly sharp that I had to drop my gaze to the toile de Jouy bedspread and concentrate hard on the blue shepherdess and her blue lover. Juno stood up and pulled the case off the bed, testing its weight.

'Oops, nearly forgot my book!'

She ducked down and slid an Ian McEwan paperback out of the bedside cabinet. Then she hoisted the case back up onto the mattress and flicked up the latches.

'You OK?'

I nodded.

'You look quite pink. You're not coming down with anything, are you?'

'Hope not.'

She studied me for a second or two. 'Sorry if I sounded ratty. It's a difficult time. Mum and I— you know what it's like when you're supposed to be feeling a certain way, and you're not. You said yourself, you didn't miss your dad at your wedding till you realized you should have, and that was what upset you. You were sad about not being sad. That's what you told me, remember?'

I nodded again.

'Do you think it's good, I mean helpful, that very often we don't know we're doing something for the last time? You asked me that. After Joe died.'

I'd once confessed it had sent me nearly mad reliving that final twenty-four hours and ticking off the things I'd never get to do even one more time; putting out his socks for the morning, reaching for his hand, squirting him in the bath with his squeezy Nemo, holding his coat so he could get his arms in, looking at his worm garden, wiping his face.

144

Another mum in one of the Internet forums told me that you have to grieve for each thing separately. I'd thought at the time, Then I'll never manage it.

'It's hard not to be able to say goodbye,' I said. 'Then again, it's impossible saying goodbye.'

But Juno was looking away, inside her own memories.

'People talk about making their peace, but sometimes it's not up to you. It's not your peace to make. Are you thinking about your mum?'

She blinked at me and came back to herself. 'Mum, Dad, whoever.'

There was a pause, then her smile came back and it was like a cloud passing away from the sun.

'But that's in the past. I'm more worried about the present; Lord knows what the girls'll get up to while I'm away this time. Soph's going through a very strange phase at the moment. Damn hormones. I feel like shaking her and saying, "Where's my lovely little girl gone?"'

From across the landing we could hear the thump of music, two competing beats from different rooms.

'She'll come out of it. I was awful with my mum for about six months after Dad left. It was as if I couldn't help myself, like being possessed. I can remember the sensation exactly, opening my mouth and horrible words coming out that weren't mine.'

'What, and projectile vomiting, and your head spinning round?'

'The works. I was foul.'

Juno was thoughtful. 'The house does feel disturbed, now you say that. It would be just like

Soph to attract a poltergeist. Look—' She came and stood near me and I could feel the tension coming off her. 'Is there any chance you could have a word with her, while I'm away? Ask her if she's OK, and whether she could pull her weight more, be more understanding? Only, she thinks the world of you. She doesn't see you as this Great Nag. She's been talking recently about mothers-who-are-more-like-your-best-mate—all her friends have them. New-generation mums. I fear I'm an obsolete model.'

I imagined Tom's voice: *You don't fear anything of the sort*. But I just said, 'Yes, if you think I can help. Of course I will.'

I went round again late that evening because I'd discovered Pascale's phone down the side of our sofa. 'I only found it because it bleeped at me,' I told her. She fell upon it with a cry like a mother reunited with her baby.

Manny was bowed over the computer and Sophie was curled up in an armchair reading *Cosmopolitan*. Pascale's homework books were laid out on the carpet. On the stereo Josephine Baker sang about her *deux amours*.

I stood for a moment and drank it all in; the dark leather sofa, the kelim rug, the witty and chic ornaments on the mantelpiece. Above the bureau hung a studio portrait of the four of them, taken last year, the girls in white blouses and Juno with her hair up so you could see her long neck and fine jaw-line.

It would be so easy to slot into this household, slide out of my own and into this life.

Before I left, I asked Manny how he was coping.

'We're fine,' he said, showing his white teeth. He looked relaxed.

'And Juno? How would you say she's doing?'

'OK, I think.' He scratched the back of his head. 'Tired, obviously, commuting backwards and forwards. Upset about her mother.'

'Yes. More upset than I think she realizes.'

'Could be.' He looked so handsome in his blue shirt, collar unbuttoned. 'And how are you doing, Ally?' His eyes roved about my face till I felt suddenly shy.

'It's a good question,' I said.

*   *   *

Kim [To camera]—I think, in the end, I got on very well with Manny. Emmanuel! He's definitely a bit—not arrogant—confident, say, very confident. Not that that's necessarily a bad thing; I wish Lee would have more confidence in himself. But Manny seems to—know a lot about the world. I thought it was bullshit at first 'cause he was playing me this weird French music and showing me this modern art that I frankly can't be doing with, our dog could do better and I said so. I said it was a load of old tat. And I thought he'd be cross that I was, you know, dismissing him, but he laughed and said I was an iconoclast. Which means I like breaking rules. Which is about right, I'd say.

Kim—So did you and Juno meet at university?

Manny—That's right. Top you up again?

Kim—Cheers. I could get used to wine every night. And you've been married—?

147

Manny—Forever! No, it'll be, how old's . . . fifteen
   years. We married straight out of university.
Kim—Yeah?
Manny—It was—ha ha—a decision that kind of
   got made for us.
Kim—How do you mean? Oh! I get you!
Manny—Of course, we were delighted, once it had
   sunk in.

Kim [To camera]—Not so clever after all, then,
   when it comes down to it.

*   *   *

The doctors felt Juno's mother was stable enough,
so there were seven of us gathered round the TV
to watch *Queen Mum*. I'd left it taping at home,
too.

   'I wish I'd had time to prepare something proper
to eat,' Juno said, carrying in another bean-bag for
Ben. 'It would have been lovely to have had
another party.'

   'You mean we're not enough for you?' said Tom
drily.

   Juno was going back out of the door and didn't
hear.

   'Stop it,' I hissed. 'She's wound up enough
already.'

   'Is she?'

   'God, yes. Can't you tell?'

   Tom shrugged.

   'Come on, girls and boy!' Manny shouted up the
stairs. 'It's time! Assume your positions!'

   The kids thundered down and settled themselves
on the floor, Soph with her bare feet dangerously

near Ben's legs. I noticed Ben glance at her and shift closer to Pascale on his other side. Manny and Juno took the big chairs and Tom and I had the sofa. Juno sat bolt upright on the edge of the seat.

'Oh my God,' she breathed as the title sequence came on.

The girls squealed. Manny leaned forward and peered at the screen.

'Oh, look! It's our house!' cried Pascale. And it was. There was our street on the screen.

'It's funny how seeing something on television almost *validates* its existence,' said Manny.

'Shut up, Dad,' said Sophie. 'Watch!'

*   *   *

Lee—Kim's my soul-mate.

Kim—Ooh, get him!

Lee—No, she is, I don't care how daft I sound. I love her to pieces. She's the only woman in the world for me.

Kim—Aah, that's nice. So, can I have another baby?

Lee—No. Have you found owt?

Kim—Nope. All clear. You can put your shirt back on, now.

Interviewer—What were you doing?

Lee—Oh, I have her check my back every couple of months for dodgy moles. 'Cause, you know, I spend a lot of time out in the sun.

Kim—He worries about skin cancer, don't you? Soft a'porth.

Lee—Not so soft. Sensible, more like. Them UV rays can be deadly.

Kim—He's always dying of summat. His health's

the only thing he ever gets really worked up about.

*   *   *

'It's our kitchen, Mum!'
   'Oh yes . . . Do you know, I'm so glad we went for the blue glazed tiles in the end—'
   'Shhh!'

*   *   *

Kim [To camera]—Bloody hell, have you seen these? I presume this is coffee—"café"—and this'll be tea, thé; sugar, sucre. But what's "farine", when it's at home? Hang on. Oh, it's flour! God. I dropped French after the third year. And this'll be . . . what's "poivre"? Peppercorns. Why can't it just say so? I can't be doing with this. I'm going to have to stick bloody Post-it notes on everything. If I'd wanted foreign, I could have gone on *A Place in the Sun*.
   Now, what's in here, no label . . . more sugar, it looks like—Jesus, what's that? There's all black things in there, eugh, God! They look like a load of little beetles. Can you see? What is it? Eeew, best get that lid on quick before they make a break for it! I dunno. Gave me a real fright. Cause it's not what you expect, is it, house like this? And it's not like she goes out to work, or anything.

*   *   *

'It was lavender sugar!' cried Juno in anguish. 'I
150

made it last summer. From a recipe in *Country Living*. Oh, God, do you think the viewers'll have understood?'

'Bound to,' said Manny. 'Don't worry. You're on again.'

*   *   *

Juno—There you go, you big slavering thing . . . Are these yours? Vita-Dog Crunchies? Okey-dokey; now, how many do you have? Do I fill your bowl right up? Nobody else in the house, so I can't ask anyone. I'll try half-filling it to begin with—Oh! Marmite! Get off! Get your nose—Hell, now look what you've made me do. God, nearly an entire box and they're all over the floor . . .

Right; I've shut him in the living room with his bowl so I could tidy up in here. There's all this biscuit-dust on the lino, and I didn't want to risk getting down on my hands and knees with that sex-mad beast about . . . They would be circular biscuits too; looks like they've rolled everywhere. I'll need to get—actually, I can see a load under the fridge. Just a sec, this won't do; it needs to come out. I'll have to pull it out. Can anyone give me a hand?

Oh my goodness, can you see that? Gosh. That's quite . . . I'm going to need some rubber gloves, I think.

I suppose with Kim working, she doesn't have the time to get right down—This is going to need a whole bottle of bleach, I reckon.

*   *   *

Across the room I saw Juno smiling.

'What a mess,' I said.

'You've never seen such cobwebs, honestly. They were so thick that there was an actual chip caught in one. An old, dried-up chip. Did you see it?'

'Yeah, but who really cleans behind their fridge?' said Tom. 'Ally doesn't.'

'Thanks,' I said.

'It's true. That time the Beko broke down and we had to replace it, we found a mummified mouse under there.'

Manny laughed but Juno wasn't listening. I thought, I'll never have sex with you again for that, Tom Weaver.

'Look, this is the scene where I had to go to Kim's office,' said Juno. I turned in surprise. 'I didn't know you went to her workplace. You never mentioned it.'

'Didn't I?' Juno was transfixed by the screen. 'Probably because it wasn't that interesting. Bloody boring, to tell you the truth.'

*   *   *

Juno [To camera]—Juno Kingston, reporting for duty at Leavis Timber Merchants and Fixing Supplies Ltd. It looks quite a busy place. You can really smell the sawdust, too. No other women anywhere. Not that I can see, anyway. Oh well, in we go.

Juno—Hello!

Manager—Hello, Mrs Kingston. Nice to have you on board. Great. I'll just have to remember not to call you Kim, though, eh? Very good. So, if I can hand you over to our foreman, Mr Denman . . .

Mr Denman—All right? There you go, through here. Come with me, love, and we'll soon get your nose to the grindstone. So, you're on *Queen Mum*? That must be a laugh.

Juno—Oh yes, very much.

Mr Denman—And our Kim's in your house? That must feel a bit weird.

Juno—I haven't had much time to think about it; you know, what with fitting in myself and seeing how everything works—

Mr Denman—Oh aye, I bet. So, what do you do normally?

Juno—In what sense?

Mr Denman—Your job, love. What's your job back at home?

Juno—Oh, I see. I manage a household and look after my children. And I do quite a lot of charity work, I do some taxiing for Age Concern and I help out in . . .

Mr Denman—You don't have an actual job, though? There's nothing specific you do, skills-wise?

Juno—I can turn my hand to most things. I have a first-class degree in modern history—

Mr Denman—Can you type?

Juno—Ahm, two-finger style . . .

Mr Denman—Can you work the Sun system?

Juno—The Sun what?

Mr Denman—It's a computer program we use.

Juno—Oh. No.

Mr Denman—Do you know how to fill out an invoice slip?

Juno—If someone'll show me—

Mr Denman—Tell you what, you make us all a nice cup of tea, and then I've got some boxes of screws you can unpack. All right?

Mr Denman [Speaking into mobile phone]—Is Karen there? Oh, grand. Karen? Yeah, it's Geoff Denman here. Y' all right? Great. Look, I know you're officially on maternity leave still, only I was wondering if you could pop back for a spell. Whether your mother could have . . . Ooh, only a fortnight. While Kim's away. Yeah, a bit of a mess. It'd take too long to explain here. But you'll come in and cover for Kim, will you? OK, you check with your mum, then, and get back to me. Terrific. Cheers.

Juno—Was it milk and two sugars? No, I remember now, it was no sugar. Not to worry, I can soon make you another. Should there be biscuits? I'll get them when I go back. There you go; there's your black coffee. Are you a coffee fan? Are you? I'll bring some Java in tomorrow for you to try.

There. Think I've got that right now. No sugar for Alan. I'll write them all down tomorrow, so I don't forget.

So. Is anyone here watching that brilliant series on medieval churches?

*   *   *

'They were such a stuck-up bunch,' said Juno crossly. 'I think the manager quite liked me, though.'

154

'Oh MY GOD!' yelled Sophie. 'They've kept the karaoke!' She grabbed a cushion and hid her face in it.

Pascale sat up, staring. 'Jesus,' she said. 'We look like we're all drunk.'

'You look wonderful,' said Manny. 'And you know it.'

For maybe fifteen seconds we watched the girls singing their sad, breathy duet, then Manny did a couple of lines of 'She' in a Charles Aznavour voice that had us all in fits. Kim sat on the arm of the sofa and smirked. Next the camera cut to an exterior shot of the house. It was night-time, but you could hear 'Club Tropicana' coming through the lighted windows. Tom nudged me and raised his eyebrows.

'You look like you were having more fun than me,' said Juno.

'I think we probably were,' said Manny. 'Oh, good Lord, it's Mrs Beale! Whatever is she wearing?'

'Have you seen her lipstick?' said Sophie. 'And she's got a snood on her hair. How bizarre.'

'I like those gloves,' said Pascale. 'I wonder if she'd lend them to me.'

*   *   *

Mrs Beale [To camera]—It was Kim's idea for fund-raising. We get the hall free anyway on Tuesday afternoons, Over-Seventies. So Kim said, Why don't you do a karaoke concert? I just laughed at her, because, I mean we've done comic poetry recitations in the past but, anyway, she said, You could do songs from the war. So I

155

mentioned it to Dorothy and she said, What a good idea. We could all dress up in Forties style and do songs from the shows. And that's what we're doing today. We're having Lord Woolton pie and vitality mould, raspberry snow, all sorts. The money's going towards the new rehabilitation unit at Forest Hills. I tell you, we have had such a laugh.

That Kim's a ray of sunshine, she really is. A bonny little ray of sunshine.

*   *   *

'That's not what you called her,' said Juno to Manny.

'Hmm?'

'You said she was—'

'Isn't this your scene coming up?' asked Tom. 'Ally? The dead bird?'

'Oh God,' I said.

*   *   *

Kim [To camera]—That sodding bloody cat! Look at it! I could kill it, I really could. I threw a watering can at it, but I missed. Just a sec—

Damn! Nearly had him then. Where's he gone?

Right, I see him now. Wait—

Caught the little bastard! Did you see? I nearly had to stick my fingers down his throat to get the bird out. Still. Look. Eugh. Poor little thing; it's still alive. Do you think it'll be all right? I hate cats, me. Because they don't eat what they've killed, do they? They play with it

156

for fun. That's cruel, in my book. God, you should feel my heart going. I'm going to sit down for a minute.

Yeah, it's still breathing, can you see? Little scrap. I wonder what I should do with it now.

OK, I'm going to pop round to that woman next door because she might have an idea, d' you reckon?

Ally—It's going to die, Kim.

Kim—I can't see any blood.

Ally—No. It might have internal injuries, though, it might be bleeding inside. Sometimes they die of fright, too.

Kim—Uh. Shall I put it back outside, under a bush or summat? Let it die in peace?

Ally—Fing'll get it for sure. Leave it here. I'll keep it quiet till it goes.

Kim—You want to stroke it, don't you? Soothe it. Or do you think that would give it more stress? Oh! Like a candle going out.

Kim [To camera]—It's terrible to watch something die like that. A tiny life snuffed out. I can't stop thinking about it. It's really upset me.

*   *   *

'Well!' exclaimed Juno. 'I call that a liberty. Throwing missiles at my cat, barging into my friend's house with a dead animal.'

'You did all right,' said Tom. 'Well done.'

I was speechless for a moment. 'They've cut it!' I said at last. 'I don't believe what they've done there.'

157

'What?' said Juno, very interested.

'She dropped that bird in the bin. Your bin! Just dropped it in, cool as anything, like it was rubbish. They've edited it out.'

'I was going to ask what happened to the body,' said Tom. 'I didn't want to dig it up by accident next time I was gardening.'

'But it's skewing the truth,' I went on. 'The way they've shown it, Kim was distraught, nearly in tears. But in real life she wasn't that bothered. Why have they done that? It's not a fair representation of the way she was.'

'That's TV for you.' Tom spread his hands and turned back to the screen. 'They don't tell the story you want them to tell.'

'But it's biased. It's going to—'

'Hello,' said Manny. 'Here's Juno again.'

*　　　*　　　*

Juno—I've been in this house over a week and I feel I hardly know you two.

Marco—That's 'cause there's nowt to know.

Chris—Have you finished with my Moonbase CD?

Marco—No. Haffy's got it.

Chris—I never said you could lend it out! Haffy never looks after owt. If he loses it or breaks it, you're buying me another.

Marco—In your dreams.

Juno—Who are Moonbase? Are they a band? My daughters like playing loud music, although I don't know whether they like Moon—

Chris—Dad! Tell him.

Lee—What? I'm trying to read this article Juno's give me about building projects in Belize.

Juno—It's actually very interesting. The local community out there have raised funds by pooling their resources and getting sponsorship from Western companies.

Chris—Why does nobody listen to me in this house?

Marco—'Cause you've got nowt to say, bozo.

Juno—I'm listening to you, Chris.

Chris—Yeah, but—You can't make him get me a new CD, can you?

Juno—We need to talk this through as a family, don't we? Firstly, how do we know that the CD is damaged?

Chris—We don't. But he shouldn't have taken it, that's the point.

Marco—You gave it me.

Chris—Exactly. I gave it to you, not your no-brain mates.

Juno—That's a fair point, Marco. If you borrow things, you need to treat them with respect.

Marco—Jesus. I'll get it back, stop whingeing.

Chris—Where you going?

Marco—Where do you think? Get your bloody CD back. 'Cause I'm clearly going to get nowt but grief till it's back in your sweaty little mitts.

Juno—There. That's solved. Marvellous what a little negotiation will do.

Lee—Oh aye, in't it? Very good, Juno.

Chris—Chur.

Juno—Pardon?

Chris—I said cheers. Ta.

Juno—No problem. Glad to help. So, Chris, tell me what you've been up to at school recently. What options are you taking? Do you think you'll stay on in the sixth form? Do you have

159

any long-term goals?

Chris—Er . . .

Juno—What options have you chosen for next year?

Lee—He's going to join me when he leaves school, aren't you?

Chris—Yeah.

Juno—As a builder?

Lee—No, love, as a circus performer.

Chris—I do a bit with my dad during the summer holidays. It's a laugh. Marco tried it but he's not bothered. You have to train up and he weren't interested.

Lee—On his own head be it. It's a bloody good trade to be in. I'm turning away work. I can have my pick of jobs. Do you know how much money we brought in last year?

Juno—But is that really what you want to do with your life, Chris?

Chris—Yeah.

Juno—All I mean is, have you explored all the options? You could stay on and get a few A2s, then you'd have more choice about where you went in life.

Lee—He dun't want choice, he wants be a builder. It's a skilled trade. It's worth a hell of a lot more than a piece of paper with a letter on it. He'll never be out of work, I'll tell you that much. Qualified builder gets treated like royalty, you can virtually name your price.

Juno—I only meant education's important, it can expand your horizons—

Lee—You're not listening, are you? He can take NVQs in Building Services Engineering, anyway.

160

Juno—I'm fully aware there's a lot of money to be made in building. But that's not the be-all and end-all of a job, is it? What about if he wanted to become an architect, say?

Lee—He doesn't.

Juno—Have you asked him?

Lee—Chris; do you want to become an architect?

Chris—No.

Lee—Happy?

Juno—I just thought—

Lee—You know your trouble, love? You come across as a snob. I'm sorry, but you do. There's no shame in manual work, especially skilled manual. Building's a respected profession.

Juno—A snob?

Lee—Yeah.

Juno—I'm not a snob! What a thing to say. Unless, unless to be interested in, you know, developing your children's ideas and personalities, and taking an interest in their education means you're a snob. Unless wanting to be around them and keep an eye on where they are, and trying to instil in them high moral standards and a sense of personal responsibility, of citizenship, and helping them grow into emotionally articulate adults is being a snob. In which case, yes, go ahead and call me what you like.

[To camera] Snob, indeed. I'm really quite hurt, for God's sake. My children go to a comprehensive. We're just ordinary, an ordinary family.

*   *   *

Kim [To camera]—Have you seen the prices of baths in here? *Country Living*, this is, one of Juno's magazines. Four thousand five hundred! For a bath. It's mad. Hundred and twenty quid for a table-lamp . . . She's got a manky old basket out in the garden, right; Manny told me it's a vintage skep, whatever that is, and it cost ninety-five quid. I was going to put it out for the bins. It's another world, it really is.

CHAPTER ELEVEN

The credits rolled and a voiceover told viewers that the phone lines were now open for voting. We had an hour to kill.

'That's that, then,' said Tom, avoiding my gaze.

I didn't know what to say: it sounds weird but I couldn't decide what I'd seen, exactly. How bad was it? Was it bad? Images from the programme shifted in my memory. An unpleasant sensation had settled in the pit of my stomach.

But when I came back from phoning my votes in, Juno seemed upbeat; Manny was his usual hearty self. The girls were completely high.

'Shall we get the karaoke machine out again?' asked Pascale.

'I know what we'll do,' cried Juno, jumping up. 'Let's do a moonlight sports day.'

'A what?'

'It's a beautiful night. Bring your wine outside, everyone. Manny, get the CD player from the kitchen. Pascale, grab the matches; Soph, run upstairs and bring down seven beanie babies. Tom, you carry the crisps out, will you? Did I see you had a second hand on your watch, Ben?'

'Can I do anything to help?' I asked, bemused. Wasn't this so Juno?

'I may need you to blow up some balloons for me; we'll see how it goes. Has Ben got a football we can borrow?'

And so for nearly an hour we played party games by the light of garden torches, with Al Bowlly singing about the girl of his dreams. If I have one snapshot memory of that time, it's of Juno's flushed face after she won the balloon relay and flung her arms round Manny. 'That's my girl,' he said, then Pascale and Sophie ran up and draped a beanie dog on Manny's head, and the CD was *Love Is the Sweetest Thing*. I thought, I wish they were filming this.

There's a gap between the way you first perceive something and how you view it later. By the time we all sat down to watch the results, I felt quite optimistic. Juno was her usual sparkly self, and I think we were all quite tipsy. Even Ben was mellow enough to let Sophie and Pascale lean against his bean bag.

The phone rang.

'I know who that'll be,' said Juno.

'Do you want me to come with you?' asked Manny.

'Actually, no, if you don't mind.' She gave us the thumbs up and disappeared out into the hall.

We saw the final few minutes of *Casualty*, then there was a trailer for a documentary on volcanoes, then the *Queen Mum* logo came on screen.

'Shit,' said Sophie.

In the studio, Kim sat on a sofa and talked for maybe thirty seconds to the presenter, Abby Cavanagh. Kim looked good, in a purple velvet dress that hugged her figure and showed off her blonde hair. Then the screen filled up with a photo of Juno's face and we heard Abby asking if she was there, and if she was excited. 'Terrifically,' said Juno's voice. 'I can't tell you how much fun it's all been.'

'And how have your friends and neighbours reacted to you being on telly?'

'Everyone's been marvellous, really marvellous. It's been a brilliant experience all round.'

'That's great.'

'I wish they'd hurry up,' said Pascale. The picture of Juno slid back so half the screen was her and the other half Abby, with Kim standing next to her. We saw Abby smile. 'And the lines are now closed, so we can give you the results. Are you ready, girls?'

'Absolutely,' said Juno.

'It's now or never,' said Kim.

'It's now,' said Abby, 'and the viewers have decided, with a massive eighty-two per cent of the votes, it's . . . Kim Stokes! Kim Stokes, you are this episode's Queen Mum!'

'I'll go through and check she's OK,' said Manny, leaping up from his chair. Abby handed over the gold envelope with the hotel details and theatre tickets in it, and then she popped the tiny crown over Kim's shiny hair. The last scene I remember was Abby with her arm round Kim's shoulders, and Kim putting her hands to her cheeks, like she was Miss World. She looked extraordinarily pleased with herself. If I could have smacked the woman, I would have done.

*   *   *

When Juno reappeared she was grinning and her face was very red.

Tom said, 'I thought you acquitted yourself well on the phone just now. Beautifully generous. Really nicely done. And now you haven't got the rest of the series hanging over your head, have you? You can just forget about it. Carry on as

165

normal.'

I reached out to touch her. 'That's right. Don't let that silly old slapper get you down.'

She shrugged me off at once. 'It was only ever a bit of fun, Ally. It's not as if it matters, or anything. Manny's taking me for a weekend break anyway, when my mum's feeling—'

'We know. That's great, smashing.'

'I think,' said Tom, 'the way to look at it wasn't that you were unpopular, it was that Kim was . . . oh, sod it. Like you said, it was a stupid TV show. So,' he was edging nearer the front door all the time, 'we'll be making tracks now, it's been a long old evening.'

'Yes; thanks very much for—'

'Ben!' Tom called. 'Time to go.'

Ben came round the corner into the hall. 'Do I have to? Pascale wants to show me a game.'

'Yes,' said Tom simply.

Outside I could see all the drawn curtains up and down the street. Behind every one *Queen Mum* would have been playing, I thought.

'They mustn't have voted,' I raged as we stepped into our house.

'Who?'

'The people in this street. Too damn posh to pick up a phone. That's it, isn't it? Kim'll have mobilized all the neighbourhood, probably got them all multiple-voting. I mean, how else could Juno have ended up with such a low vote?'

Ben disappeared upstairs in some kind of sulk. As the opening bars to 'Shamed' sounded through the floorboards, Tom slumped in the armchair and tipped his head back as if he was exhausted.

'I have no idea,' he said. 'You're the one who

166

watches it.'

'The only ones who got lower than that were . . . there was that one who kept wearing a see-through blouse, and that very tall woman who was caught pouring bleach on her rival's roses. Nothing like Juno! What I don't get is why they have to show the stupid percentages anyway. Can't they just say Won and Lost?'

'Juno did know that was the format of the show.'

'But the way it was edited!'

Tom dragged his hands over his face. 'That's the name of the game, isn't it? It's what editors do, cut sections. If that sometimes colours a scene, that's the nature of documentary. Don't tell me you never realized that before.'

'Thank you for the lecture in media studies.'

'Oh, come on. It's only someone telling a story. Say twenty people watch a sequence of events, then describe what they saw. How many different versions would there be? Twenty. There's no such thing as true reality TV, everything's edited. You know yourself how biased you are with Juno; the woman can't put a foot wrong.'

'I'd call that friendship.'

'Whatever. The point is, your mind edits real life; why should television be any different?'

I could have thrown something at him. 'God, you're so two-faced. Ooh, Juno, you acquitted yourself so well.'

'I'm not. I'm just trying to live in the real world, Ally.'

'Damn you for being so bloody grown-up,' I said, and went to run myself a scalding bath. I needed to get behind a locked door so badly I could have screamed.

*   *   *

We knew Juno was in trouble when, a few days later, she got a mention on *Have I Got News for You*. 'I'm not a snob,' the contestants kept saying. It was the running gag of the night. The next afternoon she came round to tell me she'd given up at the shop.

'God, Juno, how will they manage without you?'

'Very well, apparently.' Her tone was clipped and angry.

'What happened?'

It transpired she'd gone in as usual to find Mo and Gill smiling—smirking—over a tabloid. She'd brought the paper back for me. I'M NOT A SNOB BUT MY NAME'S REALLY JUNE said the headline, below a TV still of Juno in mid-shout.

'I wanted to show it to you, in case you thought I was hiding it.'

'What does it say?'

'Just that I grew up in a tiny house and I changed my name. Nothing criminal. Good God, you wonder what else has been going on in the world that there was room for this on page seven.'

It was true, then.

The little red-brick two-up two-down looked uncannily like our old place in Bolton. Not a stone parsonage after all.

'I think these terraced properties are becoming quite fashionable, aren't they?' I said, trying to scan the text to see what else was claimed. It mentioned the price of her current house, and then talked about the four-and-a-half-thousand-pound bath Kim had wondered at. 'Your bath didn't cost

168

that much, did it?'

'Of course it didn't. That's supposition on their part. If you read carefully, it doesn't actually say I have one.' She sighed. 'They did ring two days ago but I wouldn't talk to them.'

'Quite right too.' I read on, enthralled in spite of myself. Rags to riches; poor girl marries good, was the spin. 'I never knew you were a June.'

'Lots of people change their names,' she said.

'That's right. No one's called me Allison for years. I'm Ally to everyone now.'

'Exactly. It's not a major deal, is it? If they'd been into hospital and harassed my mother, I'd have reported them to the Press Complaints Commission—'

'They didn't, did they?'

'No. Just asked up and down the street I used to live.'

'Charming.' I handed her back the paper. 'Your best bet with this, Juno, is to line Fing's litter tray with it. That's all it's fit for. What a waste of paper.'

'Isn't it?'

'Hey, do you want to burn it?'

Juno exhaled. 'You see, Ally, this is why you're my friend. You have the best ideas.'

I wanted her to say then, 'Do you feel differently about me now?' so I could go, 'No, of course not.' But instead she asked for some matches and I went inside to see what I could find.

We dropped the paper in the middle of the lawn and I touched each corner with the barbecue lighter. Then we went and sat on the low wall to watch.

'You shouldn't stop working in the shop, though,

just because of that. I mean, Mo and Gill are OK, aren't they? I know Mo's dippy . . . I'm sure they weren't sneering—'

'Trust me, they were.'

'They were probably smiling with embarrassment; people do that.' As the flames took hold, I imagined the brown burn stain running across the photographs of Juno's face, of the house. The paper curled in agony; thin red worms of glowing red chased through the black layers. Pages swelled apart in ruffles soft as chiffon.

'It wasn't so much the article,' said Juno. 'That was the last straw. I haven't felt right there for weeks. Perhaps you outgrow a place. Time for a change. I've enough on with the PTA, although it's probably a big joke now that I lower myself to do the second-hand uniform. I might even tell Mrs Beale to sort out another lift for herself, too.'

'Juno, you can't do that.'

Crisped scraps of charred paper began to detach themselves and tumble off across the grass. The centre portion of the pages was still unmarked but a lot of white smoke was billowing upwards.

'I feel as though I need a break, start some fresh enterprises. Then again, sometimes I feel so damn weary I think all I want to do is lie around with a good book.'

'I can understand that.' Both of us were mesmerized by the smouldering newspaper.

'Have you seen how much smoke it's making?'

'You'd think we were burning a whole tree. Perhaps it's something to do with tabloid ink, the chemicals.'

'Yeah. Although the burning bit might be about

170

to go out. Can I have the lighter again?'

'It's next to you.'

She got up and walked back over to the newspaper, bent to apply the barrel. Click—June! Click—Not Juno! Little orange flames began to float over the page edges once more.

'It's like,' she called across, 'when you have a rid-out of your clothes. You know, when you go through your wardrobe and think: That doesn't suit me any more, or that's looking shabby.'

I nodded.

She looked down again at the tiny flames and the smoke drifted around her lovingly. 'I feel like that about some parts of my life. The *Mail* rang last night.'

'Wow.'

'Wanted to do an interview giving My Side of the story, the traditional mum angle. The mum trying to uphold family values in the face of a permissive society, and receiving no thanks for it, is what she said, more or less. My chance to redress the balance. Nicely spoken woman. She said they send round a make-up artist before they take the pictures, glam you up.'

'That's fantastic. When are they coming?'

'I said no.'

'Why?'

'Because . . . ' Juno slid her sole over the ash flakes that had settled around her feet, wiping them into paste. 'I don't trust them. To tell it right. GMTV wanted me for a slot as well.'

'Blimey. What did you say?'

'I told them I had too much on, with my mum being in hospital. They didn't argue. God, I'm tired. The phone's never stopped ringing.'

Nobody's contacted me, I thought. Not that I'd want them to. My kind of hell, that would be. 'I hope the girls are helping out more.'

Juno pulled a no face and came back to sit next to me on the wall. 'In, as Soph would say, my dreams. They don't know it but I had a modelling agency call about them yesterday.'

'I'm not surprised.'

'Not catwalk or anything, this was catalogue work, they said. They wanted to get both girls on the books.'

'Be ever so careful, Juno. There are some dodgy characters out there.'

'Oh, I said no. Don't get me wrong, I think it was legit, but I don't want them any more distracted from their schoolwork than they are. You know, I had no idea Pascale's results would be in the national press; thank God they turned out OK.'

'Slightly better than OK.'

'I meant, very good. We were thrilled, obviously. Anyway, the head's been excellent. He let all the senior kids watch a special screening of the show with Sophie and Pascale introducing it and answering questions afterwards. Let them have their day of fame. Then they were expected to go back to normal. But Sophie's being a little minx at the moment. So the modelling offer's just between you and me.'

Faintly, from next door, we heard the phone ring.

'That yours?'

'It will be.'

'Aren't you going to get it?'

'Can't be bothered. It'll be some media type.'

I laughed. 'It's all happening for the Kingstons,

172

isn't it?'

'Not half. Oh, I tell you what we were offered on Thursday. You'll never, ever guess.' She leaned away slightly so she could see my reaction and there it was, her *fizziness*, back again.

'Go on.'

'Some woman's mag wanted Manny to be on a calendar!'

I gaped. 'Not a nude one?'

'Not a nude one. Your mind, Ally! I can't remember whether it was *Bella* or *Best*, something like that, and they're putting together a reality TV pin-up calendar. There'll be that vicar who drives an HGV, and the guy with the ponytail from *Fitness Freaks*. And Manny.'

We were both giggling now. 'Mr January.'

'Mr June, more like.'

I thought, God, she's amazing, you really can't keep her down for long. 'What would he have to be doing?' I sniggered. 'I mean, what sort of pose would he strike? He's not going to take them up on it, is he?'

Juno shook her head. 'He is not. Although I think he was quite flattered to be asked.'

'I'll bet.'

I thought of Tom and how he would have reacted if anyone had propositioned him in that way. Instant divorce. Ben had made me promise, the day after *Queen Mum* had aired, that I'd never go on television again. 'You do understand, I'd have to leave home if you did and go on the streets,' he'd told me.

'Actually . . . ' Juno's happy expression slid away. 'I'd better go back and listen to the answerphone. In case it's hospital, about Mum. I'm back up there

173

anyway this evening, but you don't know what might happen in a few hours—'

'I'll see to the girls tomorrow, then?'

'If you would. It's such a relief to know you're around to help.'

'No problem,' I said, meaning it.

I watched her walk back across the patio, away from the black mess on the grass, her Liberty skirt rippling around her ankles. The scent of smoke was in my hair.

*   *   *

U ASK: PASCALE KINGSTON

—Did you enjoy being on TV? [Carla Hutton, age 12]

—Yes, it was a top experience. I got to know loads about what goes on behind the scenes and how a TV production gets made. I'd recommend it!

—I saw you did brilliantly in your GCSEs. Congratulations! Was it difficult to balance your schoolwork with your TV commitments? [Jake Farrell, 15]

—No, because it only lasted two weeks. I'd done my mocks and there was a good gap before my GCSEs. Mum and Dad would never have signed up for it if they'd thought it would affect my schoolwork. The teachers were pretty understanding about it, too.

—How have your classmates reacted to your being on telly? [Annabel Moran, 13]

—Everyone's been fine with it. The boy who advertises YoPlus is in my class anyway, so we're used to having celebs in our midst! I got a bit of teasing at first but it was only in fun. Mum told me it would be a nine-day wonder and she was right. Things go back to normal pretty quickly—it's like, Is X going out with Y and Have you seen Z's haircut, and it all gets forgotten in the excitement. I think young people today are so media-savvy that it's not that big a deal.

—What did you think of Kim Fox, the woman who became your mum for a fortnight? [Jameelah Almulad, 16]

—She was good fun, but we were glad when Mum came back. It's difficult when adults try to be your friend because you can only really be someone's friend when you've known them for a long time.

—Did you get to meet anyone famous? [Joel Griffin, 11]

—No. My sister Sophie tried everything to get Paul Eden's number off the producer, though!

—Would you like to have a career in television? [Jee Adams, 13]

—Not really. I want to work in astronomy. Those are the only kind of stars I'm interested in!

NEXT WEEK: CHARLIE KWAI FROM CENTURION. Email, text or write your questions for Charlie to the addresses on page 5.

[*The Funday Times*]

*   *   *

I'd only been in Juno's house two minutes before the telephone rang. The girls had gone straight upstairs to change out of their uniforms and their music was on full. I waited for a moment, not sure whether to pick up or let the answerphone kick in, then I thought it might be Juno with a message for me or her daughters, so I grabbed the receiver. Too late: the recorded voice started up:

You've reached the Kingston residence—'Hello?' I said. 'Hello? Who is that?'

—Emmanuel, Juno, Sophie and—

'Hang on while I see if I can turn—'

—all busy doing thrilling things at the moment and can't make it to the phone, but if you have something of burning importance to impart—

'I think it's nearly finished,' I shouted.

—BEEEEEEEEP.

'Juno?'

I half recognized the voice. 'Juno's away. Who is this? Can I help?'

'It's Kim. Who's this, then?'

'Ally.'

There was a pause.

'Ally from next door.'

'With the dead bird?'

'Well, you were the one with—'

'Oh yeah, I get you, hiya. Can I speak to Juno, please?'

'She's away visiting her mum.'

I could hear some talking in the background, then Kim said to me, 'Up in Bradford? Right, yeah, it was a funny do, her old house being in the paper. My aunty has a house just like that in Leyland. She's done it very nice, but it's poky. Han't Juno done well for herself, when you think?'

'Was there something specific you wanted me to pass on?' I said coolly, though my heart was racing with indignation.

'I've rang before,' she said. 'Left a message, but

176

she didn't . . . All it was, I wanted to say I hope there's no hard feelings. You know.'

I imagined for a second I was Juno. I stood taller and lifted my head up, looked down the long hall at the afternoon sun casting coloured shadows through the stained glass door. 'Of course not!' I trilled. 'Why on earth would there be? It's only a game-show, only for fun. We've all found it very entertaining, here, to see the way each person's been presented on camera. It's actually been a fascinating process to see how the medium of television filters events—' I stopped myself before a bitter tone came into my voice.

'It's great, in't it? I've had loads of papers ringing up, since. I've even been stopped in the street. They'll be asking for my autograph next!'

I made a huh sound that might have passed for a polite laugh.

'Oh, while I'm on,' she said, and I thought, here goes, I knew she'd be after something, 'our Chris was wondering if Juno could give him a reference. He's wanting a Saturday job in some shop, I don't know the details. I think it's only packing stock. But he's decided to put Juno down for some reason.'

'I'll tell her. I'm sure there'll be no problem.' Even though you are a sneaky manipulative cow.

I thought we'd reached the end and I was about to make goodbye-type noises, but then she said, 'Did Manny tell you about my course?'

'Your course. Crystal healing, wasn't it?'

'No. Film studies. It's brilliant, I've just started. He's lent me a load of books and videos to check out, 'cause he says even though it's quite a good course, there are gaps in it. Mind you, one evening

177

a week I don't suppose they can fit a right lot in. But you look at the old films, then at the modern ones and compare them, and you can see where they get their ideas from. So tell him I'm really enjoying it, will you?'

'I will. Look, I'd better go, I'm getting the girls their tea while Juno's away and I've got to pick Ben up from football later on.'

'Have yours started back already? Chris and Marco, their term starts Monday. It's all go, in't it?'

'It is indeed.'

As I put the phone down I realized how like Juno I'd been speaking, clipped vowels, breezy tone, all northernness slewed off. I hadn't done it deliberately, it had simply happened. As though I was trying to make myself as unlike Kim as possible. Upstairs the music boomed on.

I made the girls a sandwich each to keep them going till dinner and put the plates on a tray with two glasses of milk, as I'd seen Juno do. Then I went to see how they were getting on.

Pascale was already changed and doing her homework.

'How can you use a compass properly when you're lying full length on a squishy duvet?'

She grinned at me and slid the sandwich off the plate. 'Natural genius. Cheers,' she said and took a big bite.

I left her to it and went into Sophie's room; no sign of her. Across the landing, the bathroom door was closed. I went over and listened and heard running water. Back to her bedroom, then, to wait, because now was the time to talk to her about supporting Juno, being more grown-up. Now was the time to straighten things out.

I went to sit on the bed but found I couldn't cope with the stale air in the room, so I got up to open the window. Sophie's china-horse collection was still arranged along the sill, reminding me of how recently she'd been a little girl. Over the bed now, though, where the picture of trotting palominos used to be, was a poster of an almost naked man rising from the sea, water dripping from his nipples. Make-up bottles and compacts and tubes covered her dressing table messily, joss-stick ash lay in lines across the top of the bookcase. And did she expect her mum to pick those clothes up off the floor? Even Ben knew where the linen basket was.

I should have left them where they were, to demonstrate the point, but mums can't do that. It's a reflex action, the bend-and-grab. I draped a blouse and jeans over the back of her chair and went to pull the bedspread straight, because that was all hanging down over one side. Then I found all the bedclothes were rucked up underneath. I pulled them right back and started again. Fourteen and couldn't even make her own bed. I'd show Soph how nice the room could look with just a tiny effort.

But in flicking the bedspread back into place at last, I caught the edge of a glass that had been balanced on her bedside table and knocked it backwards against the wall. Coke splashed into a jellyfish stain on the wallpaper and ran its tentacles down the back of the cupboard. The glass bounced and fell without cracking, rolling in an arc towards the door. Damn and damn and blast, and that was something else that was Soph's fault because they

179

weren't supposed to have fizzy drinks except as a treat, and certainly not at night-time when the rot fairy comes.

I retrieved the glass, rubbed it on my sleeve, then placed it on the windowsill. The bedspread wasn't too marked, and the covers of her paperbacks would wipe clean; most of the drink had gone down the wallpaper. I snatched a packet of make-up-remover tissues from the dressing table and tried to dab away the worst, but I couldn't get to it all. Gingerly I tilted the bedside table forwards and saw that dark runs of Coke had gone right down to the skirting board and were pooling in a long bead there. I sighed—Soph should be helping with this—and edged the table out.

And there it was, a little packet of Durex. A dark blue box standing on its thin edge up against the skirting. Just handy. As I stared, it toppled over onto the carpet.

At the precise moment my brain registered what I'd seen, the bathroom lock clicked and the door across the landing swished open. I whipped the packet up and into—where?—where?—the breast-pocket of my blouse, then I settled the bedside table back against the wall, sod the Coke stain, and was still dithering when Sophie walked in.

'Oh, hiya.'

She was wearing an old baggy T-shirt and her hair was wrapped in a towel. I froze, very conscious of the square bulge in my top pocket, worried that the logo might show through the cotton. My hand came up to play with the chain at my throat, self-consciously bringing my forearm across over the box.

180

'I was tidying your room. And I brought you a sandwich.'

She laughed. 'Cheers, that's great. You didn't put butter in mine, did you?'

'No.'

'Cool. I've got to cook for twenty minutes, now.'

'What do you mean?' I managed. 'Do you know,' I heard myself saying, 'what I've just found?'

'I'm putting a copper tint on my hair.' She misinterpreted my lingering look of horror. 'It's not permanent, don't panic. Washes out in six to eight weeks.'

'I hope you haven't left the bathroom in a state.'

'Oops. I might have, now you mention it. Shall I check?'

'That might be an idea.'

When I heard the shower going again I ran downstairs, though the side door and back into our kitchen where I pulled the condoms out and threw them on the table. The blue box skidded then spun cheerily. When it stopped I saw there was a picture of a seashell on the front.

Little Sophie. Still only—and this was illegal, so it was serious—fourteen. Fourteen! Who with, for Christ's sake?

I touched the box with my finger and it shifted gently round on its axis. No cellophane. On a sudden impulse I picked the packet up and ran my nail under the flap, then tipped the contents out. Three condoms dropped out, wrappers intact. How many should there be? Three, it said on the blurb. So she hadn't used any! But then again, this might not be her first box. God knows how many she'd got through before now. She'd probably taken the outside plastic off for speed.

181

And what if, now I'd removed them, and she didn't realize, she got herself into a position where she needed one and it wasn't there? That would be my fault, and she could get pregnant, and some friend I'd have been then. To her, to Juno.

I ought to tell Juno. But she was so fragile at the moment I didn't think she could cope with anything else. Manny was around, would be home at seven. Could I tell Manny? Or would he simply fly into one of his tempers and do a whole lot of damage; and wouldn't Juno be upset that I'd gone to him and not her? I could hear her: 'She's my daughter, we have a special bond.'

And unbidden, a picture flashed into my head of ten-year-old Soph piping cream on dishes of red jelly to make four smiley faces, and Juno leaning over her shoulder with a handful of chocolate buttons for the eyes. I remember looking at Sophie's Breton top and her chic white pedal-pushers and thinking: What a pretty little girl. That would have been the first summer we were here, with Joe. And Ben had his first skateboard, was skateboard-mad up and down the drive endlessly and wouldn't wear a helmet, and the whole of our lives stretched away into those new-house sunny days.

The back of her bedside table; it was so ill-judged, a child's hiding place. Perhaps she wanted them to be found.

It was no good. I was going to have to tackle Sophie myself.

182

CHAPTER TWELVE

The knowledge of the condoms hung over me all evening. Even Tom noticed something was up.

'You're very distant tonight,' he said as we settled down to watch TV. 'Not still brooding over Juno's true identity, are you?'

I tried a mild lie, to distract. 'It was a shock, but I don't think any the less of her.'

'You do.'

'No. It makes her more like me, which is good.'

'Is it?'

'*Top Gear*'s on, did you know?' I said. 'Motorbike special.'

That shut him up. I picked up my library book and tried to read but the words just skidded off the surface of my mind. I kept imagining Sophie's face when she realized the box was gone. Would she go to Pascale? How much did her sister know? Was, dear God, Pascale at it too? That really would give Juno a breakdown.

The door bell went at twenty to nine and scared me half to death.

'You are in a funny mood,' said Tom as I mopped coffee from the sofa arm. 'Shall I get it?'

'No. I'll go.'

Soph stood on our doorstep under a cloud of midges. 'Can I talk to you?'

'I think you better had,' I said, and felt my stomach swoop with fear.

I couldn't take her through, past the lounge, because I didn't want Tom walking in on us, so we went upstairs. Ben's door was shut and his Do Not

Disturb sign was on the handle. Sophie hovered on the landing behind me as I pushed open the door of Joe's room.

'Oh!' she said, glancing at the Tweenies sticker on the door. 'Is it all right?'

'It's the one place that's really quiet. We don't want Ben interrupting, do we?'

I don't keep it like a shrine. It's the room I sometimes go to think, and to be alone with Joe. It's true a lot of his stuff is still here but that's more to do with not being able to let it go, not wanting to feel disrespectful. It's not that I think he's coming back, or anything.

I switched the bedside light on and we sat in non-threatening gloom, me on the bed, her on the tiny chair by Joe's mini-desk, hugging her knees.

'Have you got them?'

'The condoms?'

She flinched. 'Mmm. I saw the bedside table had been shifted, and when I checked behind . . . '

'I've got them, yes. Do you—need them back?'

She shook her head vehemently.

'Are you sure?'

'Yeah. For definite.'

God, this was difficult. I said, 'You're not going to get yourself in—a pickle without them, are you? Because that would be worse—'

Sophie began to giggle. I stared at her.

'It was that word, pickle,' she said, her voice unsteady. 'I know it's not funny.'

'No, Sophie, it damn well isn't.'

I looked again and saw she was shivering. It was nerves, she was strung out.

'Do you understand how serious this is? You're only just fourteen.'

'Are you going to tell my mum?'

'I don't know yet. It depends on whether you can reassure me that you'll stay well away from—this side of life—until you're ready, and it's legal. Fourteen! I hadn't even kissed a boy then.'

I wanted to tell her about self-respect and STDs, I wanted to explain the importance of hanging onto a time of your life that's special and uncomplicated, but I knew if I started a lecture she'd be gone. Behind her, Joe's poster of the four seasons showed snowmen, daffodils, beaches, brown trees.

'Ally, would it make you cross if I said something?'

'It depends what it is.'

She chewed her lower lip for a moment. 'Right, lots of girls my age are doing it. Loads of girls at school. They are. And when I'm with them it seems like it's no big deal. But now I'm here, talking to you, it seems like it is. Do you get me?'

I reached across and took her hand. She squeezed it gratefully.

'I think, Soph, that what people say they do, and what they actually do, are two different things. That the only issue that matters here is you, and what you want to do, and whether you feel you're ready. I'm not your mum, but I'm looking at you and I'd say you're too young. You are, Sophie.'

'But the teachers at school say I'm mature for my age. It said so on my last report.'

'Oh, come on. There are all sorts of mature, you know that. It didn't say, "We believe Sophie Kingston is now ready for full-on sexual intercourse," did it?'

She did laugh then, putting her hands over her

185

face and giving in to the horror that was talking about virginity to her mum's best friend.

'Have you had sex, Soph?'

She stopped laughing and sucked in her breath. 'No.'

'Honestly?'

'Honestly. I swear.'

'Because if I find you've been lying to me, I shall be very hurt.'

'Ally, listen, right? This is the honest truth. What it was—'

Light suddenly flooded the room.

'Jesus.' Ben stood in the doorway, his face white. 'Mum! I thought, I thought—'

'It's OK, Ben. We've nearly finished.' I tried to sound calmer than I felt. 'Look, love, can you go down and check your dad's unloaded the washing machine?'

He stood for a few seconds, still gazing round the room, then he detached himself from the door frame and we heard him thudding down the stairs.

'God,' said Sophie. 'Do you think he heard?' She looked stricken.

'If you mean, is there any chance Ben could have crept up quietly on us, then no. You've heard him; he moves around like a rhinoceros.' I smiled, trying to calm her. But she was too spooked to carry on. She was on her feet and across the room before I could do anything.

'I will tell you about it,' she pleaded, her knuckles yellow-white where she was gripping the door handle. 'I promise. You're just about the only person I can talk to, sometimes. But not now. There's something I need to work out first, in my head. Please, please don't say anything to anyone

186

else, will you? I'm begging you, Ally.'

My eyes searched her face for the truth.

'OK,' I said at last. 'I won't, for now. Don't make me regret that decision, Sophie.'

*   *   *

By the time I got to the bottom of the stairs, Sophie was closing the front door. I stood for a moment in the hall and heard Ben singing under his breath his tuneless version of 'Shamed':

'Looks like she don't love you

But she taste so good

She taste sohhhhh good—'

He jumped with embarrassment when I walked into the kitchen. 'Soph still here?'

'No, she went home.'

He'd flopped the wet washing into the basket for me and was rewarding himself with a processed-cheese slice out of the fridge. He likes to bend the little squares up into tubes first. I've told him it's disgusting. 'Is she OK? Has the grandma died?'

'She's fine. Everyone's fine, as far as I know. Sophie wanted a chat.'

'Yeah?'

I put my hand to the side of my mouth as though I was whispering a great secret. 'Women's problems.'

'Gross.' He unpeeled another cheese slice and began rolling it like a spliff.

Tom wandered in. 'Was I supposed to hang the washing out?'

'Yes.'

'That our Sophie I saw slipping out into the night just now?'

187

'It was.'

'Everything all right there?'

'Don't ask, Dad,' said Ben, waving his cheese tube in the air. 'Women's bits.'

'Right,' said Tom. 'Jolly good. Did you want this blouse on a hanger, Ally?'

*   *   *

Kim [To camera]—I said to the girls, I just said to them, Go get them uniforms off, and they said, Why? And I said, Because we're going on a field trip, that's why. You should have seen their faces. Leave the dishes, I said. Let's get going. Sophie was back up the stairs like a rocket and Pascale wasn't far behind. Where are we headed, Dad? they kept asking. But he wouldn't say. It was a mystery tour.

Pascale [To camera]—I can't believe we're bunking off school. Kim's phoned and said we have to do extra filming—just like that! I'd love to have seen Mrs Hitchins' face. Mum never lets us miss one day. You have to have, like, your leg hanging off by the tendons for her to let you stay home. And Fridays are a waste of time because we have extended assembly and RE and double games and community studies, which is a load of yawning teens sitting in a circle discussing anorexic gay drug-users. Slightly sad to miss music and English, I suppose. Soph's ecstatic because she's missing a French test, even though I've told her Mrs Davis'll only make her do it when she goes back.

    She doesn't think ahead, my sister.

188

Manny—Kim's absolutely right, there's a hell of a
    lot more to education than sitting in a
    classroom. I should know. I work every day with
    people, artists, who 'think outside the box'.
    Britain needs more people like that, challenging
    traditional ideas and roles. That's what today's
    about. Expanding the girls' horizons.
    Broadening their experience. Providing depth
    and shade to their appreciation of popular
    culture.
Interviewer's voice—So where is it you're going?
Manny—Blackpool.

*   *   *

Manny had come round to help Tom fix some
cupboards to the garage walls when it came out
about the Blackpool trip. I was supposed to be
helping Tom, originally, but I'd feigned a migraine
at the eleventh hour because we'd had the Bike
Row again and I was still smarting. There was no
way I was going to hold cupboards up for him
when he wanted to kill himself.

The Bike Row goes like this:

Tom—I think it's time I had a motorbike again.

Me—No, don't, they're too dangerous.

Tom—They're not dangerous. I'm a good rider.
You remember; we went everywhere on a bike
when you first met me. Anyway, I'll do a refresher
course.

Me—It doesn't matter how good a rider you are,
it's the bad car drivers you need to worry about.
You're just not visible on a bike.

Tom—I'll get a ruddy great Goldwing, then. No

missing one of them.

Me—You're still so vulnerable if you fall off. And I don't want Ben getting into bikes, either. I'll buy him a car outright before I'll see him climb on the back of a motor-bike.

Tom—Ally, I understand why you're worried. But you can't wrap us both in cotton wool.

Me—I can stop you deliberately making yourselves more likely to die, though.

Tom—OK, look, I know we've had one death in the family, but that doesn't mean Fate's against us. You could argue that we've had our portion of tragedy.

Me—Life doesn't work like that, though. There was a woman in the paper and she'd lost three sons in different accidents and then her husband dropped dead of a heart attack.

Tom—Heart attack, precisely. So he wasn't doing anything dangerous, was he? I could go tomorrow, any one of us could. That's why you have to pack in as much living as you can.

And so we go on, round and round. We have the Bike Row about once every twelve months, usually at the start of summer, but Tom had been distracted this year and it hadn't happened. Then suddenly we have a September warm as June, and the high-pitched engine-buzzing on Sunday afternoons from the main road gets into his head, and we're off again.

Most people believe they're lucky. I mean, if you've had a normal life with the normal kinds of losses and disappointments in it, then you tend not to dwell on your own mortality or the frailty of those around you. But those of us who are acquainted with grief see the world a different way.

190

Fate doesn't even-out your luck for you. Real life's not like fiction, where an author might feel he has to balance hope and despair for artistic neatness. When Fate's deciding whether you're going to get splatted, no unseen power tots up what's happened to you so far to see whether you've had your share of crap for the year. Every day, every moment is a blank, unconnected with the weight of what's gone before, where anything could happen. And that's what made me so angry with Tom, because he should have understood.

'You want to jump on a big Kawasaki and ride right away from me!' I once shouted at him. 'You want to escape!'

I waited for him to say, 'Who wouldn't?' but instead he smashed a wall clock. I didn't know whether that meant yes or no. That was the Boxing Day after Joe died and we could hardly bear to be in the same room.

So here was Manny, handsome even in his decorating gear, leaning in at the kitchen door and asking ever so sweetly for a drink. I fumbled the lump of cheese I was grating, skinning my knuckle instead.

'Cup of strong coffee, please. And an answer to a proposition.'

'Oh yes? Did you know you have a load of sawdust in your hair?'

He stepped back onto the patio and brushed at his black fringe. Fibres of wood fell like snowflakes onto the paving. 'Did I get it all? Has it gone?'

'Not really. It's mostly at the side. No, the other side.'

I stood on the threshold and he bowed his head while I fluffed his fringe with my fingertips.

191

'There you go.'

'A woman's touch.'

I sucked on my knuckle. 'So what's this proposition?'

'I'm planning another trip to Blackpool. We had such fun when we were there before, I thought it might cheer Juno up.'

'Right.'

'And I'd like you to come too, all of you, I mean. We'll make a family day of it, have a laugh. Do some crazy things.'

'Do you mean for the day or staying over?'

'Let's make a weekend of it. If you're game?'

I thought Tom and Ben might like that, big dipper, amusement arcades, fast food. 'If we've nothing else on, that would be great.'

' 'Cause it was excellent when we were up there before.'

'With Kim. You said. Actually, Kim and I were chatting on the phone the other day. She says you're helping her with a film course. I have to say, I think that's very generous of you.'

I meant: How can you help the woman who humiliated your wife? Tom would have been making voodoo dolls.

Manny didn't bat an eyelid. 'It's my passion. I love the arts and I love to help people access them. Kim's genuinely interested, and it's wonderful because she's always been defensive about education before. I think she had a bad experience of school. But she's a bright woman, you know?'

I must have looked unconvinced.

'No, she is. There's more to Kim than comes across at first.'

'If you say so.' I handed him his steaming coffee.

192

'But I wouldn't mention that to Juno, if I were you.'

*   *   *

We took the train, because Juno said it would be more of an adventure. Manny charmed some people out of their seats so we could be together in one big group. Us girls had one table, and the boys claimed the one across the aisle.

'Do you remember that time we went to London to see *Chitty Chitty Bang Bang*?' said Pascale, settling herself into her corner seat. 'We were in Chester, shopping or something, and she said, "Let's go and get a cup of tea at the station." '

'Which was, like, miles away.'

'Yeah. So we trooped after her and she didn't go in the cafe at all, did she, Soph?'

'No. And I was bursting for a pee as well. What she did was, she said, "I wonder where this train's going." Pascale read the monitor and told her, "Euston." Then she just, climbed on, didn't she?'

'Yeah; she went, "Shall I get on it?" and left us on the platform and shouted to us through the window. We thought she'd gone mad. But then she waved the tickets at us and told us to shift ourselves.'

Juno was beaming. 'Wasn't it a nice surprise, though?'

'There's always something a little planned about Juno's spontaneity,' said Manny. He reached into his pocket and pulled out a folded piece of paper which he passed across to her.

She started to speak, but the train moved off and the girls screeched and my bag fell off my lap. I bumped my head on the edge of the table trying to catch the tins of Fanta as they rolled by.

'Poor old Mum,' I heard Ben say.

'What's that?' asked Sophie, nodding at the paper in Juno's hands.

'A letter of support from a member of the general public.'

'That's nice,' I said.

She screwed the letter up and pushed it down the neck of an empty plastic bottle that someone had left behind. 'Yes, that's what I thought till he started going on about surveillance cameras and eugenics.'

'Have you had a lot of interest from nutters?'

'A bit.'

'I've got a game,' announced Manny. 'A train game. Each of you has to think of a famous person and imagine the kind of carriage they'd design for themselves, given carte blanche. Like *Through the Keyhole*. So, for example, I'd say, everything in this carriage is pink. The curtains are ruched pink satin over lace and there are frilly cushions everywhere, and a small white hairy dog is sitting on the table looking out of the window.'

'Barbara Cartland,' I blurted out.

'Spot on. Shall I do another? OK, then; the walls of the carriage I'm imagining now are covered in rhinestones and mirrors, and the seats are padded purple velvet with ermine cushions.'

'The Beckhams,' said Sophie.

'Wrong; anyway, I haven't finished. The ceiling is set with twinkling lights like stars and in the corner is a piano made out of finest—'

'Elton John,' I said.

'—finest ebony inlaid with tortoiseshell, and the

194

name of its owner is picked out in diamonds across the top.'

Manny looked about expectantly.

'And there's a bottle of black hair-dye in the cupboard, and a tooth-whitening kit.'

'Got it,' said Tom. 'Elvis Presley.'

'Nope.'

Small back gardens flashed past the window, then banks of brambles.

'Give up?'

'Liberace,' cried Juno suddenly.

'Bingo,' said Manny. 'Well done. Your turn.'

'Who the hell's Liberace?' said Sophie.

'A famous glitzy American entertainer.'

'I've never heard of him. What does he do?'

'He's dead now, but he used to play the piano very flamboyantly, he was popular in the Fifties—'

'Oh, wait a minute,' said Pascale. 'That's not fair. How are we expected to know someone from half a century ago? That's age discrimination.'

My eyes kept being drawn by a couple two seats down from us. Sophie was watching them too. Young and gorgeous, they could barely keep their hands off each other. The girl's skirt was so low-slung that you could see a good two inches of the waistband of her white knickers, and her boyfriend's fingers kept sliding round the flesh just above the elastic, making her squirm and gasp. No one else in our party could see the couple from where they were sitting. Sophie's lips parted in sympathy as the girl caught the boy's face between her hands and French-kissed him. 'All right, then,' Manny was saying. 'You have a go. One point to Juno, but it's Pascale's turn.'

Pascale grinned. 'OK. You'll like this one, Dad.

Are you ready? Right, the carriage I'm imagining has names all over it. It's got people's names sewn into the seat covers and painted on the roof and felt-tipped on the windows. Most of them are men's names, but—'

'Tracey Emin,' said Manny.

'Oh, rats. Was it so easy?'

'It was a clever idea, well done.'

'She could do a train carriage.' Pascale looked thoughtful. 'She could write on it all the names of the people she'd ever travelled with.'

'That wouldn't work, though, would it?' said Juno, swigging from a bottle of Evian. 'If you went on a bus, you wouldn't know the names of everyone else on board, would you? Unless you took some sort of a register. And you'd have to be quick before some of them got off. And if you went on a train like this one, imagine how many passengers there are on here today. Maybe the rail companies have records, but whether you could access them . . . Probably someone like Tracey Emin could, because she's famous.'

Manny was staring at her from across the aisle. 'It's a game, Juno. A game.'

The young girl with the tiny skirt was now sitting on her boyfriend's lap and licking his cheek. His eyes were closed and his head tipped back against the seat. Sophie's eyes were glued to the band of brown skin between her ribs and hip-bones. I prayed we wouldn't hit any long tunnels.

'I've got one,' said Tom. 'Who'd have a carriage done out entirely in brown, brown nylon, brown melamine, with about a million china animals on every surface? Eh, Ally? And plastic covers on the back of the three-piece suite, and one of those

196

signs saying *If you sprinkle when you tinkle please be neat and wipe the seat* over the loo?'

'Ha ha. Very funny.'

Juno raised her eyebrows at me.

'He means my mum,' I told her.

The girl we'd been trying not to watch got up from her seat and walked right past us. Close-up you could see her skin was glittery with bronzing powder—that'll be all over his jeans, I thought—and her long straight hair was lightened in odd strands. Lip gloss, long caramel-coloured nails; she was groomed rather than pretty, but still eye-catching. I saw Tom steal a glance at her navel as she swayed against his seat. When she reached the end of the carriage, the Engaged sign on the toilet lit up. Ten seconds later her boyfriend got to his feet and followed her.

Sophie knelt up and turned right round to watch him go, open-mouthed.

'All right, Soph?' asked Juno. 'Do you need the loo?'

Sophie slumped back down. 'No, Mum. I can control my own bladder without being reminded, thanks.'

'Pardon me for asking.'

Were they? Sophie's eyes asked me. Were they really? On a train?

Her expression made me smile, then we both started to giggle. The more we tried not to, the worse we got.

'I don't know what's tickled you two,' said Juno.

Sophie's eyes were watering, her chest heaving with suppressed laughter. She fell against me, helpless.

Pascale looked on, frowning in puzzlement.

'What?' she said. 'What?'

'Hey, I've got another one for you,' said Manny. 'Whose carriage do you think this is?'

'Bored with that,' said Juno. 'Sophie, blow your nose, for goodness' sake. Sit up. Now, a pound for the first person to spot the tower!'

I turned my gaze dutifully to the window, but all I could see was the couple in the toilet.

CHAPTER THIRTEEN

I'd been amazed when the taxi had drawn up outside the B & B. Dear God, was this it?

Juno had booked it; stick with Juno and you'll always find the perfect restaurant, tea shop, lay-by. Her family walks in the countryside always yielded sightings of wild animals, or encounters with interesting locals who gave them fresh pears from the orchard or let the girls hold newborn piglets. When Tom and I took Ben out for a day trip, one of us would get stung by a wasp, or decide to be travel sick, or we'd drive forty miles to find whatever it was closed and end up eating in a motorway service station.

So if there'd been a hotel in Blackpool with William Morris soft furnishings and the *Observer* in the guest lounge, Juno would have found it. Not this.

'I wanted to go for the authentic Blackpool experience,' she said as we walked into the pine-panelled hall.

'It smells of smoke,' whispered Pascale, wrinkling her nose. 'Why is there plastic on the carpet?'

'We like our guests to pay up front,' the little thin landlady was saying.

Why am I not surprised, I thought.

She pointed to a handwritten notice above the telephone. 'Cash, cheque or any major credit card.'

'Over to you, Manny,' said Juno brightly.

*   *   *

199

Manny—I never thought it would be so clean. The sand's like, almost like new suede. Pity about the sea being so grey. You get these fantastic blues in the Med. I do love that texture, though, that slight springiness under your soles that only damp sand has. Makes you want to run about.

Kim—Go on, then.

Manny—Maybe later.

Kim—Look at the girls. You'd think they were about eight, wouldn't you?

Manny—What are they doing?

Kim—Drawing love-hearts in the sand. Aww.

Manny—And then falling out about it. Sophie! Be careful with that stick—

Kim—We used come here a lot when the lads were small. But I haven't been back for years. It's heaving in the summer.

Manny—I've always loved the sea. The flatness of it. That straight, uninterrupted horizon, with all the different shaded bands of blues and greys; no wonder painters—

Pascale—Hey, Dad, we've found a treasure chest buried in the sand.

Sophie—An old crate. Can you help us dig it up? There might be something in it.

Kim [To camera]—Bunch of old condoms, probably. You wouldn't catch me digging around on this beach, no way. Not with what goes on under the pier every night.

Manny—There you go. Happy now?

Sophie—It wasn't even a whole crate after all. Just the lid. I wonder what was in it, originally? Jugo

200

anaranjado. It sounds like someone's name. Oh, Jugo, my love, take off your sombrero and kiss me.

Manny—I did tell you it was junk.

Sophie—Wouldn't you love to find a bottle with a message in it?

Manny—Or a chest containing a Greek hero and his mother.

Kim—Come again?

Manny—Perseus and his mum were cast adrift in a locked chest because Perseus' granddad, the King of Argos, was told that his grandson would one day kill him.

Kim—King of Argos?

Manny—But the two of them were rescued, and young Perseus grew up to become a mighty hero, slaying the deadly Medusa and rescuing Andromeda from a sea serpent.

Kim—And did he kill his granddad?

Manny—Uh-huh. Accidentally brained him with a discus.

Kim—You see, I know nowt, me. How come you know all this stuff, Manny?

Manny—Too much time reading books, not enough time on the beach.

Kim—Thought so. Take your shoes off.

Manny—Huh?

Kim—Come on, take your shoes and socks off and let's have a paddle.

Manny—The water'll be freezing at this time of year, are you mad, woman?

Kim—Get 'em off, Manny. Feel that sand between your toes. Go back to nature.

Manny—I don't think so. In the summer, maybe. This wind's straight from the Arctic.

Kim—Suit yourself. I'm going in, don't care how cold it is. You can't have a trip to the seaside and not have a paddle. Girls! Hey, girls.

Manny [To camera]—There's no way I'm putting my bare feet in that water. I might as well sit with them in the freezer compartment. She's mad.

Kim—Feel better now?

Manny—I'm admitting to nothing. Gagh, you see, I'm all gritty in my socks. I wish we'd thought to bring a towel. Juno always brings a bottle of water to rinse the sand off.

Kim—Sometimes, love, you have to just do stuff. Don't be such a wuss. It's a few grains of sand, for God's sake. Anyway, don't tell me you weren't enjoying yourself.

Manny—Oh, I'm not denying that. It's just that I don't know whether twenty minutes' frolic in the waves is worth twelve hours of discomfort.

Kim—Christ. We'll buy you some flip-flops.

Manny—Must admit, it does leave you tingling.

Kim—Well, then.

Manny—What? What are you smiling about?

Kim—That's all right, then, in't it?

*   *   *

Juno and I arrived down to breakfast at the same time, even though it was only just past seven. I'd had a bad night.

'Where's Tom?'

'Asleep still. So's Ben. I hadn't the heart to wake them.'

202

'Yes, my two are sleeping like princesses.' Juno lowered her voice. 'Did you know, Soph still sucks her thumb? She'd kill me if she knew I'd told you. It's quite sweet. By the way, I don't know what you said to her while I was away, but she's been positively angelic the last fortnight. For Soph, I mean.'

She glanced up at the door but there was no one there.

'Is Manny on his way?'

'No, he's taken it into his head to go for a walk along the beach. Banging about the room at six thirty, like it was a weekday. I said to him, "It's not Suffolk, you know; if you want windswept and deserted, you've come to the wrong place." By then, of course, I was properly awake. I said I'd go with him but he had a headache and wanted quiet. Do you think we should ring the bell in reception, or something? I'm parched.'

I wandered out into the hall and listened at the kitchen door. I could hear movement behind it, so I knocked timidly. The landlady opened it and said, 'Breakfast starts seven thirty, but I'll do you a pot of tea.'

'Is there coffee?' I said, thinking of Juno, but the door had closed again.

I went back to wait. Juno was gazing round the room as though she was at a gallery. 'Look at all the crystal animals. And the wall plates threaded with ribbon. It's so kitsch. But then that's part of the fun, isn't it? Like us eating fish and chips out of newspaper.'

I nodded. Mum had some crystal animals that she displayed on a mirror for dramatic effect. She'd have thought this place was home from home.

'Though I say it myself,' Juno went on, 'this trip was one of my better ideas. You know, that corner bureau's quite a nice piece. Look at the little ivory insert round the keyhole.'

The landlady came in then with the teapot and crockery. 'Planning anything nice today?'

'What would you recommend?'

She tilted her head and considered. 'There's no end of fun you can have in Blackpool. There's the piers, the Winter Gardens, the trams, the waxworks. Take your pick. All sorts.'

'Joe would have loved the trams,' said Juno, when we were alone again.

I loved her for remembering to include him. Tom might have thought the same thing but he'd never have said it aloud.

'That's true. He'd have been badgering for a ride from the minute we got here. And a go on the donkeys. And those drop handles on the bureau would have all been flipped up before you could say "Edwardian". I used to be forever telling him off about that.'

Juno poured the tea but said nothing. It was all right, though.

An old couple wandered in and sat at the table by the window. The man had tusks of tissue coming out of each nostril.

'He gets these very bad bleeds,' the woman explained, turning in her chair to stare at Juno. 'I think it's his tablets.' She picked up the menu but continued to look over at our corner. When her pot of tea came, she was so busy gawping she poured her milk on the cloth.

'Whatever are you doing?' said her husband.

'You chow me for mekkin' a mess.'

'Shift your plate,' she snapped.

Juno raised her eyebrows. 'What it is to be famous,' she whispered.

*   *   *

Manny [To camera]—Kim's right. I didn't do
   enough of this sort of thing as a child. Spent far
   too many hours waiting around on my own in
   huge Victorian buildings for my father to finish
   his meetings. I've got this image of myself,
   sitting on a high-backed chair under some
   enormous oil painting with my legs swinging . . .
   So, where would my mother have been, then?
   Do you know, I've never thought about that till
   this second. It was odd, wasn't it, leaving a little
   boy like that entirely unsupervised. I mean,
   there were always diplomatic staff about, but
   they were all pretty busy. So I was left to my
   own devices. I used to sit and read, mainly.
   You'd never get away with it these days, you'd
   get reported. I wonder if she took herself
   shopping?
   I must ask her about it sometime.

*   *   *

Manny made an appearance just as we were finishing our toast.

'Everything all right, ladies?' He bent to kiss Juno, then pulled up a chair between us. 'Breakfast good?'

'Lovely, thanks. I said no to the big plate of grease but Ally's had it and wolfed it down.'

205

'I can see.' Manny took the last piece of toast from the rack and, leaning across, wiped it round my plate. Then he took a huge bite.

'Really!' said Juno. 'Headache's gone, then?'

'Uh-huh.'

'Did you have a nice walk?' I asked. He hadn't shaved and his chin, as it moved up and down, was dark and rough.

He swallowed the toast and looked pleased with himself. 'I went for a paddle.'

Both of us looked in surprise at his feet as if we expected to see waves lapping there.

'It was great, refreshing. You should try it.'

*　　*　　*

Juno had decided we should go up to the top of the tower first.

'It's an intrinsic part of the Blackpool experience,' she said. 'You can't come to Blackpool and not have a trip up the tower. It's part of our cultural heritage.'

'The tower was opened in 1894,' read Pascale as we rose slowly in the lift. 'It weighs two thousand, nine hundred and forty-three tons. Ten thousand light bulbs are used to decorate its exterior. Two thousand ice creams and six thousand cups of coffee are sold in the tower premises every day.'

I shut my eyes and tried to pretend I was on the ground. Tom reached for my hand.

When the doors opened it was into an enclosed space with large windows.

'You all right?' said Tom.

'I don't think she'll be doing the Walk of Faith, will you, Ally?' said Manny, slapping me on the back. 'Come on, there's no need to be so anxious. Look, even those Brownies are having a good time.'

It was true; seven-year-old girls in yellow sweatshirts were taking it in turns to skid across the glass plate set into the floor. One of them even stopped in the middle and stared straight down at the three-hundred-and-eighty-foot drop below her little feet. I wanted to rush over and drag her to safety.

'Not coming up to the next level, then?' Manny called, already halfway up the spiral staircase.

'I will,' said Tom at once. Ben and the girls scrambled after him. I stayed by the gift shop playing with the snow globes.

'Spectacular views,' said Juno. 'You can see of all the piers, the big dipper, the ferris wheel; some gorgeous Victorian buildings too. Do you want to come to the side and look out?'

'I'm fine,' I said, and she left me alone.

On the way down to the ground floor we stopped off at the ballroom balcony and marvelled at the gold on the ceiling and the classical-style murals.

'Isn't it deliciously tacky?' said Juno, sitting herself down on one of the red-velvet seats.

I didn't think it was tacky at all. I flopped down next to her and leaned over the side to watch the elderly couples waltzing below. For some reason, I wanted to cry.

'It's like *The Wheeltappers and Shunters Club*,' said Tom. 'Look at the stage!'

Out of the floor, in front of the magnificent swagged curtains, rose a white Wurlitzer. The music flowed round the room eerily.

'That Wurlitzer organ delivers seventeen

thousand, seven hundred and forty-five numbers each season,' read Pascale. 'Between the months of July and October, four hundred and forty-eight thousand people dance in the Tower ballroom.'

'Bad taste overload!' cried Juno. 'It's *too* much. I'm off to look at the aquarium.'

I told Tom I'd join them in a minute.

'Poor Ally,' he said, bending to look in my face. 'Still suffering from vertigo?'

'Yes,' I said, because that was easiest. When they'd gone, I rested my arms on the rail and gazed around at the ornate ceiling lamps, the bunting hung at my eye level, the Sixties-style tables and chairs dotted around the parquet dance floor. It was beautiful and sad at the same time, like a violin note.

Below me, the couples danced on.

*   *   *

Pascale—Look at that, Dad, a real palmist.

Manny—Depends what you mean by 'real'.

Pascale—She's seen all the stars. Look; Myra
   Forsythe, Colin Dovedale . . .

Manny—Who?

Kim—Shall we give it a whirl?

Sophie,—Oh, yeah. Cool. Can I go first?

Manny—No.

Kim—That's right, Soph, age before beauty.

Manny—I mean, no, they're not going in. It's an
   utter rip-off.

Sophie—Dad?

Kim—It's only a bit of fun. Lighten up. I went to a
   woman in Salford one time and she was
   brilliant, knew it all. Reckoned I'd be moving

208

into choppy waters but I'd sail through.

Manny—I said no.

Pascale—Please, Dad. It's social research. We could go, check it out, and make up our own minds in an adult way.

Sophie—Go on.

Kim—Yeah, let them have a turn, you old meanie. It's three against one.

Manny—I'm not, no. I'm not going to give my permission for you to go and listen to some charlatan who's probably laughing all the way to the bank. Look, I don't mind giving you money for books or to go and see a film, but I'm not funding this rip-off. Christ, I'd rather you went and blew your savings in Top Shop, then at least you'd have something to show for it.

Pascale—Yes, please.

Manny—That wasn't an offer, by the way. Your savings are staying where they are.

Sophie—But it's our money.

Manny—Yes, and we've been through this—

Kim—Aw, Manny, let them have a go. It's harmless. You said you wanted them to have a load of different experiences.

Manny—Good God. Look, right, I'll tell you want I'm prepared to do. Sophie, Pascale, here's twenty quid each. It's yours to spend on clothes while you're here. You can buy any rubbishy old tat you want. But you don't go into the palmist's, OK?

Sophie—Wow, yeah, excellent.

Pascale—Cheers.

Manny—Christ. What a carry-on.

Kim—Ooh, Manny Kingston. That's blackmail, that is. Juno won't like that.

[To camera] She won't like that at all.

*   *   *

If Juno had some sort of agenda in Blackpool, I couldn't work out what it was. She refused cockles, but bought a paper plate of egg-and-bacon-shaped rock; we did the amusement arcades but not the waxworks.

'Why should we always have to do *worthy* things?' she said, when Manny tried to persuade her to take a look at the Sea-Life centre.

I exchanged glances with Tom. That's rich, his expression said.

Later, when Juno and the girls were strolling ahead and Ben and Manny were examining some vintage slot machines, he said to me, 'Can you not see what she's doing?'

I shrugged. 'How do you mean?'

'Everything Kim did, she's turning her nose up at. She's slagging off all the places Kim went with Manny.'

'Oh, I don't think so.' In front of us, she linked arms with the girls, her head moving animatedly.

'You watch. I never had Juno down as petty.'

The next attraction we visited was the Pleasure Beach.

'Didn't you come here with Kim?' asked Tom, his face innocent.

Manny shook his head. 'Kim doesn't like fast rides. She was in a bad car accident as a kid.'

'I want to go on the bumper cars,' said Sophie, holding an imaginary steering wheel in front of her and snarling.

I've always called them dodgems. Says a lot, that.

I waited alone at the bottom of the big wheel while they swayed a hundred feet above me on thin metal struts. To my right, a little boy was sobbing for a goldfish and his mother, or sister, I couldn't tell which, was giving him an earful. For God's sake, I nearly said as she dragged him past, give him a bloody fish and be glad about it.

After the wheel, Manny bought us all ninety-nines and Pascale told us that a man called Richard Rodriguez had used the big dipper to break the world roller-coaster-riding record, staying on for a total of five hundred hours.

'They sell forty-seven miles of hot dog sausages a year, plus enough candy floss to returf Wimbledon Stadium four times over.'

'Like you'd want to turf a tennis court in candy floss,' said Ben, pulling the leaflet out of her hands so that she squealed and pretended to fight him for it.

'I feel sick,' said Sophie.

'You *have* to go on the big dipper, though,' said Tom. 'You can't go home without a ride on that. It's the law.'

Juno looked concerned. 'Soph? Do you think you actually are going to be sick? Do you need to go and sit down quietly somewhere?'

I surprised myself by stepping forward and putting my arm round her shoulders. 'She can stay here with me, there's no need to spoil your fun. We can go get a cup of tea and find a bench somewhere—over there, by the helter-skelter, that's where we'll be. OK, Soph? And I bet you she'll be right as rain in twenty minutes.'

'It's cool but the sun's very bright. Try and get

under the shade,' said Juno, frowning.

I wondered whether she'd leave us, but I guessed she was bent on proving her fearlessness to Manny. Juno would have climbed on that roller coaster if it had been on fire. In the end she patted her daughter on the arm, and joined the rest of them in the queue. Sophie and I had, at the very least, quarter of an hour on our own.

'Well, madam,' I said.

*   *   *

Kim [To camera]—I'm not completely thick, me. I'm not Mastermind or anything, but I do have a brain. My school reports were always good, I could have stayed on if I'd wanted. But I didn't. I wanted a wage, some independence. That was my decision.

I'm not saying he tries to make me feel stupid. He just knows so much. About all sorts.

Except about enjoying himself.

*   *   *

'What?'

'You know. Have you got something you want to tell me?'

She looked blank.

'Sophie, I'm not going to waste time here; are you, by any chance, pregnant?'

She opened her mouth to speak but she must have inhaled some saliva because she started a coughing fit instead. She clapped her hand to her lips and her eyes bulged in disbelief at me as she struggled to get her breath. '*No*,' she rasped finally.

212

'God, Ally, what a thing to say.'

I walked her over the bench and all the while she was looking at me and shaking her head.

'All right,' I said. 'But you can't blame me for asking. Condoms in the bedroom; sudden feelings of nausea—'

And even as I was speaking, I was back in the old house with Ben banging on the bathroom door as I retched into the brown sink; gasping, Mummy's coming, sweetheart! between heaves. Images flicking through my head: pinning Joe's scan photo up on the corkboard in the kitchen—Ben peering over the Moses basket—cutting someone's tiny fingernails—scalding my thumb on the steam sterilizer. Please, God, don't let her be pregnant, I thought. I couldn't bear to have a baby in my life again.

Sophie was laughing, actually laughing out loud. 'Sorry, oh, Ally. I know it's not funny.'

'How do you know you're not pregnant?' Her face went serious and she answered in such a low voice I could only just make out what she said.

'Because I haven't had sex yet.'

'Right.'

'I haven't. It's true. I swear, God's honest truth.'

But there was still the tiniest smile playing around the corner of her mouth. Should I believe her or not?

'So what was the Durex in aid of?'

'OK, what it was, right, I wanted to practise. I got them out of a machine—'

'Which machine?'

'In Bruno's.'

'The coffee house? They have Durex machines in there?'

213

She sniggered. 'I know. In case you come over all horny in the middle of your latte.'

'Was anyone with you?'

'No way. I wanted to try it on my own. Oh, *God*, this is *so* embarrassing. Do you not understand? Ally, I haven't even got a boyfriend, I'm *that* sad. Right; I wanted to see, close-up, what a condom was actually like and what you did with it, so that when I did need one it wouldn't be a complete—' She waved her hands. 'I did the same thing with a box of tampons when I was about eight. I wanted to see how everything, you know, worked.'

The crowds flowed past me as I considered.

Suddenly she said, 'How old was she, do you think?'

'Who are we talking about?'

'The girl on the train.'

I thought back. 'About twenty,' I lied.

Sophie looked disappointed. 'Oh. She seemed younger to me. Thing is—'

'What?'

'It's everywhere, isn't it? Sex is all around you, you can't get away from it. Even in the sweet shops on the front, did you see? All those rock willies? Don't, I'm trying to explain. It's all over the magazines I buy, it's on TV all the time, it's in adverts for ice cream and cars and even bloody kitchen spray. It's in the Shakespeare we do at school and we talk about it in social studies, it's in pop videos for the under-twelves, family bloody sitcoms, it's on the Internet. It's like, everyone in the whole world's doing it, this huge enormous *load* of sex, so why would it be such a big deal if I joined in?'

'But you know the answer to that.'

'Yeah yeah.'

You shouldn't be so beautiful, I felt like saying. You can't cope with it.

'Ally—what was your first time like? Can I ask you that?'

I sighed. 'No.'

'Oh, God. Are you cross?'

'No.'

To be truthful, I've had three boyfriends in my life. Proper ones. The first, Robin, I fell completely in love with, would have slept with, only he finished with me before I plucked up the courage. Mark, my second, I slept with straight away, even though I didn't care about him much. We lasted about six weeks. Then I met Tom, and I knew straight away I wanted to marry him. I've edited out Mark from my history; as far as Tom's concerned, it was him I lost my virginity to. I don't like to be reminded of that painful twenty minutes spent barricaded in the coat room at Des Farris's party. I was eighteen, then: two years later I was a married woman. Far away, behind the thumping beat of S Club Seven, people were screaming. There'd been an accident last year where a girl had fallen out of a roller coaster and died, but it might not have been here.

'It's good I've got you to talk to,' Sophie was saying, head on one side, smiling one of those melting smiles she does.

'You should speak to your mum, though.'

'Oh yeah? And watch her have some sort of foaming-at-the-mouth-type fit?'

'Juno's not like that.'

'She is with me.' Through the crowds I spotted Manny's tall figure weaving towards us. 'Here they are,' I cried, jumping up and pointing. I waved my hand in the air.

'Trouble is, you don't know what she's really like,' I heard Sophie mutter.

*   *   *

We stayed till the lights came on along the sea front.

Ben wanted a last go on the Test Your Strength machine—'No way am I going home as a Lightweight,' he told us—while us grown-ups drank bottles of cider and gazed over the railings at the glittering black sea. Sophie and Pascale leaned against the iron street lamp like a couple of good-time girls, red highlights in their hair from the illuminated cupids above.

'Do you truly not have a boyfriend?' I said to Sophie as we walked back to the station. She slowed down so we could be a little apart from the others.

'Nope,' she said. 'It's dire. I mean, I have been asked out, but only by dingo-boys. There's no one in my class I fancy, they all act like they're about ten.'

'Boys mature later than girls.'

'You're telling me. Paxo doesn't have a boyfriend either, but she doesn't want one. She *says*.' After a moment she added, 'Do you think there's something wrong with me?'

I shouldn't think any boy can get a word in, I almost said. 'I'm sure there are hearts beating hopelessly all over the place for you, but their owners are too scared to come forward.'

'Yeah?' Behind her veil of hair she beamed.

216

'Honestly?'

'Very much so. Don't wish your time away, it'll happen soon enough. But do you promise me you'll be careful? You know, with *things*.'

'I promise, Ally-pally. I promise I promise I promise,' she sang. 'I pro-mise, I pro-mise.' Then she leapt up onto a garden wall and started balancing along the top like a tightrope walker. 'Look at this girl go!' she shouted.

I can't say I felt very reassured.

CHAPTER FOURTEEN

There are some scenes in life you watch that your brain won't take in. This isn't real, it tells you: think again, this can't be happening.

I'd been in Ben's room making his bed. Tom had taken Ben out to Sealand to look at some Peugeots he was interested in test-driving, and I was using the Sunday lull to catch up on housework. I'd stripped the sheets off and I was shaking out the clean ones when I spotted Sophie run out on her back lawn. She was wearing her dressing gown and Doc Martens, and she had her violin with her.

First she put the instrument face-up on the grass and stood deliberately on the body. Without moving her feet she crouched down and began to pull the neck hard towards her. It didn't break at once; she had to stand up again and stamp on it. Then she twisted the neck away—it had been hanging by a few splinters—and I think she must have cut her hand because I saw that there was blood on her palms. The main part of the violin dropped and hung by the strings, swinging. She booted it round the garden a few times, the way you'd kick a football, and then she jumped up and down on it. Her hair was flying about her face.

I was going to open the window and call, but she shot off into the house. I continued to stand there stupidly. Where were Juno and Manny, for God's sake? How much had they paid for that violin?

Sophie came racing back out, this time with a pair of kitchen scissors and some pliers. She wrenched the bridge off, snipped the strings and pulled out the pegs one by one as if they were teeth.

Suddenly there was a terrific hammering on our front door. I almost fell on the bottom step trying to get to the latch.

It was Pascale, wide-eyed and breathless. 'Can you come round, quick, Ally? Soph's gone mad.'

'Where are your mum and dad?'

'Sainsbury's. Please, Ally, quick. She's smashing things up.'

I nipped back to grab my keys from the kitchen, then we hurried down the side of her house to the garden.

'Where's she gone?' said Pascale, panting slightly. Bits of glossy chestnut-coloured wood were strewed over the green. 'Shit. I hope she's not having a go at mine. I need it for Tuesday's recital.'

She bolted for the back door and I followed. 'Or she might be harming herself,' I suggested.

Pascale gave me a scornful look.

There was no sign of Sophie downstairs so we went up to see if she was in her room.

She was. The door was locked and we could hear angry music from behind it.

'Soph? Soph? It's Ally.' No response. 'Are you all right? Can you open the door for me?' Still nothing. Pascale emerged from her own room clutching her violin triumphantly. 'This is fine, anyway.' She inclined her head towards Sophie's door. 'She'll want you to try a lot harder than that. You could be there for the duration. Would you like a chair to sit on while you wait?'

I shushed her and drew her across to the other side of the landing.

'What's the background to this?'

219

Pascale shrugged. 'Some sort of row with Mum. There've been a lot of those lately.'

'What about?'

'I wasn't listening to most of it, I've heard it all before. It started with Mum asking Soph why she wasn't dressed yet, and then it moved on to shopping, because Soph wanted some crappy fluorescent drink she'd seen on TV and Mum said she wasn't going to buy it because it was full of additives and looked like pee. Then I think it went on to how Soph should do more around the house, and Mum took her upstairs to see the mess her room was in. They must have had some kind of meltdown in there, because Mum stormed out and went and sat in the car.'

'Where was your dad?'

'On the phone.'

'What, all the time?'

'Yeah. He's always on the phone. Then Dad went and had a word with Mum, and he came back in and said it was best if they both left each other alone to cool off, and the shopping would only take forty minutes, and was I OK to keep an eye on my sister. I said yes because I didn't realize how freaked out she was. I went upstairs and she shouted at me to leave her alone. I said, had she remembered about the recital on Tuesday and she just flicked open her violin case and stared into it. Then she got this bottle of red nail varnish and, and *poured* it all over the violin, I couldn't believe it. So I said, "You'd better stay away from mine," and she goes, "I'm not interested in your fucking violin." That's it, really. You saw her in the garden, you know the rest.'

But I didn't know the rest at all.

220

By the time Juno had come back, Sophie still hadn't emerged. I'd tried talking to her through the door but she wouldn't answer except to tell me to leave her alone. I couldn't help feeling hurt. Pascale didn't seem as bothered as she should have been; now she was stretched out on the living room sofa gabbing into her mobile.

'Has Madam calmed down yet?' Juno called from the hallway.

'Uh-oh,' I heard Pascale say.

'What?' said Juno when she saw my face. 'Is there a problem?'

*   *   *

Kim [To camera]—I like them, I do, but I still say they're not normal, those girls. Too good to be true, if you know what I mean. Stepford teenagers. Like, when I was their age, I can't tell you the sort of stuff I was getting up to.

Interviewer's voice—What sort of things were you getting up to?

Kim—God! I'm not saying on national TV, what do you think I am? Just, you know, normal girls' stuff. The viewers'll know what I mean. Boyfriends and what have you. Going out, being young and a bit mad. I certainly wasn't faffing about with a bloody fiddle, I'll tell you that for nowt.

*   *   *

'I'm going to leave it for Manny to clear up,' said Juno, coming in again with another carrier. 'I'm

221

too upset to deal with it now. Pascale, go check on your sister, will you? See if she's deigned to unlock her door yet.'

Pascale slalomed obediently off through the bags of shopping that dotted the hallway.

'Where is he?'

'Manny? I left him at the library. He announced on the way back that he needed to pop in and have a word with the head librarian about an exhibition. I was supposed to wait for him, but, you know, I had this sixth sense that something wasn't right at home. So I went in to see how long he'd be and he said he couldn't tell me. I got straight in the car and drove home.' She put her hands against her temples. 'I wish I'd insisted he'd come with me, now. What a God-awful mess.'

We started unpacking together.

'What are you going to do with her?' I asked, unsheathing a French stick from its paper bag.

'Give me that, Ally, thanks. Good question. For a start, she can play Pascale's violin when it's not being used—although what we'll do about Tuesday, I don't know—and if she damages that, she's grounded till a new one's paid for. It's an awful thing to say, but I feel like giving her a good old slap.'

'Don't say that, Juno.'

She raised her brows at me. 'It's all right for you. You live with a reasonable teen. You know where you are with Ben, he's a star. But I never know from one minute to the other what Soph's going to be like. Moody isn't the word.'

She started slamming tins into the back of the cupboard with a force that made me wince.

'And I told her, and I've lost track of how many

222

times I've said this, I have not got the time or the energy at the moment to keep up with her awkwardness. It's no joke driving up to Yorkshire every few days, and not sure what you'll find when you get there. I know Mum's stable for the moment, but it won't last. The doctor's warned me.'

'Here.' I handed her a bag of fruit as sympathetically as I could. A lemon rolled off the kitchen top and fell on the floor.

'Damn thing,' she said, and kicked it out into the hall. It skipped over the tiles and ricocheted off the skirting board, coming to rest by the telephone table. I fought with myself not to run after it.

'What do you think it was that made her flip?'

Juno emptied tangerines into a copper bowl. 'I have no idea. It started with the usual stuff about how she needs to have more consideration for the family unit, I could write the script. I did say to her as well—not to go *throwing herself* at Ben—Maybe that was what sent her silly. Although if you can't give your own daughter some advice about these . . .'

I stared at Juno but she was peering into a drawer. Something about the set of her shoulders told me she was avoiding looking at me.

'Oh,' I said. My mouth went very dry and I had to swallow. 'Yes, I said I thought she had a crush on him, do you remember?'

'And I just said to her it was completely pointless.'

'Yes.'

'He's made it quite clear he doesn't fancy her. She's only making a fool of herself.'

Because Juno knows he's gay, I thought. Will she

223

say it?

'Damnation. Look at that, the bag's split. I've been trailing couscous all over the floor. Manny, where are you when you're needed? Ally, can you get the mini-hoover from under the stairs?'

I did as I was told. When I got back she was muttering about Kim.

'So I'm up and down to Yorkshire, Manny's nipping off to Bolton every other week, reckons he's got to drop off all these books and tapes for Kim's course. It's ludicrous. She can get her own books out of the library, and record all the films she wants off the TV. They've got a big enough satellite dish stuck on the side of the house.'

'Manny goes to visit Kim?' I could hear the surprise in my own voice. I didn't mean it like that, I wanted to say. But you can't start justifying yourself in these situations or it sounds so much worse.

'He's helping her with her course. I did tell you. But there's no half measures with Manny, not where films are concerned. Don't look at me like that, Ally, there's nothing going on. This is "Two O-levels" Kim we're talking about. She's about the last woman Manny would find attractive. He's just got this passion for educating people. Remember last year when Ben mentioned he liked Westerns, and Manny insisted on lending him that whole pile of so-called definitive ones? Wanted him to fill in a sheet about them all?'

'Yes,' I said. 'I had to do it for him.'

Juno blinked. 'You didn't? I am sorry. But, you see, that's what he's like.' She paused, frowning, then seemed to brighten. 'Anyway, it's sort of a reciprocal arrangement.'

224

'How do you mean?'

'I've been helping Chris with his options. He *asked* me, before you say anything. That lad's the best of the bunch, not that that's saying a great deal. He phoned me up wanting to know what Pascale was going to do for AS, so I've been outlining some courses for him. He says he might think about English language and business studies. Though whether he'll get as far as—'

Pascale appeared at the door. 'Soph says she'll come out but you have to promise not to hit her.'

Juno let out a cry. 'Oh, Ally. Oh, what a thing to say; as if I'd hurt my own daughter.'

'Of course you wouldn't. Do you want me to speak to her?'

Juno shook her head.

I stepped over and took the packet of rice she was holding. 'Pascale and I'll finish here. Go up and see her.'

She stood for a moment, then walked briskly out of the room.

'Silly little drama queen,' said Pascale, pulling out a packet of ginger biscuits and picking at the top. 'She winds Mum up and then we all get it in the neck. There's no way she's borrowing my violin, either. Pass me that bread knife, Ally, would you?'

Upstairs there was the sound of a door banging several times, as if two people were tugging on either side.

'She hasn't ever hit Sophie, has she?' I heard myself say.

Pascale stopped sawing the biscuit packet for a moment. 'Not yet. I'd say it might only be a matter of time, though.'

*　　*　　*

Because Ben's birthday's in October, we've never been able to plan anything outdoors for him. But this year there was an unseasonably warm spell that came out of nowhere and so we took him and Felix to Oulton Park and let them tootle round the mini-track on go-karts.

'Will they be all right?' I asked Tom. It had been Tom's idea; I'd have taken them to see a film, had them sit safely in the darkness for three hours.

'Look at them, Ally. They've got Kevlar back shields and leg pads and helmets, and they're fastened in with harnesses. Besides, see his face? He's loving it.'

Before we went home, Tom signed himself up for a track day. 'I can blag a bike for the weekend. Hire one, if I have to. Ally, I've got to have a ride.'

I said nothing. But late that evening, after Felix had been picked up and Ben was in bed, Tom was so tender with me that he must have known how I was feeling. He came and sat behind me and massaged my scalp, something he knows I love. Then he kissed my neck and stroked my shoulders and arms for ages. For a long time I resisted the good sensations and held on to my resentment. How dare he be so happy? But the touching continued. My anger sublimated. 'I don't want to have sex tonight,' I said at one point.

'Fine,' he said, and carried on.

At last I turned to him and he kissed me deeply. His hands moved down to my breasts and I didn't stop him. 'Oh, Ally. Thank you,' he kept saying. 'Thank you.'

*   *   *

Kim [To camera]—He's my rock, Lee is. He's my soul-mate. I know where I am with him, I can always depend on him. I love him to bits, the daft bugger. Yeah. My rock.

*   *   *

'How close are you to Tom?' said Juno.

The question came out of the blue; we were sitting behind her French windows watching it drop dark. It was Ben's night for swimming practice and he wouldn't be back for another hour and a half, so there was no point starting the tea yet. Four till six was one of those stretches of day when I hated being in the house on my own. It used to be CBeebies time. Tweenie clock, where will it stop? I have trouble with dusk, too. Juno knows these things.

'How close? Too close. I found one of his toenail clippings in my slipper this morning, and he wasn't at all contrite. I suppose that's what marriage is, when it comes down to it, an intimate knowledge of toenail clippings.'

I thought Juno would laugh, but she didn't. She said, 'But do you know the way he's going to act in a given situation?'

'Hmm. Usually. I know when he finishes a packet of something he'll put the empty packet back in the cupboard and not in the bin, which is incredibly annoying. I know he still hopes one day to be world bike-racing champion. And that he turns off any party political broadcast, by any side,

227

on principle.'

'Better than complaining all the way through it, which is what Manny does.' She sipped her wine and gazed out across the garden. 'But what I mean is, do you know him *right through*? Do you know what he's thinking, deep down?'

'Tom doesn't have a deep down. What you see is what you get. Ben's the one with scary depths.'

'You should try living with Soph.'

Yes, I thought, and you don't know the half of it.

'Maybe you don't ever really know anyone,' I continued, because I didn't want to remember the spilt Coke running down the wall and what came after. 'Let's be honest, lots of people don't even know themselves.'

'That's too bleak for me at this time of the evening,' she said, pushing her hair behind her ear.

'How well do you feel you know Manny, then?'

'We've been married for fifteen years,' she said. 'So maybe hardly at all.'

Manny proposed to Juno in the town square in Le Havre, she's told me about it. When she said yes, he climbed on a bench and sang 'C'est merveilleux' and the baker from across the street came out and gave them each a madeleine. Afterwards they went for a boat ride and she says she remembers looking up into the sky and thinking, This is where my life begins! Tom asked me to marry him while we were walking across a car park in Bolton on the way to Benson's For Beds. 'Because if we are going to get hitched, I'll order a double,' he'd said.

Pascale whirled into the lounge. 'Ally, did you know your mobile's going off in the hall? Mum, have we got any plastic bags anywhere?'

228

I was up at once, because whenever my mobile goes I assume it's going to be bad news. I shoved past Pascale and went to stand by the bottom of the stairs with the phone pressed to my ear. As Juno went by on her way to the kitchen, I turned my back on her smile.

The screen was showing Ben's number, but the voice on the other end was someone I didn't recognize and there was a rushing noise in the background that made it difficult to hear.

'What? Ben? That's not you, is it?'

'Can you come and pick him up?'

'Who is this?'

'Is that Mrs Weaver?'

'Yes! Who are you?'

'He's by the Fountains roundabout. He's had an accident and he can't walk.'

The phone bleeped and the voice disappeared. I stood for a second in front of the willow-pattern wallpaper, and my head and chest felt as if they were filling up with helium. Then I tried redial but whoever I'd been speaking to had turned the phone off.

Without waiting to explain, I wrenched the front door open and ran outside. Thank God I'd only had half a glass of wine.

As I reached the gate I heard Juno.

'Ally? Ally? Whatever's the matter?'

'Have to pick Ben up,' I called into the air.

'Hang on, let me—' she shouted, but I was over the little wall and into our garden, wrestling the lining of my handbag for my car keys, pressing, clunk, then in, throwing the bag into the passenger foot-well and the phone on the seat where I could get at it.

It would take me ten minutes to get to the Fountains, fifteen or twenty if the traffic was heavy. The tyres squealed under me; Mr Kirk, sweeping leaves at the end of the avenue, looked up and frowned. When Joe died, he'd sent a card with a country bridge on it and a sentimental verse, even though he's never spoken to us before or since.

At the end of the road, I turned left and at once heard Tom saying, No, take a right, fewer traffic lights. Too late now. Or could I try an illegal U-turn? I had ten seconds till I drew level with the break in the central barrier.

Can't walk, the boy had said. What did that mean? Paralytic again? A broken leg? Bleeding to death on the pavement; comatose?

Now: I trod on the brakes and swung the car round across the chevrons. Someone bibbed their horn at me and headlights signalled furiously, but I didn't care. I barged my way out into the stream of cars, with my heart pounding somewhere up near my neck.

I'm law-abiding by nature. I was always the one at school who waited sensibly for the teacher to come, who never turned over her paper till told to do so. It was my short-term ambition to keep out of trouble, my long-term one to be ordinary; all I ever wanted was to have a family, a quiet life.

A winking light on the other side of the road made me draw in my breath but it was only roadworks, not an ambulance speeding to my dying son.

I never took risks with the boys. Even when I was pregnant I did everything I was told to. If the midwife had said stand on your head for nine

230

months, I would have done. My babies never had cot bumpers or baby walkers, any of the paraphernalia that's now considered to be dangerous. All our sockets had safety plugs in them. Yet every day you see people walking their kids along high walls, leaving their newborns outside shops to be abducted.

The traffic round the Fountains was jammed right the way up, the lights at the top only turning green for what looked like five seconds at a time. Chester's rush hour. I let out a howl and revved the engine in anguish. What if, at this very second, Ben's blood was pooling on the ground in some dark corner of the Northgate car park? I thought I could see blue flashing lights ahead.

In a burst of adrenaline, I swerved the car off the road and onto the pavement, nudging the side of the bumper up to the wooden railings. What would they do? Fine me?

I slammed the door and darted out into the road, weaving between stationary car bonnets. In my head I heard Ben's scared voice, he'd have been six years old and we were watching *White Fang* on TV: *Anyone who's not watching this film is really lucky, Mum*. Across the central reservation the cars were moving faster but I still ran out. Trusting to luck, which was stupid when you think about it.

Then I was pounding up the hill, eyes roaming around the bushes and the low wall that became part of the entrance to the baths at the top. 'Ben!' I shouted as I ran, and saw in my mind's eye Joe lying on the tarmac. I thought of the memory board they'd had at school, where the teachers had written kind things and his classmates had drawn pictures of Joe and crosses and flowers, and afterwards, after the children had talked about death and asked their questions and said goodbye over a cherry tree sapling, we were given the postings in a scrapbook that the headmistress had put together. And as my lungs went on forcing out breath I found myself wondering what Ben's headmaster would do, and where they'd have the special assembly; and then, there he was: there Ben was, head between his knees, sitting on the coping stones just past the entrance and looking like a beggar.

I stumbled up to him, my legs shaking, and yelled, 'Where's your phone?'

I hadn't meant to make that the first thing I said to him. He raised his head and, dear God, how pale his skin was.

He reached stiffly into his coat pocket and pulled his mobile out. 'Oh. It's not switched on. No, battery's dead.'

'So, what's the matter with you?' Relief had evaporated within seconds. I couldn't believe how angry I felt. 'That—who was it on the phone?—said you couldn't walk.'

Ben cast me a sorrowful glance and lifted up his foot. It took a moment to register what was wrong.

'Oh, Jesus.'

I'd assumed he was resting his shoe on a piece of wood, for idleness. But when he moved his leg, the wood came up too.

'It's a nail,' he said, grimacing. Looking again had made him weaken. I could tell he wanted to cry, his voice had that little waver in it. 'It's gone through my sole and into my foot. I didn't want to pull it out on my own.'

I was pressing my hand over my mouth and staring. But that was no good, was it?

'Does it hurt?

He let out a sob-laugh. 'What do you think, Mum?'

'Stay where you are, I'll get the car.'

'Like I'm going anywhere.'

The triage nurse saw him straight away, but after that the board in A&E said it was a two-hour wait to see a doctor. The smell of the place was the smell of Joe dying.

'So tell me, how the hell did you get a nail through your foot when you were swimming?'

'I haven't been swimming, Mum.'

I phoned Tom and gave him the bare facts; I knew if he got home to a dark and empty house he'd have a fit. I played it right down. Ben's hurt himself at the Northgate, I said. Nothing serious, but he'll need a tetanus shot. I know, it's a nuisance. So, there's some fish in batter you could just stick in the oven, whatever you can find. See you when I see you.

We sat in casualty and watched the news on a TV mounted near to the ceiling. A car bomb had gone off somewhere but the sound was turned so low you couldn't follow the story. It might have been the Middle East.

After half an hour Ben was sick on the empty seat next to him. I tried to mop the fluid up with a magazine but it had pooled in the plastic dip towards the back and the pages weren't absorbent enough. I had to go and get pleated green paper towels from the toilet. No one seemed to be around to help.

'So where have you been?'

'Blacon.'

'Blacon? Why? Doing what?'

'Seeing Ian Nuttall. Playing footie on the building site near his house.'

'Ian *who*?'

You'd think that if a patient vomited in the waiting room, it might bring forward his appointment time. I went over to the receptionist. 'My son's in a lot of pain,' I said.

'Yes, his notes are here,' she said. 'You'll be seen as soon as possible.' What kind of an answer is that? I wanted to shout. It wasn't her fault, but I still itched to grab her by the hair and scream abuse into her eyes. No wonder they have protective screens in these places now.

'Ian Nuttall, used to go to my school, left after Year Seven.'

'The one who went to live in Spain?'

'Yeah. He came back, well, him and his mum did, and he goes to Gladhills now. I saw him at the baths.'

'Did I ever meet him?'

'Dunno. Don't think so.'

'So how long have you been going to his house?'

'About four months. I've been going there instead of swimming.'

'It's a good thing you didn't try to remove it yourself,' the doctor said when we were finally called through. People try—' he shone a light on the tender puckered flesh under Ben's curled foot—'to take foreign bodies out and often end up causing even more harm. Hmm. It's gone right through, can you see? You didn't just step on this did you?'

'No, I jumped onto it,' said Ben wearily.

234

'Trying to be Superman?'

He's fifteen, I could have said, not five. But it wasn't the doctor's fault we were here.

'It's going to hurt,' said the doctor, writing on his clipboard, 'I can't pretend it won't. What I need you to do is stay as still as you can. Perhaps hold Mum's hand, if you feel—'

Ben looked at me, gulped and began to heave again. I held the cardboard dish under his chin for him.

'That'll be shock,' said the doctor. 'I'll give you a minute.'

'So, let me get this right, Ben; you've been saying you were at the Northgate when in fact you've been going somewhere else entirely?'

'Yeah.'

'And instead of swimming, you've been going to this Ian's house?'

'Not all the time.'

'Where, then?'

'All over. The shops, the building site. Nothing illegal, in case you're wondering. I haven't been doing *drugs*. I'm not stupid.'

'Why not tell me where you were? I wouldn't have stopped you.'

'You'd have been—'

'What?'

'Like you are now.'

'What's that supposed to mean? Ben?'

Afterwards, the doctor gave him his tetanus jab and a bottle of antibiotics. 'Because we don't know what kind of nasties might have been living on that nail, do we? The wound was quite, mmm, dirty. And these are painkillers, take as necessary but not more than four in a twenty-four-hour period; and

235

I'll get you a pair of crutches before you go. I'm assuming you'll want to be back at school as soon as possible?' He smiled at his own joke. 'Crutches will help you get around till it settles down. You shouldn't need them for more than two weeks. Is Mum OK with changing the dressing? Any problems, pop down to your GP. And no more playing around on building sites. Hey, Mum?'

Thanks, Doc, I could have said, I wasn't feeling nearly inadequate enough.

'Ben, talk to me.'

'I wanted to be on my own.'

'But you weren't, you were with this Ian.'

'Yeah.'

'Tell me about him. What kind of a boy is he?'

'*You* wouldn't like him.'

'Why not? You could bring him back to our house, better then playing on a manky old building site. He could come for his tea.'

'I don't think so, Mum.'

A nurse dropped by with a leaflet that explained about flesh-eating bugs and another that was all pie charts about why it was important to return NHS equipment. In the rack outside our bay there was a new booklet on bereavement that I took in case Juno might need it.

'What makes you want to spend so much time with Ian?'

'He's a laugh. We were mates in Year Seven. I was sad he left, I was glad he'd come back—God!'

'Some mate, leaving you sitting on your own with a nail through your foot.'

'Ian didn't leave me. He took me to his house but his mum wasn't in, so his brother gave us a lift to the Northgate because I told him to, I thought it

236

would be easier for you to find me. But Ian was with me up till you came.'

'So where was he?'

'He ran off when he saw you coming. He thought you'd be angry.'

I wanted to slap his face so damned hard it made my whole arm tingle. My jaw ached from being clenched and I knew my expression was murderous. Forcing my face into a smile, I said:

'You like being with your other friends, Felix, Jase. When you go round to theirs, I know where you are.

'I wanted to be . . . away.'

'From what? Me?'

'No. Just *away*. I wanted to be—out of the loop.'

'What's that supposed to mean?'

'Well, look at you now, Mum, the way you are with me, this interrogation.'

'So it's my fault?'

'It's—'

'What? Don't turn away from me like that.'

'I think I'm going to be sick again.'

When we got home the kitchen windows were running with condensation and the smoke alarm was going off because Tom had gone up for a shower and forgotten the tea. Ben flopped on the sofa and reached for the remote, but I shouted at him to leave the TV off. I gutted the alarm of its batteries and slid the charred fish out of the oven, burning myself on the glass door in my haste. Tom found me standing by the sink with my arm under the cold tap.

'You in the wars again? Ben's in there looking like thunder. Did he get jabbed in the bum? What did the doctor say?' I took my arm out of the

237

stream and began folding kitchen towel into a pad.

'Ally?' Tom's face dropped.

'There's more to it than I said on the phone.'

'Oh, hell, is he really hurt?'

'It's not his foot. You need to hear what he's done, you won't believe it.'

The air was clammy with steam. If I had a motorbike, Tom's expression seemed to say, I'd jump on it this minute.

CHAPTER FIFTEEN

Juno—So, firstly, thanks for all being here. Marco?

Marco—How long's this going to take?

Juno—It depends how much people want to say. Why?

Marco—Because I said I'd be down the leisure centre by eight.

Chris—You boarding?

Marco—Yeah.

Chris—I thought they'd finished that for the summer. I thought it was aerobics now, or summat.

Marco—No. What would you know about it, anyway?

Juno—The longer we spend in general chat, the longer it's going to take. Lee, where are you going?

Lee—Forgot to feed the dog. I won't be two minutes. You start.

Juno—Right, what I wanted to ask was whether you could give me some kind of run-down of your movements for the week, so that I can plan around them, and also so I'll know where you are at any particular time. Jot them down on this calendar, I'll hang it in the hall. Contact numbers too, please.

Marco—You what?

Juno—So if you know, like tonight, that you're going to be at the leisure centre, jot it down on a piece of paper for me a few days beforehand.

Marco—Why?

Juno—I've explained why. Courtesy, in part.

Marco—Yeah, but, that won't work, will it?

Juno—How won't it work?

Marco—'Cause sometimes you just decide on the spur of the moment to go somewhere. Or a mate rings up. How can I tell on a Monday night where I'll be on the Friday?

Juno—If we can—

Chris—You'll be hanging round the arcade like you always do.

Marco—I might not. Better than you, Saddo, stuck in your room reading your dirty mags.

Chris—I don't! I go out loads, me. I'm out tonight.

Marco—Where?

Juno—Yes, where?

Chris—Frankie's.

Marco—Oh yeah, your little bum-chum.

Chris—Sod off, Marco. You're always on t' same thing. You're like a broken record. You're obsessed.

Marco—Who are you calling obsessed?

Juno—Lee? Lee, have you finished in the kitchen? Look, boys, it's a safety issue as well. It's no good just having a general idea of where I might find you. Is it, Lee?

Chris—Git.

Lee—They've never come to harm yet. I can always nip round in my van if there's a problem. And they've got their mobiles.

Chris—You can't hit people in a meeting, it's not allowed.

Marco—Watch me.

* * *

Tom took Ben upstairs for a man-to-man chat. 'I

think it's best,' he told me. If you stay out of it, is what he meant.

By the time he came down again I was beside myself with temper.

'So?'

'I'm not absolutely sure.'

'Was it my fault?'

'No,' he said straight away, because yes, or even a pause, would have destroyed our marriage at a stroke.

'It's not the fact he hurt himself, though God knows, if he'd fallen on his face—'

'I know, I know.'

'But it's the deceit. He's never been a liar, Tom. Did he use that phrase "out of the loop" with you?'

Tom nodded.

'What does it mean?'

'What it is—' He came and sat next to me, put his arm round my shoulder. I stiffened my muscles under his touch. 'I don't want you being upset, but it's good if we can get this out. He should feel he's able to tell us things, shouldn't he?'

'Go on.'

'He says he wants more freedom.'

'So it is my fault.'

'Why do you assume that?'

'Because you think I stifle him.'

'I don't.'

I laughed bitterly. 'Yeah, right.'

'All I'm saying is, I think there's room for manoeuvre. Yes? Don't go all brittle on me. Please, Ally.'

Which one of them was it used to come to me all the time with Lego bricks and ask me to un-stick them? Whatever I was doing, even in the bath,

241

they'd follow me round. Perhaps it was both of them. When I took the bricks, they were always slippery with spit and covered in baby toothmarks. I used to dream of a time I'd be able to sit and read a book or eat my tea without constantly having to get up. I've poured a million cups of squash, emptied a thousand packets of baby wipes. But in the end, you know, you're redundant.

When Tom stroked my arm that night in bed I jerked it away. Whatever he was after, sex, forgiveness, forgiveness-sex, I wasn't interested. If I was a useless mother, I might as well be a useless wife. At about 2 a.m. he suddenly said to me out of the darkness, 'You don't think it's drugs, do you?'

You know all the bloody answers, why ask me? I told him silently. He must have thought I was asleep because he didn't speak again.

I woke up still furious.

'Are you going to phone school and tell them Ben won't be in today?' Tom asked me.

'Why don't you do it?' I snapped.

I'd dreamt we were both standing on the edge of an orchard; we might have been looking over a fence or a wall. Juno was under the trees picking fruit, although, now I thought about it, they were rowan berries she was pulling down. They're poisonous, aren't they? I didn't register that in the dream. And Manny was there too with Soph on his shoulders, but she was about four, tiny, like the ones I work with at nursery. I'm not sure where Pascale was, or Ben, or Joe. I wanted to go in and help Juno gather berries but Tom was complaining all the time about needing to go to the garage and pick up his car because he'd had those monster truck-type wheels fitted to it. He wouldn't let me

242

go to them over the wall. In the dream I hated him.

'Mr Hannant's promised me they'll swing a few room changes so he doesn't have to go up and down stairs so much,' Tom said when he got off the phone. 'But they'll need a day to sort it. I've told him Ben might be in tomorrow unless his foot suddenly gets a lot worse. He was scooting round the kitchen last night like an old pro on those crutches. I said to him, "There's not a lot wrong with you, is there?" '

'I'm glad you can laugh about it,' I said sourly.

Tom glanced at his watch. Then he registered I had my nursery tabard on over my blouse. 'You going into work?'

'Yes. Why shouldn't I?'

He exhaled noisily. 'Oh, Ally. I could have done with knowing . . . All right, I'll have to phone Mattison and tell him I'll be in after lunch, although he's not going to be pleased, because we're just into a new project with Jensen.'

'No,' I said. 'You don't get it. Go into work. If Ben's old enough to "have some freedom", he's old enough to be left for three hours on the sofa, with plenty of drinks and the remote and his mobile. He can call me if his foot drops off.'

Tom looked defeated. He went pointlessly to the bottom of the stairs, then came back.

'Ally, don't be so angry.'

'I'm not angry.'

'You bloody are.'

He stood for a moment, debating with himself. I turned my back on him and went into the kitchen to assemble an invalid tray. I heard his feet pounding up the stairs, then the quick bib of Juno's car horn out the front.

243

'That's terrible,' she cried when I went out to explain why Ben wouldn't be needing a lift that day.

I started to pour out the tale of what a rubbish mother I was, but she just talked over the top of me.

'Building sites should be well fenced-off, locked up. I should think you've a case for suing. Which site was it? Do you want me to ring the council about it?'

'Yeeowch,' said Pascale. 'Right through his foot? So it was sticking out the top?'

'Can I go see him?' asked Sophie, opening the car door.

'We haven't time,' said Juno.

'Gotta go get my French book anyway, forgot it was Wednesday,' she chirped, and was gone, sprinting across the drive, her tie flapping over her shoulder.

'Look at that. She's been shortening her skirt again,' said Juno.

*   *   *

There's no one at nursery like Joe, but some of the things the little ones do remind me of him. They churn out the same scraggly drawings, figures with legs like tentacles and hands like pincushions. The boys all fiddle with themselves continually, dreamily, looking up with mild surprise when you tell them to stop. They all ask questions, all the time, and they tell interminable stories in a machine-gun delivery that carries them through all other activity, e.g. going to the toilet.

I try to treat them all the same but you can't help

liking some more than others. Favourite last year was Ella Greaves, whose mum had been killed in a car accident when Ella was only two. I used to brush her hair for her, even though it didn't really need it; I'd say, 'Your bobble's coming out,' and then I'd pull the elastic off and smooth the strands down with my fingers. We used to have to take her out of the room when the others made their Mother's Day cards. Her dad had a kind of absent, shell-shocked quality to him that made me wonder what he was like with her at home, and once I saw him put one of her pictures in the bin on the way out. I ran after him with it into the car park, pretended I thought he'd dropped it by accident. Later, Geraldine told me he'd got a new girlfriend who Ella liked. I was relieved about that.

This year my soft spot was for Charlie Castle, a red-headed boy who'd had a lot of trouble with his hearing and been in and out of hospital. It was difficult sometimes to tell what he said. In fact, Geraldine reckoned I was the only one who could make him out properly. His ears were more or less OK these days but he was seeing a speech therapist, and he still didn't always take notice if you gave him an instruction. 'He'll have to learn how to listen,' his mum told me. 'You need to be patient with him if he doesn't respond straight away.' So I never shouted at Charlie if he didn't do as he was told, I'd squat down so I was on a level with his face and make eye contact, then speak.

'You've got the gift with him,' Geraldine commented one lunchtime as I helped him wash his hands. 'You know he used to have the most awful tantrums in the other room? Louise was at the end of her tether.'

'I expect it was frustrating for him, not being able to join in. He's never any bother for me, are you, Charlie-boy?'

Charlie made a fart noise and ran off. It was a nice thing for Geraldine to say, though.

This morning he was being a nuisance with a long cardboard tube that he'd filched out of the modelling box on his way through reception.

'No, Charlie,' I said, but I didn't look at him directly because I was supposed to be playing letter-match with Jules and Megan. I was dimly aware of him stomping round the room saying he was an elephant after that, I suppose the tube would have been his trunk, thinking about it. I should have stopped and taken it off him. The next thing was, Charlie lying on his back yelling with his hand over his eye and Geraldine staring in through the open door.

I jumped up, letter cards everywhere, and ran to him. He was incoherent with grief.

'Can you take your hand away from your eye, sweetheart?' asked Geraldine.

I pulled gently at his arm and we saw to our relief his eye was fine. There was a curved red mark underneath on the cheekbone, though.

'He was playing pirates,' said Jules, helpfully.

'I think,' said Geraldine, wiping Charlie's face with a tissue from her pocket, 'he had the tube to his eye and I knocked the end when I opened the door. His eye's all right, though, isn't it?'

'It looks OK. Probably needs a magic ice pack, though.'

'I'll go and get one from the kitchen. And an accident form, while I'm at it.' She chucked him under the chin. 'You'll be fine in a minute, won't you?'

Geraldine left us sitting on the mat, Charlie sobbing against my chest, and the moment slipped and became nine years ago with Ben, in the garden at the old house, crying into my blouse because he'd fallen over the step and burst his nose: melted again and became me, lying on the ground screaming, holding my arm while the bike wheels spun in the air and my father waved uselessly, a dot in the distance. Charlie's hair tickled my collarbone and his elbows dug into my stomach.

When Geraldine came back I told her I thought I had a migraine coming on.

'It wasn't your fault, it was a classic accident,' she said as she knelt down beside me to examine Charlie's progress.

'I know.'

'I don't want you going home and worrying.'

'No. I do feel grim, though.'

'I'll get Mo in from Big Toddlers. Off you go.'

She's a good woman.

I could have rung Ben but I needed to see him, check for myself he was all right, perhaps talk some more. I had to be at home with my son as quickly as possible.

Some bouncy theme tune was playing on the TV as I walked through the front door. I dropped my bag by the hall stand and went straight through into the lounge. No Ben, but a whole lot of Penguin wrappers round the sofa and an empty can of Coke on its side. I righted the can without thinking, then turned and ran up the stairs.

'Ben, are you OK?'

What if he'd collapsed in the bathroom and the door was locked? No, he was in his bedroom, I

247

could see the crutches on the floor and his foot sticking out.

'Ben?'

But it was Soph I saw first, sitting on the bed and pulling her school shirt on over her head, her bra strap flopped down over her bicep, her navel ring glittering. Pulling her shirt on?

'Sophie?'

She looked completely terrified of me. I watched in amazement as she grabbed her tie and her shoes, then bolted past me.

'Fuck,' said Ben. 'Oh fuck.'

*   *   *

Kim—This is nice, a girly day out. I could shop for England. It's good to have a sit down, though. God, my feet. It's lovely that top you got, Pascale. I'd have liked one for myself but they didn't have it in my—Shift those bags; there, we're sorted. Now, what are you having?

Sophie—Just a Diet Coke for me.

Pascale—And me.

Kim—Yeah, me and all. Do they come to your table? Oh yeah, I see. Catch his eye when he comes past, Soph, you're good at that. No, I thought that top was gorgeous. And I liked your earrings, Soph. I wish I'd had girls. Instead I get these two lumbering great lads. Not that I don't love them, but there's nobody ever changes the toilet roll except me and the seat's always up.

Pascale—Mum reckons girls are higher maintenance.

Kim—Does she? I'm surprised at that. At least girls talk to you. You can't get anything out of boys. 'Cept grunts. I bet you tell your mum all sorts, don't you?

Sophie—We don't talk to Mum all that much, do we, Paxo?

Pascale—Shhh.

Sophie—No, but we don't, do we? Not about personal stuff.

Pascale—I'm not sure.

Sophie—We don't.

Kim—Get away. Why not?

Sophie—'Cause she never lets us get a word in. She kind of takes over—yes she does, Paxo, you know she does. She's always been the same. You start to tell her something and she just comes in with what she thinks you're saying but she doesn't listen.

Pascale—She does. She listens to me.

Sophie—Oh, yeah, she would listen to you—

Kim—Hey up, look at those cakes with the strawberries on. Over there, on the next table but one. Probably about a million calories in every mouthful.

Pascale—Meaning, Soph?

Kim—So are we having one or not? Are we? Let's go mad. Waiter! Hey, Excuse me!

Soph—Yeah, let's go mad.

*   *   *

If Ben didn't talk to me now, I was lost.

'Well?'

'I'll do a deal with you,' he said, his cheeks still burning. 'I'll tell you the truth, and you don't mention it to Dad.'

'No deal,' I said.

When I first had sex with Tom it was in a hotel room in Manchester. He booked it so we didn't have to feel rushed, he said, or spied on; it was such a thoughtful thing to do. He paid for it out of his Saturday job. And everything went OK, considering. It was a nice experience. He claimed he was a virgin, but then, so did I, so who knows?

Later on we used his bedroom, then the halls of residence, but never my mum's house. I couldn't, it seemed wrong when she was all alone, disrespectful. I often lay in Tom's arms afterwards and wondered how she coped without this closeness.

Now this, in my house; this deceit.

'Was it planned?'

Ben rolled his eyes. 'Like I planned to shove a big spike through my foot.'

'So help me!' I burst out, throwing my arms up in anger.

'Sorry,' he said at once. 'Mum?'

I'd turned away and was gripping the edge of the shelf that held his PlayStation games. 'Give me a minute,' I said.

When Tom and I first slept together he was so careful and restrained. I think both of us kept our eyes closed while we were doing it; at least, his were closed whenever I peeped. He asked me three times whether he was hurting me. Afterwards he held me very tightly and told me he loved me. That's what it should be like.

'It wasn't planned. Not on my side, anyway. She did a dodge to get off school when she knew I was stuck at home. First I knew was when she rang the doorbell.'

I turned back round so I was facing him. 'How

250

did she get out of lessons?'

'Forged a note on her mum's headed notepaper, she said.'

'You seem very ready to shop her.'

'Why should I stick up for her? She's dropped me in it.' Ben's foot twitched with annoyance, or embarrassment. 'I *told* her she'd be in deep shit if anyone found out.'

'But aren't you having a relationship with her?'

'No! No way. She's a mate, she's . . . Sometimes I don't even know if I like her all that much.'

'You must have known what she was after, coming up to your bedroom when everyone was out. I did tell you she had a crush on you.'

Ben put his fingers through his hair, then looked angrily at me.

'She came round here, right, and there was nobody else in. What was I supposed to do; ring you up to come and save me? Leave her standing on the mat? So she came in and she spun me this story about being upset because she'd had a row with Jaclyn or somebody, although I didn't believe her because she didn't seem that fussed and she didn't go on and on about it the way she normally does when she's teed off. She made herself a drink and then she said she wanted me to show her a new PS2 game, so we went upstairs.' He paused. 'Don't make me tell you any more.'

'Keep talking,' I said coldly.

He sighed and hung his head. 'She took her shirt off, just took it off. I never even touched her. She was asking me if I found her attractive—'

'Do you?'

'Not really, but—'

'How come?'

251

'Dunno.'

'And yet you were going to have sex with her?'

'Well, you know, when it's offered on a plate like that—'

I stepped across and slapped his face.

'*Mum!*'

'Do you have *any* kind of morality, Ben Weaver? *Do* you?'

He stroked his cheek in bewilderment. I hadn't hit him hard but he was so shocked he couldn't speak. I'd hardly ever smacked either of the boys, even when they were going through the tantrum stage. Even when Joe hurled a cricket ball at my mouth and laughed when it connected. Once, when we were on holiday in Devon and before Joe was born, I walloped Ben's legs for going too near the cliff edge. But that was fear; that was love.

'I didn't mean to do that,' I said.

I knelt down so I was eye to eye with him, the way I did when I talked to Charlie Castle. Then, keeping my voice as steady as I could, I said: 'I shouldn't have hit you, it was a rotten thing to do. But tell me now, Ben, for once: *what's going on in your head?*'

Close to I could see the unevenness of his skin, a little smudge of biro ink by his ear, a minute crumb caught on his sweatshirt collar.

'Sometimes—' he began.

'Yes?'

His eyes darted round the room and his lips moved.

'Please, Ben. I need to know.' You owe me this, I could have said.

'Sometimes,' he said slowly, 'I get this total shut-down of feelings. Like an emotional coma, nothing. So everyone else is racing about cheering, or sobbing in the aisles and I'm just standing there, watching. Then . . . '

I wanted to ask him about the times that had happened but I didn't dare interrupt him.

'Then there are other times, you know, when I feel this—' he spread his arms wide like the hare in *Guess How Much I Love You*—'when I feel this *rage*—do you know what I mean?'

'About Joe?'

'I suppose so. There are so many . . . '

'What?'

'I don't want to say it.'

'Go on, Ben.'

'There are so many *wankers* out there who are still alive, and Joe's not. See, there you go, I can't talk about this with you, Mum, because it's upsetting you.'

'It's not, carry on.'

But I knew he was remembering a time when we didn't talk about Joe. In particular he'd be thinking about an afternoon when I'd picked him up from his new secondary school, and I was hanging round the gates with some of the other mums making that halting, cheery chat you do in the playground. Juno wasn't there that day, or I'd have been all right. Ben was kicking gravel, wanting to go home, but one of the women was telling us about her daughter's eye operation and I didn't want to walk off in the middle of it in case it seemed callous. She paused, and then another woman spoke to Ben. She asked him which school he'd been at before, and whether he had a brother in Year Nine because there was another boy who looked like him. I knew what he was going to say, I knew because I'd heard him explain to other adults, watched them scrunch and freeze. The counsellor had said it was healthy for him to do this. But that day I couldn't cope. I wanted us to appear undamaged for one more afternoon.

So I pulled him to me and, like someone in a weak comedy, clamped my hand over his mouth.

They must have thought I was mad. I'll never forget the look of surprised dismay in Ben's eyes as I dragged him away, his confidence in both of us knocked flat at a stroke. We drove back home in ringing silence. It was an appalling thing to do. And now I was asking him to talk to me.

He dropped his arms to his sides. 'I don't know how to explain it any more, Mum. Do you get what I mean?'

I used a line that the doctor had given me years ago. 'It's normal to feel extremes.'

'Do you?'

'Oh, yes.'

'So how do you cope? 'Cause there are times when I want to go berserk. Smash things. Even now.'

I slid myself up so I was sitting beside him. My knees hurt and my back was stiff; I felt old. Sometimes I don't cope, I could have said. There are days when I want to draw the curtains and not move ever again, and days when I could throw scalding coffee over your father's head for even smiling.

'I focus on you and your dad, and Grandma,' I said, finally. 'I concentrate on loving. I don't know that there's anything else to do. Love's the way out—'

'But what if the person you love doesn't love you

254

back?' he cried, his face flushed again. 'What then? 'Cause that's just, shit. Sorry. But it is. Love makes it worse as far as I can see.'

My heart had given a great leap. 'You have a crush on someone?'

'Not a crush. Don't say that, that's patronizing.'

'Who, Ben?'

He swore again under his breath. I thought, he wants me to know, I just have to ask again.

'I think I know who it is.'

'Yeah?'

'Is it—Ian Nuttall?'

It must have been the tension of the moment; Ben laughed out loud and thumped the duvet with his fist.

'No it bloody isn't! God, Mum, what is it with you? Do you *want* me to be gay, or something? *Jesus*-wept! Ian Nuttall? Jesus. You haven't said anything like that to Dad, have you? Or *Juno*?'

I shook my head vigorously. 'I don't know why I said that.'

'No, I don't either. You better not have said anything. Bloody hell! What goes on in that hot little brain of yours, eh?'

There was a kind of insane smile on his face, not entirely pleasant.

'I promise I haven't mentioned it to anyone.'

'Good!'

'So who is it, Ben?'

The smile shrank away and he looked miserable again. 'You won't tell?'

'Never.'

'Huh,' he said. 'Like I trust you.' But I could feel the words coming. 'It's Pascale, Mum. And she hates me.'

CHAPTER SIXTEEN

By the time Tom came home that evening, I'd established that Pascale didn't Hate Ben, but she was never going to go out with him. 'She says she thinks of me like a brother, how sick is that?' he told me despairingly. 'She doesn't have a boyfriend but there's someone in the Upper Sixth she fancies. That's what Soph reckons, although she might just have said that to put me off.'

Both of us needed to get out of the house, so we'd limped down to the weir. The water twisted below us in freezing ropes. I tried to make sense of my son.

'I knew Soph was coming on to me,' he said. 'I'm not blind. But I thought it was a wind-up. Then I decided it was to get at Pascale, because she was jealous or something. I never thought she was serious. Maybe she isn't. Soph's so weird it's difficult to tell what's going on with her.'

Ben also wanted to know what was going to happen to him. 'So what you going to do? I'm already grounded for the next *year*, aren't I?'

'I'm going to pass it on to your dad,' I said. 'Again.' Although Tom would probably give him a whisky and shake his hand. Well done, my boy. Welcome to the World.

'I hate the way you do that, make me tell it all twice. It was bad enough going over it with you.'

'You should have thought of that before. I'm out of my depth, this is men's talk.'

Besides which, I was going to have to go and tackle Juno about Sophie. And what in God's

256

name was she going to say?

*　　　*　　　*

LET 'EM FLY!

Queen Mum's KIM FOX tells Carrie Wallace why she thinks we should let our children get on with growing up

I think it's a mistake to keep your kids artificially young. In the olden days the boys would have been going off to battle when they were fourteen or fifteen, to fight and kill. The girls would have been married and even had babies, and you can't get a much more responsible job than that! There was no such thing as adolescence. You just went straight into being an adult member of society. You were expected to contribute to the community alongside people twenty or thirty years older than you.

My point is, people haven't changed. It's society that's moved the goalposts.

If you watch old films about the past, it's clear that children were often expected to work and make decisions from being very young. In David Lean's version of *Great Expectations*, Pip is put in the forge when he is hardly even a teenager. And in Franco Zeffirelli's *Romeo and Juliet*, the hero and heroine behave in a more mature way than their parents.

Young people can show amazing wisdom and resourcefulness if you give them a chance.

This current generation of youngsters work

257

hard for their exams, so they should also be allowed to play hard and develop their interests outside schools. There's more to life than sitting in a classroom, especially these days with so much competition for places. More students should be looking at alternatives to the examinations rat-race. There are lots of ways to succeed in life and not all that many are to do with getting a certain letter on a piece of paper. Parents who tell their offspring that the only way forward is through qualifications are not seeing the bigger picture. Where would Richard Branson have been if he'd spent his early years chasing grades?

Teenagers have to be encouraged to take part in local events and develop their individual talents, stretch themselves. Adult life is full of challenges and youngsters need to be equipped to meet those challenges and turn them into opportunities. And yet the older generation often spend their time complaining and knocking them—why? For example, both my sons like to use their skateboards, which is a harmless and healthy activity requiring a lot of skill. But there are some people locally who want the skate-park shutting in the evening as they say it is a nuisance to residents. So the community is sending out a message to its younger members that they have no place or rights. No wonder there is a problem with vandalism and petty crime when teenagers are excluded from their own environment.

It's my opinion that if you treat your

children like adults then they will behave like adults. If you mollycoddle them then they will not be confident enough to stand up for themselves in the big wide world. Mothers who are on their children's backs 24/7 will not get any thanks for their trouble and they could be storing up problems for the future. If you are constantly laying down the law then your kids will never be equipped to make their own decisions. If you are forever organizing their time for them, they'll never learn to manage their own daily schedule when they get a place of their own. Or they might never leave home, and how sad would that be?

The most important job we as parents can do is to toughen up our kids so that they can stand on their own two feet and take their place in society. Youngsters grow by their mistakes and a teenager cannot spend his life looking back over his shoulder to check with mummy if what he is doing is OK. That is no way to shape the next generation.

I want my boys to be men and I'm not afraid to say it!

Do you agree with Kim's views? Have your say at carrie.wallace@galsmagazine.net

*   *   *

When I first woke I thought I was in the back bedroom at our old Bolton house. I could hear traffic, which you can't at Cestrian Park, and the light coming in through the curtains was different. I kept my eyes closed and listened to the room while I remembered. Against my cheek there was an unfamiliar satiny bedcover, and there was a clock ticking hollowly. The smell of the place was like very old faint perfume or the face powder Mum kept in her handbag for years. Juno's parents' house.

There was also the sense of someone beside me, but when I did open my eyes, the pillow next to mine was empty.

I threw back the covers and shivered at the chill. Juno had found me one of her mum's bathrobes and laid it across my chair the night before. 'You're not squeamish, are you?' she'd said.

I'd told her no because I didn't want to hurt her feelings and anyway, she was so strung out. Now I was stumbling along the narrow landing in a dead woman's dressing gown, with pieces of last night coming back to me in no order.

Juno opening the front door, clicking on the light, and sniffing.

'Don't you think you can smell when a house is empty of love?' she'd said. That's only damp, I'd thought. There was mould round the door jamb.

I'd made myself go and face Juno over Sophie's behaviour. I hadn't done it at once, I'd waited two days, on the grounds that delay would make me more rational. I rehearsed what I was going to say until I sounded like a talk-show host. And then, when I got there, Juno was packing.

'They want me in Bradford.' She held a blouse up to the light, then dropped it in the case. 'The hospital. They think this is it.'

If it had been anyone else, I'd have known what to say. But the coldness was coming off her in waves.

'What can I do to help? Do you need to get away right now?'

'They said—Well, I do.'

'OK. I can collect the girls for you, they can stay at mine till Manny gets home.'

She pulled some boots out of the bottom of the wardrobe and a brown stiletto fell on the floor. Instead of picking it up and putting it back, she kicked it under the bed. 'Manny's away. Damn him.'

'Oh, Juno. How long will it take him to get back?'

She shook her head. 'He can't get back, at least not straight away. He's in bloody Ireland, a Celtic bloody arts festival. Trust him.'

I wanted to say, 'Then I'll go with you, Juno, so you won't be on your own.' But someone had to have the kids.

She stopped packing for a moment, checked her watch and frowned. 'This is so like my mother. She always made her own time. We were late for everything I wanted to go to, but when it was a place she liked, we were always there on the dot. She was in charge of time. Everyone else did the running around. I should have known that this was how she'd die, hanging on and on, then a last-minute rush. Serve her right if I missed it.'

I drew in my breath. 'You don't mean that.'

'I do. Gohhhd. Where *is* my sponge bag? It was right here a minute ago.'

I leant across the bed and moved the case lid. 'There. Look, Juno, you'll make yourself so you're not fit to drive.'

'Ally—'

'Why don't you book a taxi, for once? I know it'll

261

be expensive, but it'd be worth it. I could maybe come and pick you up tomorrow, or Tom could. He wouldn't mind.'

In the pause I had a sudden memory of Joe waving a Lego hammer. 'Mummy, you say, "Hello, monster," and then I hit you.' Juno was leaning towards me. Her eyes ranged over my face, pleading. 'Ally, will you—I can't believe I'm asking you this—'

'What?'

'Will you come with me? It's just that I can't bear the thought of being in that house on my own. It should all be over by tomorrow.'

She looked so lovely and sad. I'm always surprised no one's ever painted her.

Juno's mum had a brown suite in her bathroom and pink and white towels in the airing cupboard. The water from the hot tap was freezing; maybe you had to switch an immersion heater on. I splashed my face anyway. It had been past two when we'd got into bed.

In the medicine cabinet, behind bottles of prescription pills and a tin of Ralgex and three types of cough medicine, I found a box of aspirin and took a couple. I wondered how Juno was feeling and when we were going home.

When I got downstairs Juno was sitting, dressed, at the minute fold-down table in the kitchen drinking murky coffee.

'You shouldn't have come,' she said at once. 'Tom'll be cursing me.'

'Stop it, Juno.' She'd said the same thing on the drive over, again just after her mother died at midnight, and later, when we were trying to make some kind of meal from the poor collection of tins in the kitchenette. 'It won't have done Tom any harm to take the reins for once, work owes him some flexi days. Are you sure you don't want him to bring the girls across, though?'

She shook her head emphatically. 'I don't want them missing school.'

'Not even for their grandma?'

'She's dead now. What good would it do? Anyway, they'll have to take time off for the funeral.'

What did your mum and dad do that was so terrible? I wanted to ask. It wasn't Juno, this coldness; Juno was warm and kind. It was a relief when she announced, 'I've had it with this nasty powder, I'm going down to the garage to get some proper milk. Want anything?'

'Some hot water, if there is any. What's the trick?'

'No trick. It's broken. Something else for me to sort out,' she said, pulling on her coat. 'If there's any point. Look, I've got to go back to the hospital this morning and pick up the death certificate. Are you in a rush to get back to Chester, or can you hang on till after lunch?'

'I'm fine. Milk would be good, though.'

'You're such a friend,' she said, from the hall. The door banged and she was gone.

I got dressed, then I settled myself in the fat armchair next to the table with the crocheted mat on it, and phoned Tom.

'Everything's OK here. Yep, got Hop-along and the girls off to school, and now I'm going to get that pile of bricks shifted from behind the shed. It's needed doing for ages. How's Juno's mum?'

'Died last night.'

263

'Shit. Were you there?'

'Outside in the waiting area. I didn't think it was right to be at the bedside. I thought Juno would want some time to say, you know, goodbye.'

'So how is Juno?'

High, I could have said. By the small hours, hyper. I wondered briefly whether to say we'd shared a bed, but he might have been smutty about it.

'This morning she's icy, like she is when she mentions her dad. It's weird. Not what you'd expect.'

'Must be her way of coping. When will you be home?'

'Mid-afternoon, I'd guess. Juno needs to sort some things out.'

I dragged the cushion out from under my back and hugged it to my chest for warmth. When I got off the phone I was going to put my coat on. I don't suppose there'd been any point heating the house while it was empty.

'Take it steady on the roads, don't go rushing.' Tom's voice sounded far away.

'That's my line.'

He laughed. 'Hey, you'll never guess who I met last night.'

'Go on.'

'Our friend Ian. Ian Nuttall.'

'How did you manage that? Did he come round to our house?'

Tom gave a little snort. 'Are you worried he'd nick the silver? Joke, joke, Ally. He's a nice lad. I went with Ben to check out this famous building site—'

'With Sophie and Pascale?'

264

'No. I dropped them off at a music lesson. There was quite a row about that, because Soph didn't think they should have to go with their mum away but Pascale wanted to. I wasn't arguing, I just bundled them all in the car. So, while we were over Sealand way, I thought Ben could show me where he had his accident. And when we pulled up, Ian was on there kicking a football about. I called him over and we had a chat. He's all right, you'd like him.'

There was something very slightly patronizing about the tone of this.

'I'm not saying I wouldn't. Who said I wouldn't?'

'Ben thinks Ian's not posh enough for you.'

'Well, Ben's wrong. You can tell Ben that his mother judges people on their individual merits, and not by which estate they happen to live on. How could he say that? Where does he think his own roots lie?'

I could hear Tom laughing again.

'It's not funny, Tom.'

'Of course it isn't. I'll pass the message on. Anyway, I've invited Ian round sometime.'

'Fine.'

I squirmed irritably against the chair back and the antimacassar fell across my shoulders. Bloody house.

'And it's been good to have some time with Ben. I've enjoyed talking to him, just us two; he's a sensible boy. He really is ashamed of what happened with Soph, you know. He's positively allergic to her presence now, it's quite funny to watch.'

'Is it.'

'Although, she needs some sorting out. I suppose

265

now's not the time.'

'I wouldn't have thought so.'

'Oh, come on, Ally,' Tom said. 'I miss you. We miss you. Glad when you're back.'

'Yeah. Mid-afternoon, teatime, I should be home. We'll have a takeaway tonight.'

'Great.'

'See you.'

'See you.'

It was only as I was putting the receiver down that I thought to ask if there'd been any sign of Manny.

I went into the dingy hall to get my coat and there, on the inside doormat, was a two-pint carton of milk. Juno must have dropped it off then gone straight on to the hospital. How thoughtful was that? I picked up the carton, and took a moment to survey the view down the hallway into the dim sitting room. Juno would have come in through this door every day when she was growing up. There were photographs of her on the wall, lots of when she was little and plump but just the one of her grown-up; an unmounted wedding photo in a cheap white plastic frame. It looked as if her parents had lost interest in her after about seven.

In the back bedroom, where I went next, it was so gloomy that I had to flick the light on. An elder branch was shading the window frame and the pane itself was filthy. Thin grey moth bodies lay across the sill. The rail held no curtains.

I was looking for evidence of a little girl, and I found it. Half the floor was covered with boxes and the only furniture remaining was a table with a sewing machine on it, but you could see by the circular dents on the carpet where a bed had once been. Two feet off the ground, in one corner, someone had stuck a whole lot of pictures of animals cut from magazines. Dogs in baskets were favourite, followed by horses, but there were some chicks and a couple of kittens. I could imagine the bedhead underneath, girl-Juno lying there and gazing up at her collection of ragged-edged pets. The wallpaper around had fruit on it, as though it had been meant for a kitchen.

Near the door was a box of *Jackie* annuals and a pot of make-up brushes. Had the Clairol hairdryer in the brown-and-cream box been hers too? What had she looked like, back then? Impossible to imagine her awkward and gangly; all I could conjure was my Juno but in school uniform.

In the corner there was a black-framed mirror propped against the wall; it must have once hung from the hook hammered into the plaster above it. Teenage Juno getting ready to go out, listening to the top forty on the transistor radio that sat on the windowsill. She'd have done her homework up here, probably. Did she have friends round, giggling together? Is this where she had her first kiss?

I went back downstairs to turn on the television, any-thing to break the quiet. I also pulled the curtains right back, nearly off their rail, but it was as if the sunlight stopped at the entrance to the yard. There was a lot about this house that reminded me of where I grew up, and of our first married home. I'd cooked for years in a kitchen that cramped, and I'd hauled myself up stairs just as steep and narrow, and yet this place was so much gloomier.

When Tom and I first moved in together, we

painted our walls cream and had pine and bamboo furniture because it was cheap and compact. Later, the place was strewn with toys and baby paraphernalia in a cheerful, crowded way. I couldn't imagine this house feeling so happy. It wasn't the old-fashioned decoration here, either; Mum likes her lacy mats and flowered carpets, but however kitsch she goes, the overall effect stays cosy.

There was a lamp in the corner with a tall, thin shade made of orange hessian. Someone had glued coils of brown string to the cloth in an abstract decoration. I switched the lamp on for the extra light, and wondered at its ugliness.

It was a TV choice between news, news, programmes for schools or fly-on-the-wall in a children's ward. I watched thirty seconds of a little girl being given an injection before I turned over to *Come Outside*. This week, Aunty Mabel and Pippin the dog were investigating what happens to all the rubbish we put in our dustbins. Aunty Mabel took Pippin to the council tip and looked at all the different piles of waste. She talked about recycling and fly-tipping. One of the council workers gave her a guided tour. When it was time to go, though, Pippin had disappeared. Aunty Mabel searched and searched, calling Pippin's name, but there was no sign. Eventually she decided that the dog had fallen in the crusher or something because she said again what dangerous places rubbish tips can be, and went home alone, hanging the lead up by the door and wiping her eyes. But wait! Just as the door was swinging closed, there was a joyful bark and who should come round the corner wagging her tail etc. To my embarrassment I found there were tears running down my cheeks. Thank God Juno wasn't there to see. Crying over a TV dog and dry-eyed over my best friend's mother.

I mopped my face and went to make a drink, remembering now, out of nowhere, the way Mum had dealt with Dad leaving us. What she'd done was to establish new routines, so that instead of waiting for him to come home from the Labour Club on a Saturday night before we had our supper, we had our fish and chips early and watched the sort of film we wanted right the way through; no more changing over for *Match of the Day*. The food-shop route was different too; we didn't go down the beer aisle at all. Instead we bought extra chocolate, and took our time over the magazines and toiletries. Easter we could spend at home, baking and reading, not trailing up to see his sister in Dundee. Sometimes it seemed as though time had been suspended or even gone backwards because Mum would do all the things I loved as a child, like reading aloud 'The Robin Family' in *Woman's Weekly*, and buying mallow wafers and playing hangman. I reckon I got an extra three or four years of childhood out of my dad going.

*   *   *

Kim's mum—For all she's my daughter, I have to say she does like getting her own way. Always has done. Ever since she was a little girl she's had her own agenda. You know, if she saw a doll in a shop and made up her mind she wanted it, she'd go on and on till we got it her. I suppose she was spoilt, in a way. Now I look back. It's

269

hard to know what's best for your kids, in't it? I'd say she was the stronger one in the marriage. Lee's nice but he's too easy with her. Not that I say owt. Only get my head bitten off. But they make a good team because she leads and he follows, more or less, it suits both of them.

Interviewer—Are you close to your daughter?

Kim's mum—Are we close? Well, I only live two streets away! No, we see a lot of each other. I'm round here now helping her make inroads into this pile of ironing, because she works full time and the lads never lift a finger to help. I don't mind. I like ironing, me. I like the smell off the clean clothes. See, like that. Do you ever do that, sniff your laundry? It's a lovely smell.

Interviewer—What about emotionally? Are you close to Kim emotionally, would you say?

Kim's mum—Em, that's a good question. I'm not sure we are. I think the world of her but she does kind of hold herself apart, if you know what I mean. She dun't often confide in me. I feel sometimes there's a lot going on under the surface with Kim that I never get to know about. Good job an' all, I expect. Now. Look at that collar, work of art.

Kim—Me and my mum, oh yeah, we're like that. Very close. Very.

*　　　*　　　*

Juno looked awful when she walked back in, like she was sick. I made her sit down while I hunted for hard liquor. Eventually I found some in the sideboard; two bottles of Harvey's Bristol Cream,

270

one unopened, a half-bottle of Scotch and some Bailey's. Dust flew out when I moved them around.

'Mum and Dad weren't big drinkers,' she said, watching me pour Scotch into a mug.

'I can see that. You want this topping up with coffee?'

She nodded, and the shadows under her eyes deepened as her head dipped forward.

After a minute she leant down to her bag and drew out the death certificate. She smoothed it out, then tossed it onto the table.

'There it is,' she said. 'All done now.'

I said, 'Did you get to say goodbye? I think that's important.'

It sounds mad but we hadn't talked about it last night. On the way out of the hospital Juno had been completely silent, and then in the car she'd started going on about food and how hungry she was. When we got into the house she went all giddy and we ate our bangers 'n' beans reminiscing about stupid Seventies TV adverts. Part of me was thinking, I should ask her about how her mum went in the end. But there was something so sharp and glittering about Juno in that hour that I didn't dare. I thought she might fracture, like a mirror.

'I don't know how you do say goodbye.' Now she hunched round her mug and focused on the steam wisping above it. 'I talked to her, don't know if she was listening. It was too late in the day to say a great deal.'

'I think I understand,' I said cautiously, though I wasn't sure. 'If my dad died tomorrow, I don't know what I'd feel.'

'Mmm,' she said. I got the feeling she was a long way away.

271

'It's the weight of expectation, isn't it? Knowing how you're supposed to feel and then, if there's a gap, it's as if you're inadequate. Someone should tell you there aren't any rules.' The wail of a siren came through from the road at the front; police, ambulance? Someone in trouble, somewhere.

'It's like, people expect me to be getting over Joe, I'm sure they do—'

'Ally, they don't. No one thinks that.'

'—making veiled references, it's time to move on. But it wouldn't matter if I believed them. Some mornings I wake up and it's the same as the first day after, just as raw.' I knew I shouldn't be talking about Joe, here; it was Juno's time. But he'd become my reference point for almost everything. I tried: 'You know how some scientists believe everyone sees colours differently? Your blue might be my red, neither of us would ever know, and grief's like that, I'm sure it is. There's no point trying to measure yours against someone else's because we all see our own—colour.'

'What do you mean, Ally?' Juno put her mug down on the chair arm as if she hardly had the strength to hold it. All last night I'd felt her moving beside me, sleepless or in the grip of unhappy dreams. Twice I'd reached across the bed and stroked her arm, and she'd gone still for a while. 'It's perfectly normal,' and I was remembering an American woman I'd seen on a counselling video saying this, very earnest, very deliberate, 'not to feel a certain way after someone dies. There are no "shoulds". It's a very confusing time. There may be a lot of hate about; you might even think you hate the person for leaving you and not trying hard enough to stay alive, even though you know that's

272

not logical, but it doesn't mean you—'

'You don't understand.'

'What?' My mind was still with the American's row of pearls and blue round-neck blouse. She'd been sitting in a wing chair with a vase of flowers on a table next to her. When I'd read the credits it said her son had died in a sailing accident. I was trying to imagine her rolling about on the carpet, screaming her throat raw, digging her finger-nails into her own cheeks.

'You've got it the wrong way round,' said Juno flatly. 'My parents hated me.'

I heard what she said but I couldn't make sense of it for a second. I must have looked simple, sitting there frowning at her. 'No.'

'Yes, Ally. They really did hate me.'

'But, Juno,' I burst out. 'You're the most lovely person—why would anyone, least of all—'

She cut me off, almost shouting: 'Because they blamed me for my sister dying.'

She was on her feet.

'Oh, God, I'm sorry, I'm sorry. I didn't even know you had a sister.'

Juno with a sister!

'I hardly did. She was only around till she was six. Wait.' She walked quickly across the room and into the hall.

'Does Manny know?'

She came back carrying two photo frames. 'Here. I presumed you'd seen her pictures. I half thought you might say—although we did look similar, so . . . This is me, the thin one, and this is Diane, two years younger. Like me but plumper.'

'Christ, Juno, I thought that *was* you.'

'Her name's at the bottom; oh, no, only on the

back. But this is her. June and Diane.'

She propped the pictures up on the table.

'You look so alike.'

'Yes. I think that made it worse.'

The clock struck four notes, quarter past one. I'd been going to heat up some soup.

'How did she die?'

Juno sat down on the edge of the chair, looking at the photographs, her arms folded across her chest. I thought she was never going to answer. I had in my mind a road accident, Juno taking her sister to the shops, telling her to cross without checking, I saw the street and the lorry, I saw Joe.

'Meningitis,' she said.

'Meningitis? How was that your fault?'

'It wasn't. I was eight. But they wanted somebody to blame.'

'That's not fair.'

'What's fair, Ally? Whoever said life is fair? All right, not blame. I don't know how it worked. They closed up the day my little sister died. They took no interest in me any more, I might as well have ceased to exist. If I'd run away from home, I don't believe they'd have noticed. You don't question these behaviours when you're a child, you just learn to adapt. I can see now they were desperate, but I still can't forgive them; we lived alongside each other, and I left as soon as I possibly could, to make my own family.'

'That's terrible.'

'I used to wish I was at boarding school. I think I'd have thrived away from home. I had all the Malory Towers series.' She did a sad, fake laugh.

'It is pretty desperate for the parents, you know. They might not have thought—'

274

'But the way you are with Ben, you're so good, it's made me realize. You understood Joe dying was his loss too, and he saw professionals. Whereas my parents took all the grief for themselves. They left me—stranded.'

A vision of a tiny Juno standing crying on an empty beach. 'I can't understand why your mum and dad would react like that.'

'That's because you're a good person, Ally. I wouldn't have expected you to get any of it. Your mind doesn't work that way. Look how you've been with Ben, amazing.'

'Not really. Not such a good person, when you get down to it.'

'Oh, you are.'

Down the hallway, the letterbox snapped and we both jumped.

'Free paper,' said Juno. 'I'll have to get that cancelled, one more thing on the list.'

'I thought it was someone coming in,' I said stupidly. 'Tell me about Diane.'

'No, I don't want to go over it; don't look like that. It's not you that's upset me, just forget it. Only, do you understand now? About my reaction, my mum dying?'

I nodded.

'*You* mustn't be upset, Ally, it's not your fault.' She picked the photographs up casually, the way you'd pick up empty glasses after a party. 'I'll hang these back up. They'll all be going with the house clearance soon, anyway.'

'Oh.'

'What?'

'You shouldn't throw those photos away.'

Juno turned, the pictures clasped against her

sweater. 'Do you want them?'

'If they're going in the skip. Are you really not keeping them?'

'I have copies at home, in an album,' she said.

I was so relieved to hear she was being practical, not callous.

'OK, I'll have them.'

Everyone has their own way, I reminded myself, as I leant the frames against the front door.

Juno did some telephoning while I packed, and then we got in the car.

Key in the ignition, I paused, looked across at her strained face. 'Do you think I'm a good person?'

'Absolutely. Better than me,' she said.

We didn't talk much on the way back. I was seeing Diane lying on a sofa, her mother giving her junior aspirin in a glass of water, telling Juno to stop making so much noise and go draw the curtains. I wondered whether Juno had been asked to do something and failed, phone a doctor—but you wouldn't make an eight-year-old do that. Perhaps Juno knew her sister was ill for hours before she told anyone; maybe she saw the rash and didn't say. But the rash only comes later. She could have had nothing to do with any of it, except in her mother's head. I imagined Diane being carried through hospital doors in a man's arms and doctors rushing about, Diane laid out on a trolley with her legs all mottled. But it probably wasn't like that at all. I saw Joe, and gripped the steering wheel. His feet were pressing again into the back of my seat.

Did you know, Juno, I wanted to say, that I stopped Ben from talking about Joe as if his brother was something to be ashamed about, and I did it in the most humiliating way I possibly could? And he's never forgotten it, even though he doesn't say. He'll take that scene with him to his old age.

Did you know that when Joe's teacher, Mrs Daly, left me alone with the class memory board, I unpinned one of the pieces of paper and wrote a nasty message on it? There was a drawing by a boy who'd tripped Joe up deliberately in the playground, and another time had stolen his afternoon snack so that he had nothing to eat at break. This boy had drawn a sun and two figures, I don't know who they were meant to be, they were very poor. Joe could draw a lot better than that. Mrs Daly had felt-tipped 'Heaven' along the top. And I was so angry that I scribbled over the paper with a wax crayon and wrote *hypocritical bully* in letters so hard they ripped the surface of the paper in one place. Then I pinned the picture back up. I suppose Mrs Daly took it down. It was never mentioned, so I presume none of the kids saw it. I hope they didn't, I hope she just threw it in the bin. Did she show it round the staff room?

It began to rain and all the cars and lorries were putting their lights and wipers on.

'It gets dark early now,' I said.

Juno didn't reply but she had her eyes closed and she might have been asleep.

The worst thing I've done was to watch Mr Peterson dying. No one knows I did this.

After Joe was killed I couldn't get Peterson out of my head. At the inquest it was suggested that he might be too old and infirm to continue driving, but a doctor's report gave him the all-clear.

Nevertheless, he claimed he would never get behind a wheel again.

He lived locally. I used to go round to his house to check whether the car was there; it always was. His wife couldn't drive. At one point I was going across town every day to look, hoping I'd catch him out then I could attack him. I used to imagine watching him lower himself into the front seat, then I was going to launch myself at his thin body, screaming, pummelling his chest, dragging him out onto the ground. It would have been easy to attack him, he was very frail.

One day Tom had the small ads open because he was looking at motorbikes. In those days he was interested in buying a project bike, one that needed loads of work. He wouldn't be riding it, just fixing and reselling. I was going through what he'd circled when I spotted Peterson's phone number. He was getting rid of the car. I called and pretended to be someone else and his wife told me that her husband was too ill to drive. At first I thought she was making it up, but he turned out to have terminal cancer. She was very upset.

This is how premeditated it was; I actually hired a wig and plain glasses from a costume shop. I drove to the ward she'd said he was on and I told the nurse at the desk I was there to see him. But instead I went and sat by the bed of a man who was asleep and listened to Peterson's wife talking to a visitor, another old man. She said they were waiting for a private room or, ideally, a place in a hospice. She said this in front of her husband, so he must have known the score.

After twenty minutes the visitor said he was leaving and Mrs Peterson said she'd walk with him, go down to the shop for some tissues. I waited till they were out of the door, then I made my move.

He saw at once who I was. I'd been going to lean down and say, 'What a shame you didn't die last year,' or 'You bastard, I hope you're in pain,' but in the end I just stood and looked at him till he cried. Then I went home and made the tea.

In the seat next to me, Juno jerked her head forward and snorted; so she had been dozing. 'Was I snoring?' she asked.

'No. Not too much longer, now. Another half hour and we should be home. Do you want to call Tom and let him know?'

'Sure. God, I need a hot bath.'

She rummaged in the footwell for my mobile.

'Do you want to try Manny too?'

'I tried him earlier,' she said. 'But there was no reply.'

'When did you say he'd be back?'

'Anytime,' she said, the phone to her ear. 'Oh, it's ringing, shhh. Tom?'

In the event it was three days before Manny returned, and then it was me he came home to.

CHAPTER SEVENTEEN

Kim—Lee's diamond. I love him to bits. He's my rock.

Lee—That's nice.

Kim—My little stick of Blackpool rock.

Lee—Now now, less of your little. Giant-sized, more like. Jumbo.

Kim—In your dreams, love.

*   *   *

Manny was waiting for me in the nursery car park. I ran across and, never thought, just gave him a hug.

'Thank God you're here,' I said into his neck. He smelt of Paco Rabanne.

'Hmm?'

'Juno must be so relieved, she's had the most awful time. How long have you been back? Couldn't you get a ferry any earlier? Or did you fly?'

He held onto me longer than I expected, and when he did let me go all he said was, 'Can we go somewhere and talk?'

'Home?'

'Not yet.' He checked his watch. 'Can I take you to lunch, Ally?'

'What about Juno?'

'I need to speak to you first.'

'What's the matter? Has something happened?'

'Nothing to worry about. I just need your advice.'

I think I knew even at this point something was very wrong, the way his eyes flicked past mine. But I thought I'd go along with it. This was Manny, after all, my friend.

'OK. Let's go to Algarve, it's easier to park.'

'Hop in with me, then we only have to worry about one vehicle,' he said. 'I can run you back here afterwards. Come on, it'll be a lot less hassle.'

He took me by the arm like a Victorian gentleman and led me to his car. His cheeks seemed pinkish, slightly wind-burned. I wondered if the Ireland project had involved camping.

When he started the ignition the CD player blasted into life. I frowned, trying to place the sweeping intro; then the vocals started.

'*Foreigner*?' I asked him, amazed. I'd have soon as expected a Foreigner CD in Manny's glove box as a live salamander.

He pushed the car into gear. 'Great, isn't it? I missed out on a lot of this Eighties stuff with moving backwards and forwards to France. I love this track. It's kitsch but it rocks.'

It rocks?

I said, 'Juno's been terrifically brave, you know.'

'Yeah?'

'Yes. She has. Having to make all the arrangements for the funeral and look after the girls as well—'

Manny turned his head to me, his eyes wide. 'What funeral? Oh, shit, not her mother?'

'You didn't know?'

'No.'

'She didn't ring you?'

'No, she fucking didn't.' He swung the car through a too-narrow gap. I fell against the door,

281

someone bibbed their horn at him.

'But didn't you ring her? I mean, they have phones in Ireland, for God's sake.'

'Who told you I've been in Ireland?'

'Weren't you at a Celtic arts festival?'

'Lord, no. Oh, fuck. How could she not tell me about her mother dying?'

He flashed a look of appeal at me but I didn't know how to answer. I couldn't follow this at all.

'Haven't you been back home yet, Manny?'

'No. I told you, I needed to see you first.'

My heart began to thump.

'All right, I'll tell you why she didn't let me know about her mother,' he grimaced, taking a corner so badly that he bumped up onto the kerb momentarily. 'She'll have done it to make me look bad, I know the way she works. To make me look even more of a heel than I am.'

'She phoned you, I know she did, she told me.'

Manny shook his head but said nothing. The car was full of 'Waiting for a Girl like You'.

'I don't understand what's going on,' I said over the music.

The car swerved into a gap at the side of the road and Manny pulled on the handbrake, switched the engine off. Then he put his hands on the steering wheel, straight out in front of him. He had on a khaki shirt I'd not seen before, Indiana Jones style, and he'd rolled the sleeves back. In a different moment I'd have wanted to reach across and stroke his forearm.

'Look,' he said, 'I could see as soon as you came over that Juno hadn't told you what's happened.'

'What about?'

'Me. I've left her, Ally.'

*   *   *

Interviewer—You got married quite young.

Juno—I was a child bride.

Manny—A student one. God, we were innocents in those days, weren't we? I think we got ourselves married before we even realized it.

Juno—*Non, je ne regrette rien . . .*

Manny—I've always hated that song.

Juno—You never said.

Manny—No.

*   *   *

I could feel Juno's pain slamming into me like the impact of a car crash.

'For good?'

'No. I don't know. I felt I needed to get away and mull things over. I've been up in the Lakes, near Windermere, walking. The scenery's so marvellous there, it really makes you think inside yourself, kind of examine your interior landscape. Do you know what I'm saying?'

'No.' I was thinking, How could she not have told me this. 'Interior landscape? Manny, what's going on?'

He shrugged.

'I wanted some time alone to take stock of my life.'

Tom says there's no such thing as the male menopause. He says it's just an excuse for middle-aged men to dick about.

'Have you told the girls?'

'I wanted to see Juno, talk to her before we said

283

anything to Pascale and Soph. Ally, I thought you might understand. I've always thought of you as having tremendous emotional intelligence.'

In spite of myself, my neck prickled. 'Have you?'

'Oh, yes. You, of all the people I know, you have real depth. I thought there was a chance you might understand what I can barely articulate for myself.'

'I'll try.'

He sighed, pressed his palms against the vinyl curve of the steering wheel. 'I feel, if I carry on as I am, in the same life, I'll have missed— experiences—people—I want to interact with. If I don't change direction, then I'll know now where I'll be in ten years' time, twenty, thirty. And who wants a life like that?'

Me, I thought. 'Can't you find another job? Why does it have to be Juno's fault?'

'It's not Juno's fault. It's about who I am. I'm looking on the break as a sort of relationship sabbatical.'

'So you're coming back.'

Juno on her own; it was unthinkable. On the other side of the windscreen, the first drops of rain spattered against the glass and trickled jerkily down. The CD wanted to Know what Love is.

'I never intended to get married so soon,' he said. 'There were a lot of places I had in mind to visit first. Places less safe than Chester.'

'You're still wearing your wedding ring.'

He looked down at his hand and splayed his brown fingers. 'So I am.'

'You can go travelling when the kids are older.'

'Ally, I'm tired of always doing the right thing. I married Juno when she got pregnant because it was the honourable course of action.'

284

'But you loved her. You'd have married her anyway.'

'I'm not denying that. People change, though. Juno and I don't feel together any more. Haven't for a while, now.'

Something, I don't know what, made me ask, 'Manny, has this got anything to do with Kim?'

'I'm not sleeping with her,' he said immediately.

Kim in her high-heeled boots, Kim dropping the bird into my bin, smiling. 'Oh my God.'

'It's nothing like that. Ally, calm down, I'm telling you the truth. I am. I haven't made any secret of the fact that I've seen Kim since the show, she's so interested in the arts—'

'Like bloody hell she is—'

'She *is*. She wants to learn. No one's given her the time till now. Do you know how nice it is for me to be able to teach something to someone? To be with a person who doesn't know everything? It's a friendship that's opened me up. And she's teaching me stuff too. It's crazy, but the last time I took some videos over for her we ended up having races on the boys' Space Hoppers.' He said this as though he thought it was an immensely clever thing to have done. 'Don't turn your nose up, it was fantastic fun. We were laughing so much it was like we were drunk. Kim's mad, she doesn't care. She's always dancing, just dances to the radio, anytime; she eats what she likes, where she likes, when she likes, completely spontaneous. Juno has this need to be in charge all the time, it's exhausting. And there's more to life than having matching door plates and sitting down to organic bloody courgettes.'

I thought of those happy mealtimes we'd all sat

round their big kitchen table cracking jokes, me coveting Juno's big Provençal salad bowl, someone's smooth arm stretching out and gold bangles clicking, the sound of wine being poured.

'I think Kim's very deliberate in what she does,' I said coldly. 'I got the feeling she was an extremely manipulative woman. Juno might fuss sometimes, but at least she's honest.'

Manny was shaking his head. 'You haven't got it at all, have you? You're under the impression my wife's some kind of saint.'

'She's been a damn good friend to me.' I was swallowing constantly with nerves and fury. 'The bottom line is, you want me to sanction what you're doing, don't you? That's why you wanted to see me. You thought you could justify yourself and, what, take the message back to Juno? *Ally agrees with me, you're too controlling, the poor man needs a break?* Eugh! You *can't* be having an affair with Kim, she's so, not nice—'

He struck the dashboard suddenly with his fist. 'I just said I wasn't, didn't I? Jesus!'

He turned the key in the ignition. The music cut out, then blared again.

'Where are we going?'

'I'm driving you back,' he said. 'I'm clearly not going to get any sense out of you. I don't know why I ever imagined I would. You're Juno's clone, that's all.'

He drove as though he was in a rally. We screeched into the entrance of the car park and he stamped on the brake so that I jerked against the seat belt and fell back. As I reached shakily for the door handle, he said, 'You think she's so damn perfect? Well, I'll tell you something, one of the things she's done.' I scrambled out but he leant across the passenger seat and looked up at me with angry eyes. 'Did you know she used to post in a bereavement forum for parents who've lost their children? I mean, pretending she was one? So what do you think of *that*?'

I said nothing. As soon as I'd slammed the door, he drove away. There were tyre marks across the disabled symbol for days afterwards.

*   *   *

Manny [To camera]—So, Kim's been in the house for nearly twelve hours, and what are my first impressions? I think she'll need to speak up for herself a little more, she seems pretty quiet at the moment. I hope she's going to be the joining-in type, because we are . . . I hope she'll be up for new experiences, open-minded. I'm looking forward to discussing her tastes in film and literature. No good playing charades tomorrow night if she's never heard of *Asterix* or *Don't Look Now*. Talking of which, she's left a book on the arm of the chair, shall we check it out?

Hmm. *Symphony for the Heart* by Eveline Roswell. Nice embossed cover, lovely. Why do they do that on romance books? Is the very title meant to be throbbing with passion? And there's your standard heaving-bosomed heroine, and the masterful hero looking down her cleavage. Terrifically patronizing, isn't it? At the very least, passé. I'm always fascinated to know, why do women read this pap? Correction; some women, you wouldn't catch Juno picking up a novel like this. I must ask Kim why she brought it, what she gets out of a read like this. Maybe I'm missing something. In the meantime, I'll see if I can get her on to some Emily Lincoln. She writes northern stuff. I'll tell her it's like *Coronation Street*, that should do it.

*　　　*　　　*

I drove straight to Juno. I imagined putting my arms round her slender waist while she wept on my shoulder; Manny and Juno on a park bench in Honfleur, surrounded by flowers; Kim's grinning face.

When I got there, she was done up like a Fifties housewife in a flowered pinny and a headscarf, bright as anything.

'I had this idea, in the small hours, that I'd repaint the bedroom,' she said, re-tying the scarf around her hair more tightly. If I wore something like that round my head I'd look like Mrs Overall: Juno looked like Ann Blyth in *Kismet*. 'So when I'd dropped the kids off I called in at Laura Ashley and got some stuff called Deep Cowslip, it's absolutely gorgeous, it'll light up the whole space. But it's a bigger job than I thought. I was hoping to have it finished by the time the girls came home, but that's not going to happen—'

'I've seen Manny,' I said.

*　　　*　　　*

Kim—Top Gun, An Officer and a Gentleman, Titanic. Catch Me If You Can is pretty good too. Have you really not seen them?

Sophie—We've seen *Titanic*.

Pascale—Yeah, and you bought the single.

Sophie—Shut up, Paxo.

Manny—Interesting treatment of the class angle in *Titanic*, I thought. If you compare it with the 1957 version, *A Night to Remember*, now that's a fine film, but its emphasis is very different. Much more factual, less romantic but still terrifically moving. A product of its time. As is every film, of course, and every work of art. I don't suppose you've watched that one?

Kim—Don't think so. Is it a black and white? I like anything with Tom Cruise in. I wouldn't kick Mel Gibson out of bed, either.

Manny—You can't just like a film because you fancy the lead actor.

Kim—Why not?

Manny—All right, you can, but—

Kim—Who's to say what I can like and what I can't? It's my personal taste. Isn't it?

Manny—Yes, I suppose it is.

Kim—That's what taste is, your individual preferences. You can't go saying this is right and that's wrong. Anyway, if they weren't any good then they'd never have done so well at the box office.

Manny—Of course, the commercial aspect of a film—

Kim—Know what? You want to watch some of these films before you condemn them. You might be pleasantly surprised, Manny Kingston.

*   *   *

She'd been leaning against the newel, but now she

sank down onto the second step. 'Where? Where did you see him?'

'He was waiting outside the nursery. We only spoke for a couple of minutes, then he drove off.'

'Is he coming here?' She looked around wildly.

'I don't know. I don't think so, not at the moment.'

'Oh God. What did he say? When's he coming back?'

'He's angry with you for not telling him about your mum.'

'He didn't *deserve* to be told! Who's got the right to be angry here, hey?' She paused and I saw the first shine of tears.

'Oh, Juno—'

'What else did he say?'

'That he's been in the Lake District, he's been taking stock of where he's going in his life, he doesn't like being able to predict where he'll be in twenty years' time. He feels he's due some kind of sabbatical. That was the gist of it.' Oh, and I'm your clone, I could have added. I was trying not to let my voice shake.

'Is that all?'

'More or less.'

'But he is coming back?'

'I'm sure he is, at some point . . . '

'Did he say he was with Kim?'

'He's not with her, Juno. He says he's been on his own. I'm convinced he was telling the truth.'

'How would you know to believe anything he says?' she cried, pulling off the scarf and throwing it on the carpet. 'I don't know where I am any more with him. I mean, why did he choose to speak to you and not me? What was that all about?'

I went cold. 'I think he was testing the water. I don't know. You're not—'

'No, not really. Shit, my head's just such a mess. I'm going to phone him, that's what I'm going to do. He can come round here himself and damn well explain face to face, like an adult. Fucking sabbatical. We'd all like one of those.'

She ran up the stairs and I heard a door slam. I stood in the hall for a few minutes, debating whether to stay or go home. I thought of watching Dad leave, seeing him walk down the path with his suitcase, and the way I'd wanted to run after him and thump him hard or catch him by the trouser leg and pull him back to us. Then I remembered that he'd left during the night while I was asleep. So where had that scene come from? God, I could see it, and yet it never happened.

I wandered into the living room and picked up a half-empty mug of cold coffee, took it through to the kitchen. As I rinsed it out, I scanned Juno's wall calendar and list of useful contacts. And there was Kim's home phone number. It was like Fate giving me a great big nudge.

I used my mobile and I dialled 141 first, to make sure she couldn't trace the call back. A woman's voice said flatly, 'Hiya.' Was it her? I couldn't be sure.

'I wondered if I could speak to Kim, please?'

'Speaking.'

I nearly shouted out, I was so relieved; instead I squeezed the end-call button so hard I nearly cracked the phone casing.

I ran up the stairs, desperate to tell Juno the news. Her bedroom door was closed, so I listened for a moment, then knocked gently.

'Come in,' I heard her say.

She was sitting on the bed, her hair mussed up, her shoulders drooping.

'Have you finished?'

'Hardly started. He said he'd come back for the funeral and I told him if that was his only reason then he could go fuck himself. Then I hung up.'

'Try him again. He probably didn't mean it to sound that way.'

'Can't. His mobile's switched off, the bastard.'

I waved my phone at her. 'I've just rung Kim's house—don't worry, I didn't say who it was. She's there, Juno, in Bolton. So Manny was telling the truth.'

She put her hand to her mouth, then began to cry. Her back sagged, then she collapsed sideways on the bed and sobbed. I sat next to her, stroking her arm and wiping her cheeks where I could reach them, smoothing her hair over her shoulder. Tom's done this for me in the past. You just have to wait. Soon her whole face was wet and her nose slobbery, and the embroidered white bedspread smeared with lipstick. 'Oh God,' she kept wailing.

At last the crying wore itself out and she lay quietly, taking juddering breaths every now and then. Her eyes were tight closed and when I stood up, she rolled her face away from me, back into the bedcover.

I went downstairs to wait for Ben and the girls.

CHAPTER EIGHTEEN

I ended up cooking for everyone that night. Juno broke the news to Pascale and Sophie and then brought them straight round; I don't think she could cope with just the three of them together. The girls sat in front of the TV, whispering, and Juno and I chopped veg in the kitchen. Ben hung around us for a while, then disappeared off to his room.

Tom we told as soon as he walked through the door. 'Shit,' he said, and put his arms round Juno straight away, but she stiffened and pushed him back.

'It's just,' she said, 'I don't want you to start me off again. I'm fine till someone's kind. The girls—'

'Yep,' said Tom. 'Understood. Jesus, though. Ally, get a bottle of wine out. We all need a drink.'

Afterwards I took some leftovers out to the dustbin and found myself mesmerized by the view through my own lounge window. Was that my life, there in that lighted house? I tried to look at it without the dull filter of familiarity. That medium-height, pleasant-looking man; my husband. That beautiful adolescent boy; my son, and in a different night, a different moment of conception, he'd never have existed. If I'd married Mark Walters. Or if I'd never met Mark, or even Robin before him, I might not have been ready to love Tom. All the ways these things that were now might not have ever happened.

I looked at Ben again and saw how he was with the girls. When I was a child I'd had, one

Christmas, a little pair of plastic ladybirds. They were magic, because when you put them on a smooth surface and tried to push their heads together, they'd spring apart. Or the one you weren't holding would edge backwards all on its own as its partner drew near. That was Ben and Soph at this moment, performing a subtle repulsion-dance around the room, constantly checking each other's position to ensure the distance between them.

Then, as I watched, Juno said something to Tom and he came over to the sofa and embraced her. Her head lay against his shoulder and his lips moved in soothing shapes. He patted her hair gently, which is what he does for me sometimes. I knew I could trust him: how much is that worth?

Later, in bed, Tom picked up his book, frowned at it for two minutes, then put it down again.

'Waste of time, I can't take it in,' he said.

I reached for his hand under the covers.

'You were really good tonight, at the meal and afterwards. I know Juno gets on your nerves sometimes, but she doesn't deserve what Manny's done.'

'No. Life's a bastard.'

I had a flash of Joe sitting watching his brother play on the computer, bobbing up and down in his chair with excitement.

'It's so awful that she feels she needs to keep it a secret, though. I still think she could have told me, I wouldn't have breathed a word to anyone. Unless she thought that not talking about it would make it less real. Do you reckon she's right, that the tabloids would stick it on the front page?'

'I do, yes.'

'Surely they wouldn't be so insensitive; I mean, with her having lost her mum so recently. That would make them look mean, wouldn't it, like they were victimizing her, and then they might lose readers.'

Tom slid his fingers from mine, sighed, and put his hands behind his head. 'Possibly. But you have to remember, the Kingstons stepped into the public domain when they signed up for *Queen Mum*. Juno's a bright woman, she always knew that.'

'But she didn't know her marriage was going to fall apart.'

'Ahh, no. She went on the programme because she was confident under media scrutiny. But that's not the case any more. And it's too late, now. She can't wipe herself out of the nation's consciousness. She's in there like the Bisto kids or *Pop Idol*. Branded.'

*   *   *

Kim's mum—I'd say she's always enjoyed getting attention. She always put a hundred per cent into school plays and what have you. Even if she was just an Indian dancer at the back, she'd be swaying more than anyone, flirting her veil around, you know. One year she was in a group singing at the front and she'd made up a load of actions to go with the words, I don't think she was supposed to, nobody else was doing them. I've got it on video somewhere. It was hilarious. Oh, and I'll tell you summat else she used to do; she loved to mime in front of *Top of the Pops*. Do you remember a song called 'I Think We're

Alone Now'? I forget who sang it. That was her favourite. She had a whole routine worked out to go with that one.

Lee—See I never had a mum, not properly. She was around when I was very little, then she left, only they told me she was ill, then she came back, I'd have been about eight, then she went again. It was my Aunty Joan who brought me up really, my dad's sister. And she wan't always that nice with me 'cause she had a lot on her plate with looking after her mother and her husband working away. My dad was around but he wan't that interested. Remote, you'd call him. He's really remote now; he lives in Ireland. We telephone once in a while. I don't miss him. What's to miss?

So my family's very important to me. My lads. My wife.

I might not be one of these blokes who comes home with chocolates and flowers all the time, but I do love her. She does know that.

*   *   *

I was up again at 1.30; too much going on in my head. Mum had rung earlier with a story about a missing toddler and I'd only stopped her from delivering the punchline by threatening not to go up next week. These things get into your head and drive you crazy. I left Tom sleeping and went to make a drink of milk. Through the kitchen window the stars were very bright: Orion, Ursa Minor, Ursa Major, Cassiopeia. You can't help thinking about heaven on a frosty night.

296

As I passed the front room I spotted what I must have missed when I went past before; a faint light around the door frame. When I stood still I could hear the hum of the machine working, too.

'Ben?' I pushed the door open and he started guiltily. His face seemed hard in the glow of the computer screen. 'Ben! What are you doing up at this time? It's getting on for two o'clock in the morning. You've school tomorrow, you'll be wrecked.'

He was busy clicking windows away, but I could see before they vanished it was some bizarre porn.

'Oh, God, was that a dog?'

'No,' he said, shutting the screen down rapidly. 'It wasn't anything. Jesus, you gave me a shock. Why are you up, Mum?'

'Never mind me. What on earth did you think you were doing on there?' I put the main light on and he blinked and shielded his eyes with his arm.

'It was just a joke.'

'What was?'

'Jeez, don't make me tell you. It wasn't anything, honest, mucking about.'

'Ben.'

He lowered his arm and sighed. 'You won't want to hear. All it is, it's a stupid joke we've been having at school, sending dodgy links to each other. It's like a competition to gross each other out. We find twisted sites and mail them to each other.'

I was thinking, You used to sing the theme tune from *The Snowman* and make your grandma cry. You used to stand on the bed in your little pyjamas and ask for an extra kiss for Chiffy in case he got scared in the night-time.

'It's not all porn,' he went on. 'Some of it's, like, sick humour. There's this one cartoon site where they have kittens being chopped up with a chainsaw, body parts flying around. It's not real. Obviously. But it is quite funny.'

'Go to bed, Ben. You're right, I don't want to hear.'

The computer did its final closing-down buzz and went silent.

'There. All gone. I couldn't sleep, that's why I was down here. You know what it's like when you're lying there and all your thoughts are going round and round. I had this idea I'd surf the Net for a bit till I was properly tired. I'd been looking at fossils on eBay before.'

'You haven't been in any chat rooms, have you?' He hitched his boxer shorts up round his skinny waist and I thought of Sophie touching his tender skin. It was an outrageous image; I vanished it at once.

'Chat rooms're for saddos. Waste of time. People are never who they say they are, so it's pointless. I know all the stranger-danger stuff, so don't start.'

'And what about the danger of giving out personal email addresses to hundreds of sick websites, so we're all flooded with vile nasty spam? I don't want to fire up my emails and get a load of offers from strangers to wee on me, thank you very much. No, it's not funny. Our blocked-senders list is like an encyclopaedia.'

He came up and put his arms round me. 'I'm taller than you, now.'

'What's that got to do with anything?'

'Dunno. I'm glad you and dad are my parents, and not Juno and Manny.' Why? I wanted to say, but he'd already detached himself and given me a peck on the cheek. 'See you, then.'

'I should be cross with you,' I called after him. 'I am cross. It'll have to stop, you know, craze or no craze.'

'Night, night,' I heard him say from the landing.

I sat down and fired the computer back up.

* * *

Interviewer—What would you say you've learned from your mum and dad about how marriage works?

Marco—How do you mean?

Chris—I've learnt that you have to let the woman do more or less what she wants, 'cause she's like the centre of everything, family life. Plus, she can't half sulk when she dun't get her own way.

Marco—I won't be so soft when I'm married. My wife's gonna do what she's told.

Chris [Laughs exaggeratedly]—Yeah, right. And who'd marry you?

Marco—Who'd marry you, gay-boy?

Chris—'My wife's gonna do what she's told' . . . You're priceless, you are. Watch out, girls, bloody hell; here he comes.

Pascale—I'd say they've been pretty good role models—

Sophie—Yeah, mostly, although—

Pascale—What?

Sophie—Do you not think Mum bosses Dad around? You know, with all her schemes. Like, if she wants a pergola in the garden, we just get one. Everyone else has to sit round and discuss

299

their plans, but Mum charges ahead.

Pascale—Yeah, but do you actually care if we have a manky old pergola in the garden?

Sophie—That was only an example—

Pascale—We're pretty lucky to have a mum and dad who are still married, if you think about it. So many couples are splitting up, it's like half of all marriages end in divorce or something, so they must be doing something right.

Sophie—Suppose. I still think Mum wears the trousers.

Pascale—I disagree.

Sophie—That's your thingy, your . . . what's the word? Perogathingy. Per . . . ?

Pascale—Pergola.

Sophie—That's right. It's my pergola. And I'm sticking to it.

*   *   *

There are lots of sites about bereavement, thousands of people wanting answers. Mums like me, sitting at the screen in the small hours, searching for they don't know what.

It was eighteen months since I'd been in a forum, but I'd been so obsessed with this one place that I had no trouble remembering my username and password. You clicked on a little tree to get in.

There were threads for mums, for dads, for siblings, for grandparents. I had to go back a long way to find my last post, about dreams. Were dreams helpful, I'd asked, or were they merely upsetting, churning your mind up at the one time of day when it could have been resting? I'd had pages of responses. People whose children had told

300

them messages in a dream, comforting dreams; nightmares where the loss had been repeated only with awful twists; dreams of failure and reproach and guilt and simple madness. I read them all again, and all the friendly supportive posts with their (((hugs))) and crazy smilies.

Then I went to the member list. I was looking for Juno.

No Juno; June?

There was a JunePlus, but when I checked her posts her tone wasn't right, and her phrasing. Her avatar was a cartoon mouse in a hat. Juno's would have been something like a sunset over Ulverston, or a painting by Delacroix.

I went up and down the lists again. SuperKingy; was that her? How about Diane66? Chestermum? She might not even have been on this site; there were others.

At last I stopped clicking. Say I found her, what would I do then?

Bloody Manny.

When I checked my watch it was nearly four. I shut the machine down and tiptoed up the stairs. Ben's door was open and I put my head round it. He was sound asleep with his duvet on the floor, and a half erection poking out of the fly of his boxers. I pulled the door quietly to and went to bed.

*   *   *

I stopped off at the garage on the way back from work the next day to buy some flowers for Juno. They were on the ropey side so I took them straight round.

The front door opened before I got there.

'Can you step over the porch?' asked Soph. 'I've just this minute mopped it.'

'What are you doing home?' I made a leap for the mat. 'You're not sick, are you?'

'Mum came and collected us, right out of lessons. The secretary took us down to the foyer and she was there, waiting. I thought Dad had had an accident.'

'He's not, has he?'

'Nah. She had a postcard from him this morning, it was there when she got back after dropping us off. It had his hotel number on it so she phoned him up and they had a long talk, and then she drove back to school and brought us home to tell us what the situation was.'

'Where's your mum now?'

Sophie gestured with the duster she was carrying. 'Upstairs, asleep. She was awake all night. She looked awful; hey, Paxo, didn't Mum look like death this morning?'

Pascale nodded. 'I told her to go and lie down, and when I last checked she was out for the count. We're tidying round as a surprise.'

'I've never seen you with a duster,' I said to Sophie. 'Was it a novel experience?'

'Yeah, tops. Shall I put those in a vase for you before they fall apart? I wouldn't want you dropping petals where we've hoovered.'

Pascale took me though to the lounge and offered me coffee. She is so Juno's daughter.

'No thanks. Just tell me what the latest is on your dad coming home.'

She turned and checked to see if her sister was behind her. Then she lowered her voice. 'Soph thinks he's having some kind of holiday, I don't think she gets it at all. According to Mum, Dad's got to get something out of his system and then he'll be fine and we'll all be together again. But you know the way Mum talks, sometimes she sounds more confident than she is.'

'There.' Sophie walked in with a green pottery vase, my flowers leaning over the rim like passengers in a hot-air balloon.

'For God's sake, stick a mat under it,' said Pascale, as Sophie plonked the vase down on the naked dining table. 'Look, you've got water all over.' Sophie held the vase up in the air and water dripped from its base onto the carpet. On the waxy dark wood was a broken circle of liquid. Pascale stepped forward and wiped the surface with her sleeve, leaving an arc of tiny droplets. She tutted and tried again using her other cuff. 'Give them here, I'll sort it.'

Sophie rolled her eyes, then beckoned me through the doorway. 'Ally, can you come and check out the washing machine for me?'

We went into the kitchen and Sophie knelt down on the quarry tiles so she could peer through the porthole. I don't know what she was expecting to see. 'Don't say anything to Paxo but I think I might have broken it,' she said. 'I've turned it off but the door won't open. It's jammed.'

'That's because it's in mid-cycle. It's a safety device. If you opened the door now, all the water would flood out.' I pressed the on switch and the machine jurred back into life. 'Why did you want to open it up anyway?'

' 'Cause I filled the plastic ball with detergent and then forgot to put it in with the clothes. I left it

303

on the top, here. Don't look at me like that, there's a lot to remember when you're doing housework.'

She turned to rest the small of her back against the edge of the unit, holding the ball in her two palms like a crystal.

'So what it is, Dad's having one of those little crises that middle-aged people have,' she said. 'He's fed up with his job and he feels he's getting old. Basically, he's gone off to sulk. When he's got it out of his system, he'll be back. We've not to mention it to anyone because it's not worth mentioning. He's having a crazy blip, that's all.'

'Is your mum going to go up and see him?' I knew I should have waited to ask Juno this.

'No. She says that would make him cross and confused. He's got to work it through on his own and then he'll be fine. Bloody washing, though. I can't believe I forgot to put the liquid in. What a div.'

'You'll have to wait for this load to finish, now. Just bung the detergent in as soon as the dial gets to zero and set it off again. There's no harm done.'

'Yeah. As long as the machine isn't bust, eh?'

'What was that? What's bust?' shouted Pascale from the hall. 'What've you been doing?'

'Nothing,' I called back. 'I was telling Sophie about the time Ben thought he'd broken our washer.'

I saw Sophie transfer the detergent ball to one hand and give me a discreet thumbs-up.

Pascale came to the doorway. 'So everything's OK in here?'

'All under control,' I told her.

'Right, I'm going to go up and have a shower now.'

304

Sophie raised her palm and waggled her fingers. 'Missing you already, Sis.'

When Pascale had gone, I went over to the sink and pulled the dishcloth off the tap. The trouble with teenagers is that they never see a job through. It was true the girls had washed up, but all the tops needed wiping down, the sink needed swilling, and although they'd dried the plates and cups, the cutlery was still leaking in the drainer.

'Knives and forks don't count,' said Sophie. 'Or glasses. Didn't you know?'

'Do they not?'

She sighed and hung her head. 'You're so nice.'

'I am.'

'No, you really are. I never apologized properly about upsetting Ben—'

'And upsetting me.'

'And you. And betraying your trust. I felt so crap afterwards. I will never, ever do anything like that again, I promise. I know I promised before but I do mean it now. I've finished with sex. That's it.'

'Is it, now?'

'God, yeah. If I'd known how bloody difficult it all is—' She flicked her hair back over her shoulder and I saw the tendons move under the smooth dark skin of her neck, imagined someone kissing her there. 'It seems like a lot of hard work, being an adult.'

I laughed. 'That's true. There are compensations, though.'

'Are you going to tell Mum about me and Ben?'

'No, Sophie. You are.'

Her eyes went wide. 'You must be—'

'I don't mean just now, but when things calm down, you're going to have a good old chat to your

305

mum about everything that's been bothering you, ask her all the questions that you need answering, because that's what mums are for.'

'I couldn't.'

'You have to.' She didn't reply but I thought I detected a faint nod. Or it might just have been her shifting against the machine. The dial clicked round and, after a pause, the drum inside began to spin. When Joe was a tiny baby he loved to sit in his bouncy chair and watch the clothes going round. Spin cycle was his favourite part.

Sophie stepped forward, away from the jolting washer. 'Ally?' She was still holding onto the plastic ball. 'You know Dad being away and having his little holiday so he can sort his head out and come back to family life feeling refreshed and all that shit.'

'Hmm?'

'Is that all it is, really? Is Mum telling the truth? Is she?'

I didn't hesitate. 'Of course she is,' I said.

*   *   *

A strange thing is happening to my memories of Joe. It might be normal; the books say everything's normal. Crying; not-crying. Starving; bingeing. Wanting to scream your other children away. Not wanting to let your other children out of your sight. Keeping toys and clothes; giving them to a charity shop; bundling them into black bags and throwing them on the tip because you can't bear the thought of anyone else using them. Phoning the Samaritans repeatedly and then putting the phone down.

I'm remembering times I'd forgotten, it's as if

306

I'm discovering a whole new Joe. Going round the supermarket, for instance, and him spitting on the floor and laughing. I told him not to but he carried on. I had raging toothache that day, and period pain on top, and all I wanted was to down some painkillers and sit in a bath. I said, 'If you don't stop this minute, Joe, I'm going to have to smack you. And Ben, I will smack you too because you're giggling and making him think it's funny and it's not, it's horrible.' Then Joe spat into the carrots and a lady saw us and pulled a disgusted face. I didn't smack him, but I yelled at him so hard that my voice went thick and I could see other customers faltering in what they were doing, listening to the mental woman with the maladjusted son. Afterwards Ben said, 'I don't think I'll go shopping next time, Mum,' and I snapped at him, 'So how do you expect us to get food into the house, the bloody Tesco's fairy?'

And once, when Ben had been poorly with an ear infection and up for two nights on the trot, Joe wouldn't come out of the bath and I yanked him out and he was so slippery he wriggled out of my grasp and banged his head on the airing cupboard. Then, as he lay on the lino and sobbed, I shouted that it was his own fault for not doing what he was told. Tom came in and took him into his bedroom and dressed him in his pyjamas for me. Tom did his story too because Joe didn't want Mummy that bedtime, but I was so fed up and tired I didn't care.

If I'm honest—and it seems that now I'm able to be—there were days I felt so hassled that when they were squabbling I went into another room, shut the door and left both boys to cry.

My brain's only now giving these things back to

me, drip-feeding me the whole picture. I must have been too fragile during the first couple of years; I presume it's the subconscious protecting you. And yet I'd rather have these memories than not.

I think it's happening to Tom too. We were in the supermarket together, and in the stationery aisle Tom suddenly said, 'Do you remember when Joe begged for that packet of multicoloured erasers, and you bought them for him and then when he got in the car he said he wanted what Ben had instead, an Action Man ruler, was it?' He shook his head, half smiling. Yes, I thought, and what came next: me tearing the packet out of his hands, opening the car door and sending them sailing across the car park, Joe's amazed eyes following them. Tom saying, 'There was no need for that, Ally.'

'He could be a little sod, couldn't he?'

Tom picking the cellophane packet of erasers by one corner out of the muddy gutter, wiping the cardboard hanger at the top with the edge of his hand as he walked back towards the car.

'I can't think about it, Tom. It makes me feel too bad.'

He put his arm round my shoulders. 'OK.' He turned his head and kissed me swiftly on the cheek. No one else in Tesco's was kissing that day; several people looked. ' Hey, shall we treat ourselves to a bottle of wine tonight? It would be nice, just the two of us, get Ben ensconced on his PlayStation with CarAttack 3 or something. Unless you want your clone round.'

'Bastard,' I said mildly. 'I'll never confide in you again, you know that, don't you?'

Could Manny be right? I'd asked him, waking

him in the middle of the night, because mad accusations seem so real when it's dark outside and you're the only one in the world who's not asleep. Is that all I am, I'd whispered, a poor imitation?

When Tom had understood, he laughed loudly, then threatened to punch Manny in the mouth next time he saw him. 'I can't believe you've lain here worrying about that. The man's having some sort of brainstorm, you're just a casualty of his guilt.'

I sighed and wriggled against him gratefully.

'I suppose it is true,' he continued, 'that you've constructed a Juno to your own requirements, one that ignores a lot of her little faults and plays up the good sides. It's not like you copy her clothes or anything. Just this edited image you hang on to. It's harmless.'

I should have said, 'But that's what we all do. It's what's necessary to keep certain relationships on track.' I'd thought of a good phrase, the sort of thing Manny would say: the Dynamic of Prejudice. I liked the sound of that. You have to believe that somewhere, in another place, the perfect family exists, or true love does, or that life is fair. That's why people go and see films with happy endings, or read *Hello!* magazine. Otherwise, what else is there to aim for?

But I hadn't said any of this. I'd left it in my head for another day.

'I'm not a copycat,' I said now, in the wine aisle, next to a tall man with grey hair who thought I was talking to him and jerked his head up in surprise.

'Hmm, I can't choose; what sort of wine would Juno drink?' said Tom, taking my hand, grinning.

The tall man moved off and my mobile phone

rang. I grabbed for my bag, alert for disaster at once. The house was on fire, a neighbour was calling to tell us Ben had fallen out of the window, had been spotted sniffing aerosols, some brand of doom. I saw Tom go tense.

'Yes?' I clutched the phone tight to my ear. 'Hello?'

'I thought it was you,' said a cold voice. 'It's Kim here.'

*   *   *

Interviewer—Why did you apply to go on *Queen Mum*?

Lee—Because I was told to!

Interviewer—What were you hoping for when you applied to go on *Queen Mum*?

Kim—Fame! No, seriously, I had this idea it would open a lot of doors, that it would be a great experience in itself, but it might lead to other things. Like, I suppose I thought I'd meet some famous people, maybe, and I might get asked to go on other shows like the people in *Big Brother*. Some of them have stayed around, haven't they? I could imagine getting a mention in *Heat*, or, say, one of those makeovers they do on morning telly. I've always been interested in TV and what the stars are like when you get them backstage. I thought it might be an opportunity.

Interviewer—I really meant, to what extent you thought it might improve your family relationships.

Kim—Oh, yeah, that as well. Yeah.

310

*　　*　　*

Tom must have seen the colour drain from my face because he shoved the trolley to one side and mouthed, 'What? What?'

I waved him away.

I'd tried Kim's number again that morning, but only got Lee. That had made me twitchy, so I'd tried several times since, each time dialling 141 beforehand; or so I'd thought. I must have become careless. You do when you're worried.

'Why have you been phoning my home all the time and putting the receiver down?'

'I haven't.'

'Don't be so soft,' she snapped. 'Who else would it be? It's not your friend's style. I've been keeping a log, you know. I can go to the police and claim harassment and they can check your mobile, it's easily done.'

Tom was still hovering at the edge of my vision. I put my hand to my temple, partly to block him out, partly to steady myself.

'OK,' I said. 'I won't do it again.' How feeble did I sound? 'I just needed to ask you something.'

'What?'

'Have you seen Manny this week?'

There was a long pause. 'No,' she said finally. 'Not this week. I wondered if it was that you were after. The last time I saw him was ten days ago when he dropped another load of tapes off for me.' Thank God, I thought. 'He's gone, has he?'

'He's having a holiday,' I said.

'Yeah, right. Extended break, is it?' She laughed nastily. 'I'll tell you something, Ally, and this is true. I could have had Manny Kingston if I'd

311

wanted. I chose not to, that's all. But I could have had him, you tell your friend.'

'Like hell I will,' I heard myself blurt out, and the blood rushed up into my cheeks and make them prickle. Tom came forward and took the phone from me. 'Switch it off, quick,' I said, 'for God's sake.'

He pressed the button and the screen went dark. I was leaning against a pillar with one hand clutching my collar, shoppers moving past me in both directions. All at once I felt incredibly heavy, as though at any moment my weight could send me crashing though the vinyl floor.

'Are you going to faint?' said Tom.

I swallowed. 'No. Let's just get out of here, OK?'

We left the half-loaded trolley where it was and darted down the aisle and though the checkout, dodging bodies. The people queuing stared as we ran through the doors, waited for the alarm to go off.

'Funny turn?' said Tom as we stood at the edge of the drizzling car park.

'Something like that. Can we order on the Internet this week?'

'Only if you tell me what you've been up to,' he said.

*   *   *

In Ben's email folder were three new messages: Get a Monster Cock, Free Granny-Sex, and an offer for prescription drugs. I deleted them all, then moved Tom's *Motorcycle News* 'Best Trackday Crashes' supplement—*OUCH! SMACK! CRUNCH! SLAM!*—out of the way and found the Post-It

312

notes. 'Upgrade Spam Blocker' I wrote, then 'Set Parental Control', but scribbled it out. Ben would only work out a way of getting past it. Better if Tom could speak to him. 'You going to say anything to Juno about Kim ringing?' Tom had said as we'd driven home in the rain.

I just gave him a look.

Now I wished I had gone round, tried to clear a path in case Kim took it upon herself to call Juno, but it was 3 a.m. and I was only in my dressing gown.

I pulled the cord tighter around my waist and the sensation brought back unexpectedly one of the nights I was up with Joe when he'd had croup. I'd sat on the toilet with the lid down, Joe on my knee, the bathroom door closed and the shower full on hot. Steam trickled down the windows and the tiles, and my hair stuck to my face. Joe rasped and wheezed against my chest. 'It's not as bad as it sounds,' the doctor had told me. 'He'll be running about in week or so.'

Then the computer's message-alert noise sounded, which on our machine is something like a gunshot. I brought my hand up too quickly and caught it on the edge of the desk, sloshing my cup of milk so that some splashed out onto the keyboard. In the pocket of my dressing gown I found a tissue and dabbed at the space bar irritably. Down in the cracks between Alt and Z there were long beads of liquid; and I was remembering Tom telling me when we got our first computer, 'One thing they don't like is hot drinks, Ally,' and another time Manny telling me keyboards are so cheap these days that they throw them away at the council offices if they get messed

313

up. And somewhere in the middle of this, don't ask me how it happened, but there was one second when my throat went tight and I knew this email was from Manny.

CHAPTER NINETEEN

"Being on TV Spring-cleaned our Marriage"

Queen Mum Kim reveals how reality television brought the spark back into Fox family life

It's part of normality, the way you stop seeing what's in front of you. Kieran, the producer, told me that right at the start.

He said that the role of reality TV was to make you look again at what you thought you knew, through a different lens, so that you can discover an inner truth. He said this was as true for the participants as for the viewers.

I was married at 20, a mum straight after that. Sometimes I look back and I'm horrified that I took on those kind of commitments at such a young age. But I was convinced I knew it all, and let's face it, I could have done a lot worse than marry Lee and have two healthy boys.

Only, even when you're happily married like I am, you come to a point in your life where you think, 'Is this all there is, or have I missed some chances along the line?'

I had my dreams, like anyone. I was a smart girl when I was at school, but I never got any encouragement off my mum. I always fancied one of those arts academies, they look like a real blast. Then Lee came along and I fell in love, and suddenly my dreams looked silly against the day-to-day business of getting

315

somewhere to live and saving up for the wedding.

So there you are, trotting along, nothing really bad happens but there's just that something niggling in the back of your mind, what could have been. And people from my background, we knuckle down and get on with it. We don't go running off to therapists or weekend retreats so we can 'find ourselves'. The working classes have to get up in the morning.

The TV opportunity was a gift in every sense. It shook us all up, in a good way, and it was amazing to see myself on screen, rolling my sleeves up and getting stuck in. I was blown away when the programme aired and I won. Mind you, I do think I did some good in the two weeks I was with the other family. The viewers must have thought so too, because I've had some great fan-mail.

The boys were overjoyed to have me back. They appreciated the freedom I give them a lot more after it had been taken away from them for a fortnight. If there's one thing you mustn't do with teenagers, it's patronize them. Marco says, 'You treat me like an adult, Mum, and I'll behave like one.' And he has grown up a lot recently. He helps out more around the house now, which is nice. Nothing spectacular, but he buys us a takeaway once a week (I give him the cash but he goes for it himself) and he puts his dirty clothes in the basket.

Chris has been through a funny phase but he's more settled now. He told me once that he didn't feel he 'fitted in any more'. That's teenagers, though, isn't it? His dad reckoned it was probably woman trouble, but actually Chris has got a nice girlfriend at the moment, we met her at parents' evening. Her mum's a solicitor! So we shall have to mind our Ps and Qs when she comes round.

One thing that saddens me about agreeing to take part in the filming is that having a stranger in the house seems to have upset the bond between the boys. People got the impression from the programme that they fought all the time, but they think a lot of each other in real life. It was only ever in good fun, lads will be lads. In a way, you could say Marco's teaching Chris to stand up for himself.

Lee couldn't wait to have me home. He used to joke that I was bossy before, but now he sees we have a good relationship based on give and take. *Queen Mum* spring-cleaned our marriage, you could say. Although he was a bit threatened initially by the press interest in me, he's come round and on the whole he's been supportive about my new media course and my review spot on the Film4All website.

But the best thing that's come out of being on television is that Lee's agreed for us to try for another baby in the New Year. We've been able to talk about the effect a baby would have on our marriage and address his fears in a much more constructive way then ever before. I think nowadays Lee appreciates what he's got. He said to me the other evening, 'It's so easy to take people for granted.' I'm glad he's come to understand that.

317

I'd have said before I went on *Queen Mum* I was happy. Now I know I am.

* * *

The address was a Hotmail one I didn't recognize but I knew the style. '*Abject Apologies*', the email was headed. There's something copperplate about Manny's writing, even when he's using Times New Roman.

I'm so, so sorry, Ally, for the thoughtless way I spoke to you when we last met. I'm aware I must have hurt you deeply, but the words came out of the cloud of confusion that's shrouding me at the moment and I was angry and disappointed that you couldn't seem to understand how I was feeling. And yet, how could I have expected you to understand the state of my mind when I can't fathom it myself? I behaved abominably. Rest assured, our encounter was at least as painful for me as it must have been for you. If I could take back those words, leave them unspoken, then I would. Your friendship over the years has been invaluable to us all.

My leaving is not about Kim, you have to believe that. But you should also know that Kim is in love with me. And I felt for a while as though I had some kind of responsibility to that. 'Lovers be wise, and love for love return,' as the saying goes. But we did not have an affair. When the crisis came, I told her to go home and get on with her life, and she has done so.

Where does that leave me? Have I the courage to go back? Have I the courage to stay away? The

truth is, I don't know. I guess I need a little more
time. The constellations are whirling about my
head and I am no longer in control of my own
identity.
    I wait on time.
    Love,
    Manny

'Up himself as ever,' I could hear Tom's voice
saying. But I was touched Manny had bothered.
'He's lonely,' said Tom. 'That doesn't matter,' I
said aloud, and my voice sounded small in the
quiet. I pictured Manny sitting in a hotel room,
scrolling up and down his laptop by the light of an
anglepoise. Part of me longed to send an answer,
reassurance. Then I thought of Juno lying sobbing
across the bed and the girls' bright, brittle smiles.
My hand was hovering over the mouse as another
email shot in.
Dirty Boys Need Correction, it said.
I shut the machine down and went to run a bath.

*   *   *

Sometimes I wish that I'd kept a diary of the years
I had with Joe. Not just with Joe; of when Ben was
little, the early days with Tom, the best bits of my
childhood. You forget so much. A scene you
thought you'd lost comes back, but another drops
out of your head. I think Joe, or Ben, or Tom and I
get a different jumble of images every single time,
like shaking a kaleidoscope.
    A diary might spoil that because it would fix the
images more firmly. But what slips away from you
is terrifying: what if the memories that you lose are

the important ones? Under the lip of the wooden bath panel my fingers touched an irregularity, a slight bump under the progress of my fingernail. I climbed out of the water and crouched down on the mat to see what it was. A tiny red smiley sticker, beginning to curl at the edge; must have been there over four years, pulled off Joe's school sweatshirt and stuck down secretly while I was turning his trousers right-side out for the linen basket, maybe. And a whole series of pictures flooded back: of a Well Done sticker on a number workbook, backwards 2s in thick pencil; meeting Joe from school and telling him not to stretch his jumper out of shape because he had his arms down the sides and the sleeves flapping loose; Ben wearing a price ticket on his face and Joe copying him; scrubbing temporary tattoos off their arms in foamy bathwater. I could imagine Joe now, peeling the sticker carefully from his sweatshirt, eyeing the bin and rejecting it, keeping his eyes on me while he reached across and pressed the smiley face upwards against the veneer. I expect he giggled as he did it. Perhaps Ben spotted him and tried to tell me but I stuck a toothbrush in his mouth, or there was a missing bath-toy crisis, or I just wasn't listening. I knew the reason I'd never felt the sticker before was that it was only now starting to lift away from the wood, but it was hard not to think Joe didn't put it there for me yesterday.

Tom found me at the computer when he got up at seven.

'Don't tell me you've been there all night?'

'I stopped for a bath at four.'

Tom shook his head. 'You must be shattered.'

'Not too bad. It's less exhausting to get up do

stuff than lie there fretting that you can't get to sleep. I'll be tired tonight.'

'I bet you will. What you doing, anyway?' He came and stood behind me, putting his hands on the back of my chair, and I tensed. 'Oh.' I felt his body sag slightly as he saw what was on the screen. 'Please, Ally, not that forum again. As far as I can see, that place only drags you down. I know you said it was helpful, but you used to get so upset after you'd been on it. And it was like you were addicted, you were on there all hours. Don't start all that again, love.'

'I'm not.'

'If you say so.' He took his hands away and went across to the door.

'I'm really not. All I'm doing is taking some of my old posts and putting them into Word. See? To save them.'

But he'd gone.

I heard him shout Ben twice but I carried on cutting and pasting till he came back with a cup of coffee and some toast. 'Eat. Drink. Get your blood sugar up.'

'I'm writing a diary,' I said. 'Look.' I shrank the web page down and opened the title up. 'Joe' I'd typed in 72 point Arial. 'I'm going to paste in a picture, the one of him in his uniform. Then inside I'm going to write down everything I can remember about him. I don't want to lose anything, Tom.'

'Why start now?'

'Because now's the right time.'

I clicked everything away and got up, pushing my chair away, to hold him.

'Let me, Tom.'

'I'm not stopping you,' he said. There was no anger in his voice.

*   *   *

I'd taken a plate of oatmeal cookies round because Juno always raved about the recipe and I couldn't think what else to do to cheer her up. But biscuits are a poor substitute for a husband.

'Mmm, you're a treasure,' she said, taking down her French farmhouse tin with the anemones on the lid. 'I shall hide these from the girls or they'll be gone in two minutes.'

'Are you eating properly?'

'Yes. Stop clucking. Still no news, but life has to go on.' She still looked fantastic, in her Hobbs cord jacket, her hair twisted up off her face. What did Manny think he was playing at? 'Hey, you know you only just missed Mrs Beale?'

'How is she?'

'Not so good. Her husband's died. But she's holding it together, she said she did a lot of her grieving while he was ill.'

She popped the lid down on the tin and stretched up to replace it on the dresser.

'Don't start feeling guilty, Juno. Grace Hopkins was giving her lifts, Tom's seen them driving around on several occasions. She didn't come round to have a go at you, did she?'

'Absolutely not.' She perched herself on the edge of the table. 'She wants me to read at the funeral. She says I have the nicest speaking voice she knows and there's a poem that no one else could do justice to.'

'Are you going to?'

'Yes.' Juno sounded surprised. 'Why shouldn't I?'

'I didn't know if you were up to it, that's all.'

'I couldn't let her down. Honestly, Ally. My husband's away for a while, that's all. I'm not stricken with illness or anything.'

I felt foolish for a moment, but she took me by the arm, pally as you like, and led me through to the lounge where we sat facing each other.

'I told her about Manny,' she said. 'I didn't mean to, it slipped out. Swore her to secrecy, but she won't tell anyone. It's difficult when you're feeling vulnerable and someone's offering you their confidences—'

'I'm sure she won't say a word.'

'No.'

She could have been a Vettriano painting, sitting there with her ankles crossed and her elbow resting on the sofa arm. If Tom ever left me I'd walk about in my nightdress for days and never brush my teeth.

'She said she never liked Kim.'

'Did she?' I was thinking of the war-time karaoke and Mrs Beale's cheeks glowing with rouge and approval.

'She said Kim was the sort of person who made a great first impression, but that you wouldn't trust in the long term. All show and no substance, she said. Which was right, wasn't it?'

'She was a nasty piece of work,' I said, using one of my mum's favourite phrases. 'She did a lot of damage.'

'I let her. Was it my fault, Ally?'

'What?'

'The way everything changed. Got twisted

323

round. Soph becoming so uppity, Manny's fit.'

'Don't start talking "fault". That way lies damnation; believe me.' I saw the blur of Joe's face, the panel of the car flashing in the sunshine.

'Do you think Manny's in love with Kim?' Juno asked, and her face looked so young and naked that I wanted to throw my arms around her and rock her better. 'Tell me truthfully, please.'

'I don't believe he loves Kim, no.'

Juno started to cry. 'It's kind of you to say so.'

'No, I really believe he doesn't.'

'Thank you. I needed to hear that. I sometimes—You know how, in the night-time, you lie there thinking—I sometimes feel I trapped him—'

Through the patio windows I watched the trees shudder in the wind. The water in the stone bird bath rippled and the reflection of the sky broke for a moment.

Afterwards she went to wash her face. I stooped to pick up a tissue she'd dropped and it was then that I saw all the torn-up photos in the bin and the screwed-up notes.

*   *   *

Juno—It's been the most amazing experience. Not always easy, but terrifically illuminating. People, viewers, don't realize how much happens off-camera, that the show you see is only a tiny fraction of the experiment. I don't think it's overstating the case to say being in the programme's changed my life. What? Why are you smiling like that? That superior smirk; stop it.

Manny—Well, do you really think so? Changed
  Your Life?
Juno—Yes. I do. Do you not?
Manny—How can we say our lives have been
  changed if we can't see into the future?

*   *   *

She was gone ages. I could have reached down,
taken out one of the crumpled balls and smoothed
it legible, read the pleas to Manny that I knew
Juno had scrawled there, or drawn out two halves
of wedding photo and matched them. I could have
done this, listening for the pipes to stop hissing and
the lock to snap open on the cloakroom door, but I
didn't.

Tom had said to me after the programme, all
those months ago, 'Juno wasn't a victim, you know.
No one put those words in her mouth.' I'd hated
him for his callousness and because I knew he was
right. But TV had shown a Juno out of context,
and context is everything. You need at least a
lifetime to assimilate it.

*   *   *

Saturday afternoon, a bright clear day for the end
of the year. I was working on my Joe diary when
the doorbell rang. I waited for someone else to stir
themselves, but no one did. Juno tapped on the
window by my shoulder.

'I'm not coming in,' she said, when I opened the
front door.

She looked sensational. 'Have I seen that outfit
before? Are you going to an interview?' Her

325

narrow frame was draped in grey lambswool and there was a wide fur collar around her shoulders. She could have been a Forties film star.

'It's new,' she said shyly. 'Does it hang all right?'

'It's wow. Where are you going in it?'

'That's what I came to say. The girls are in town but I've left them a note to come round to yours when they get back. That's OK, isn't it? I'm going to go and get him, Ally, and I don't know how long I'll be.'

She was wearing little pearl earrings and plum lipstick, immaculate. But her fingers were ugly red and white where her car keys dug into the flesh. I wanted to tell her that I loved her and admired her and that everything would work out, but I said, 'Have the girls got a key?'

She licked her lips. 'Yes. And I've reminded them to feed Fing if I'm not back tonight.'

'They can sleep in our spare room,' I said. 'Or I'll sleep at yours. It's no bother.'

She didn't protest. We walked to the car and she got in, swinging her legs elegantly across the sill. When she turned on the ignition, the CD began to play 'La Mer'. She wound the window down and I could smell her perfume. 'Wish me luck, Ally.'

'You know I do.' I stood and watched her go, my mind's eye playing a vision of her car from above winding through high-hedged lanes, with Charles Trenet's voice swelling in the background.

After a few minutes I went inside to my family. The men were watching TV together, but Tom was also dismantling a piece of bike on some newspaper spread out on the carpet. If this had been a film, I'd have gone up to them and we'd have had a group hug. I'd have said something sentimental and profound. But it wasn't a film, so I went into the kitchen and started to make the tea.

CHAPTER TWENTY

We were stopped for petrol on the way back from Wrexham. Tom was walking stiffly in his leathers towards the shop, his crash helmet under his arm. I'd seen him indicate and wondered at once whether something was wrong with the bike. The brakes were failing? A wheel was loose? 'The salesmen never put much fuel in the tanks these days,' he said when we'd both pulled over. 'There won't be enough to get me home.'

'I'll wait,' I said. I wanted to follow and keep an eye on him, though I knew it was a luxury I'd probably never have again.

I leaned against the car and remembered. 'Why now?' Tom had said, trying not to show his glee. 'After all this time? Don't get me wrong, I'm made up, but it's come right out of the blue. I thought you were dead against the idea?'

'I don't know. But sort it quick, before I change my mind again.'

'It's better,' he'd explained, 'safer, to buy from a dealer than from a private individual, even though it costs more. You never know if a privately owned bike's been crashed, or nicked—'

'Just get on with it,' I'd said. I'd never seen him so happy.

Cars shot past me now, going too fast, and juggernauts that could crush your skull in a second. A lorry hooted and made me jump; when I looked up, the driver bibbed again. What was he playing at? I saw his grin as he thundered past. 'Oh!' I said out loud, then laughed. When was the last time that happened to me? I almost looked round for Juno; she gets bibbed all the time.

Tom was coming across the forecourt. 'It'll take us about half an hour from here, so we'd best get on with it,' he called. 'You all right to find your way back?'

'I think so.'

He pulled the crash helmet down over his head and flipped the visor up with clumsy gloved fingers. 'See you at home, then. And thanks.'

I stepped forward to hug him but he'd turned away and the helmet blocked me out of his peripheral vision. I let him go, anyway.

I stuck behind him for three miles, till we came out of town. Then the road widened and the speed limit went up. He shifted in his saddle, then suddenly he was off, powering up the hill and leaning into the corner. Leaving me behind. My heart squeezed with fear for a moment, but I slowed my breath down and put the radio on.

It was going to take some getting used to.